Allah's Spacious Earth

Middle East Literature in Translation
Michael Beard and Adnan Haydar, *Series Editors*

Select Titles in Middle East Literature and Translation

For a full list of titles in this series,
visit https://press.syr.edu/supressbook-series
/middle-east-literature-in-translation/.

Allah's Spacious Earth

Omar Sayfo

Translated from the Hungarian by
Paul Olchváry

Syracuse University Press

This book was originally published in Hungarian as *Allah tágas földje*
(Budapest: Kárpát-medencei Tehetséggondozó Nonprofit Kft., 2017).

First Edition 2023

23 24 25 26 27 28   6 5 4 3 2 1

∞ The paper used in this publication meets the minimum requirements
of the American National Standard for Information Sciences—Permanence
of Paper for Printed Library Materials, ANSI Z39.48-1992.

For a listing of books published and distributed by Syracuse University Press,
visit https://press.syr.edu.

ISBN: 978-0-8156-1155-4 (paperback)
       978-0-8156-5586-2 (e-book)

Library of Congress Cataloging-in-Publication Data

Names: Sayfo, Omar, 1982– author. | Olchváry, Paul, translator.
Title: Allah's spacious earth / Omar Sayfo ; translated from the Hungarian by Paul Olchváry.
Other titles: Allah tágas földje. English
Description: First edition. | Syracuse, New York : Syracuse University Press, 2023. |
    Series: Middle East literature in translation
Identifiers: LCCN 2022054096 (print) | LCCN 2022054097 (ebook) |
    ISBN 9780815611554 (paperback ; alk. paper) | ISBN 9780815655862 (ebook)
Subjects: LCGFT: Dystopian fiction. | Novels.
Classification: LCC PH3382.29.A94 A7813 2023 (print) | LCC PH3382.29.A94 (ebook) |
    DDC 894/.51134—dc23/eng/20221125
LC record available at https://lccn.loc.gov/2022054096
LC ebook record available at https://lccn.loc.gov/2022054097

Manufactured in the United States of America

Wasn't Allah's earth spacious enough
for you to emigrate and find refuge?
Koran 4.97

Contents

Acknowledgments

This novel is a result of a decade of reading and wandering the streets of Europe. My first gratitude goes to my wife, Anna, who supported me all along the way, especially during the emotionally challenging writing process. I would like to express my gratitude for the encouragement of my Hungarian publisher, János Dénes Orbán, without whom I would not have thought of writing a novel, and Attila Sipos, who did his best to guide me through the bureaucracy of publishing. I am indebted to my translator, Paul Olchváry, and my editor and pen friend at Syracuse University Press, Michael Beard, who made the English version of *Allah's Spacious Earth* happen.

I am grateful for the inspiration of Zoltán Páll at the Austrian Academy of Sciences, Martin van Bruinessen at Utrecht University, Jan Jaap de Ruiter at Tilburg University, Martijn de Koning at Radboud University, and all the colleagues working in the field of Islam in Europe. Also I am indebted to Miklós Maróth and the Avicenna Institute of Middle Eastern Studies, and to Zoltán Szalai, Tamás Dezső, and Viktor Marsai at the Migration Research Institute.

Most important, I am sending my gratitude to all the inspiring people I have met during my visits to Saint-Denis, Clichy-sous-Bois, Rosengård, Mjølnerparken, Wedding, Kreuzberg, Neukölln, Höchst, Griesheim, Molenbeek, Favoriten, Luton, Tower Hamlets, Newham, Tottenham, Schilderswijk, Bijlmermeer, De Pijp, and many other neighborhoods across Europe, who contributed to the formulation of the characters and enriched the plots of this story with their own experiences.

Last but not least, I would like to pay my sincere respect to all those in Europe and beyond who are waging the greater jihad to maintain their sense and humanity in a time of fragmentation and paranoia.

Allah's Spacious Earth

1   One more time, I figured, I would climb up to the lookout tower, perhaps for the last time. A paved road wound around the oak trees, and after a twenty-minute walk it ended as a little parking lot. Overfilled trash cans around the concrete benches of this panoramic space marked the signs of the picnics that had unfolded here. Cardboard boxes and plastic bags had faded, and fast-food bags moldered under the warm May rains.

From here only a gravel-strewn dirt path led up to the onetime television broadcast tower. When the unused structure had been transformed into a lookout tower, a wide road had been built on the other side of the hill, together with a rubberized track beside the sidewalk that wound its way up so sports-minded people could get up here in comfort alongside tourists. From our side only those gravel steps led up.

It had been twenty years since I'd been here last. The first time, when I was six, it was my grandfather who brought me up, a couple of weeks after the lookout tower's dedication ceremony. Together we ambled up the gravel steps, his right hand holding my hand and his left hand twirling the *misbaha* as he went on about our family history. From then on the lookout tower became our favorite place. Our first venture up was followed by countless others: our joint Sunday afternoon ritual. With time though I sought entertainment with the promise of excitement; after that my grandfather climbed the hill alone.

This time around the gravel crackled under the soles of the old sneakers I'd chosen for the occasion, and I began gasping for breath. More cardiovascular exercise was in order. The steps had not been such a challenge twenty years earlier.

I can't be such a wimp, I thought, huffing and puffing, quickening my pace even though I knew that I'd have sore muscles the next day. Shameful. Back then my grandfather was nearing seventy, and still he took those high steps effortlessly.

The concrete square around the onetime TV tower hadn't changed much in twenty years. Only the people had disappeared. When I came

1

with Grandfather, we had to stand in line to get up to the top of the tower. Now the only other person there was a runner stretching his leg on the guardrail on the other side of the square. Back then the elevator had zipped us up in moments, and as we stepped out onto the viewing deck the first time we went up, a cool breeze caught my hair. Now there was a lock on the door at the bottom of the tower, and the worn metal rail circling it was wound with yellow-black official ribbon.

The terrace beside the tower afforded an exquisite view all the same. The sprawling bushes behind the ashlar fence running along its edge were not too tall, so I could clearly see the river below, which seemed to run right into the bottom of the hill. The early afternoon sun glittered on the towering office buildings along its left bank. The Zone stretched out on its right bank. In the middle of the terrace was a cracked concrete block, on the top of which screws protruded where a bronze model of the city had once stood.

"So, which is the cathedral?" Grandfather had asked that day, poking a hand in the direction of a twin-spired building on the bronze model. I found it easily, pointing proudly into the distance.

"And City Hall?" This was harder, but I got it too. It was also on the left bank, not far from the cathedral.

"A clever boy you are, Nasim," said Grandfather, running his fingers through my curls.

Squinting into the sunny sky, I looked at the faraway buildings, then glanced back at the sculpture, and once more into the distance.

"And where is our building?" I asked.

"That's not on it," he replied.

"And the other tower blocks?"

"Those aren't either."

Nor did the model seem to show Al-Nour Mosque. Though its minaret rose almost as high as the steeples of the cathedral on the opposite bank, I still had to strain my eyes to discern it. With its minimalist style, it blended unnoticed into the pastel sea of the tower blocks all around it.

Even before the Loyalist Act, since expanded into the New Loyalist Act, the minaret hadn't been used for calls to prayer. It had been built solely as a spectacle, one that at dusk might even have been mistaken for some oddly shaped factory chimney. Only the green light that lit up at its top after the evening prayer made it clear just what this structure was. I always had found it odd that the green lights that lit up at dusk not only on the mosques but in numerous shops and tower blocks in the Zone never bothered anyone. While the Patriotic Front and the more apoplectic conservatives attacked the Arabic inscriptions and store signs as symbolic of Muslim territorial expansion, the green lights melting into the cityscape proclaimed Allah's glory and the slow but steady increase in the number of his followers unperturbed.

My father must have been a little kid when the Al-Nour Mosque, originally known as the Al-Fatih Mosque, opened. The Peace Foundation, which had overseen the project, had received enough money from the oil-rich sponsor nations, but construction dragged on for seven years all the same. Though the Patriotic Front protested most vocally of all, in fact it was the residents of the Zone who, with all sorts of notices and petitions, had put obstacles in the way of construction. Back then, after all, everyone had their own places of prayer, and no one had a favorable view of this competition. Those from the Maghreb were suspicious of the square-shaped minaret on the blueprint, not to mention the Maghreb-style mosaics, which they saw as proof positive that the Al-Fatih Mosque would seek to lure away faithful from their ranks. But the Turks were anxious too. The economic crisis had by then emptied out Turkey's coffers in Ankara, and that nation's leadership focused increasingly on internal strife. With its budget shrinking year by year, Turkey's Ministry of Religious Affairs sent less and less money for the building and maintenance of mosques and places of prayer in Europe. The Turkish community was especially upset about the name Al-Fatih, which they interpreted as a reference to Mehmed Al-Fatih, or Mehmed the Conqueror, who'd conquered Constantinople, and they were indignant that a mosque led by Arabs bore the name of an Ottoman hero.

The Patriotic Front had an entirely different issue with the name. To them, Al-Fatih, which means "The Conqueror," was a symbol of the spread of aggressive Islam. The Peace Foundation countered by noting that Al-Fatih, or rather, al-Fattah, was in fact one of Allah's names, meaning "The

Opener," and suggesting that Allah in his infinite mercy opens people's hearts to faith. The Patriotic Front, which had learned about Islam from the Internet, shot back that Allah had ninety-nine names, so if the Peace Foundation's aims were truly peaceful, they might easily have found an alternative. The mosque might have been al-Halim, for example, meaning "The Forbearing One" or "The Nonprecipitate One," which would have been far less given to misunderstanding.

The government—a coalition of the Socialist, Liberal, and Green parties—steered clear of the debate. When asked by reporters, the spokesperson said simply that the state stood on secular foundations and its laws applied to all, and as long as they were not violated, the state had no intention of intervening in matters pertaining to religious communities.

The Peace Foundation didn't even suspect that it was building a Tower of Babel. As if Allah, for some incomprehensible reason, did not look favorably upon the minaret proclaiming his own glory by reaching up toward the clouds. This debate of the deaf took the whole country by storm, raging throughout the construction process. When the mosque finally began operating, there were more journalists at the first Friday prayer than there were faithful. The latter did not grow much in number later on, either. All the way until the Loyalist Act cut off the inflow of foreign funding and banned foreign-trained imams, and then the New Loyalist Act just made things worse. The Peace Foundation collapsed and handed over the running of the Al-Fatih Mosque to a foundation that had long been operating in the Zone and that was even recognized by the Interior Ministry. That is when the mosque was renamed Al-Nour, or Light, which is likewise one of Allah's many names, but a far less problematic one. Moreover, the new name represented continuity with that of the Zone's old Al-Nour Mosque, which my grandfather had attended. The old, universally liked imam and his team moved to their new home, and finally there was enough room for all the faithful, who previously had clashed there each Friday. Back then it still seemed all would be well.

The climb back down the hill went faster, and my thighs bore the descent better too. The possible events of the coming days kept whirling through my mind. I didn't even notice that the gravel steps were behind me and that I was already at the bottom of the road. I had nothing to do. I walked across the bridge and headed aimlessly down the row of shops on Pater Street. The ban on public gatherings had yet to take effect, but hardly anyone was on the street. The surveillance drones were patrolling a good thirty feet above the buildings. Since the undersides of the newer models automatically projected an image of the sky above them, their constant presence wasn't even noticeable anymore. Their buzz could be heard only if the remote pilot had them descend in among the tower blocks when their telescopic lenses noticed something suspicious.

A racket could be heard from the direction of the pastel yellow cube of the school building. The high concrete wall blocked my view of the children running amuck in the yard. Rami, Husam, and the others and I had once gone there.

Rami was two months younger than me, but on account of his size everyone always thought he was at least a year older. We'd grown up together. Like brothers-in-arms we kept secrets from home, awkward family matters that we would not have told or confessed to strangers had our lives depended on it. There were two of us male cousins, and because I was Grandfather's favorite, Grandmother naturally sided with Rami. Together we experienced holidays and average days, great big family lunches, and our grandparents wrangling with their sons. When, because of some trivial difference of opinion, our fathers weren't on speaking terms, we were invariably summoned as mediators; this allowed them to save face while retreating from conflicts that neither one of them desired but their conflicting personalities harried them into again and again. Our own relationship was never affected by family disputes. Rami was the only person I could keep no secrets from. We were unified against our families by the outside world, and against the outside world by our families.

There was one thing Rami and I didn't see eye to eye on. That was our relationship with Husam, who lived with his family in the neighboring tower block. His parents had immigrated to Europe, and since his father's first workplace had folded, my father found him new work to keep his residence permit from being revoked. Husam's father was therefore forever grateful to our family, and indeed he commanded his son to seek my friendship. Husam was thin, and he was smaller than me. Maybe on account of his size, maybe because of his strict parents, but missing from him were the balls that were requisite to every other boy of our age in the Zone. Chasing his parents' dreams as a child, he wanted to be an engineer or a doctor. Of course he didn't study well enough to have a shot at either. Rami would have preferred to shake off Husam. For my part, I was fond of him from the start. Like me, he was into reading and interested in the world, and in my heart of hearts I envied him for his always having peace at home. But when we moved about as a gang, Husam was indeed a bit like a bicycle bell. When he was there, it was good, but when he wasn't, it's not as if we missed him much.

In school all three of us wound up in the same class. Unlike them I actually liked school, which was in part thanks to the head teacher in the lower grades. Miss Christina was strict, and everyone thought it best not to kid around with her. Back in my father's day she'd taught him too, and on account of that he trusted her, and even as an adult respected her unreservedly. When she had any complaint about me, Father didn't even ask me for my side of the story. But that happened rarely. Miss Christina was fond of me. When she saw that I wrote well, she suggested that I write for the school newspaper. How I loved to let my thoughts ripen, shape them into sentences, and then polish them and pour them into their final forms. One time I even got a free ticket to a local rap concert so I could write a review. To my great surprise a few students in higher grades read it, and then being chummy with them was really cool in the eyes of my peers. That's when I decided to become a journalist. For years I kept that dream alive within me. But then Miss Christina retired, and I did not become a journalist.

On Strauss Square I bought a hot dog and sat down on one of the benches by the remains of the statue. The hot dog was just as awful as usual, smothered in so much ketchup that I had to lean forward to keep the gooey red sauce from dribbling onto my pants. Graffiti tags and bird droppings covered the morbid, bronze, truncated statue of a human figure on the concrete foundation.

Under the cover of darkness one night some twenty years earlier, a local group of fundamentalists called the Tawhidis had fallen upon a statue of the former president and chiseled away the face. I remember the day, for the story was all over the news. The Patriotic Front called a demonstration by the statue for the next day. After boxing training the guys and I went out to see what they were up to. Actually I hate boxing and hated the Golden Glove Club, which I was a member of. Not only because my nose was constantly bleeding, but also because I wasn't talented enough, besides which, the whole thing bored me. Sure, it was cool when I was warming up to run in the park with the others, in a loose-fitting tracksuit and bandaged hands, but when it came down to it I went there only because my father insisted on it, saying that a man had to learn how to defend himself.

The two real stars of the Golden Glove Club were Nizar and Adnan. Both must have been six or seven years older than me. Nizar was a tall, lanky, brown-skinned kid. Adnan was quite the opposite: of medium height, massive in frame, and with light ruddy skin that virtually erupted in flames while he was sparring. The highlight of each practice was when the two of them went at it. Master Thomas deliberately always had them go last. At such times bag training ceased, jump ropes were lowered, and all eyes were fixed on the ring.

They must have weighed about the same, but on account of their different shapes, their fighting styles were different too. Nizar used his long arms to keep Adnan at bay and send jabs his way, which Adnan deflected with technical flair as he tried edging close enough so his short arms would be to his advantage instead. Of course that rarely worked. Nizar rarely let him take control. And yet his long arms had a drawback too: since they started off at a distance, Adnan had time to dodge them. Their matches were generally well balanced, often neither of them managing to get in clean shots.

They respected each other, but they didn't hang out with the same crowd. Among the younger kids they had fans who accompanied them to the matches. I was in Nizar's camp. He called me his friend, and since we lived in the same direction, sometimes he gave me a ride home on his motorcycle. I never did understand why he was so kind to me, what such a tough and yet intelligent guy could see in me. Maybe he was good to me out of respect for my father, and maybe he was simply impressed that in contrast with the others I was interested in more serious stuff. Maybe he too had read my review of the rap concert.

When Nizar turned eighteen, he stepped out of our lives. He applied to the police academy and was accepted. No one dared confront him face to face, but behind his back he was seen as a traitor. His name often came up in the dressing room and the billiard room, and never in a positive light. At such times I pretended not to hear the scornful remarks. The notion that my father would have taken on the world for a friend's honor didn't give me a moment's rest. But I wasn't him.

From then on, Adnan became the best. He became the great hope of the Golden Glove Club and an Abu Sa'id Scholarship holder, but then even his career came to end. He was arrested on suspicion of violence against the state. That day the Patriotic Front had called for a demonstration by the Strauss statue. The police came out in full force, blocking off the road leading from the subway to the square with a cordon two men deep. Everyone moving in the Zone was squeezed in there, pressed to the edge of the square. The Front members arrived on a subway train, dressed in black and waving red and white flags. As soon as the head of the first one popped out of the underpass, we began shouting invectives. Police flanked them in front and behind.

"Martin Strauss was wrong, but we are here to defend him from the barbarian statue destroyers," a woman began her speech. They had a megaphone, but all the shouting meant no more than that could be heard. The police locked eyes with us.

That's when the trouble happened. A firework exploded by the feet of one of the police officers. The next one hit his helmet. The crowd was raging, and the police, raising their shields, closed ranks. Meanwhile commotion ensued in the crowd. As I learned later, four cops in civilian clothes who'd blended in with us had grabbed hold of the young man thought to have thrown the fireworks. They tried dragging him off behind the police cordon, but he resisted. He took to shouting, flung himself on the ground, and, clutching the leg of a bench, tried to stay put. The crowd opened up before us. We shouted, berating the cops.

"Fucking traitors!" someone yelled. That told me that the undercover cops were not white. That was logical too, for it would have been hard for someone with creamy white skin to blend in with the crowd.

Passions were aflame, but no one dared touch them. That would have had brutal consequences, as everyone knew full well. The undercover cops didn't bother themselves with us, no, they only continued what they'd begun. One of them sent a fist repeatedly into the ribs of the fellow, who curled up from the blows, allowing the other two cops to hoist him up off the ground. They were all set to head with him toward the police cordon when a hooded figure burst from the wall of people surrounding them. Shoving aside those in his way, he grabbed one of the cops from behind and effortlessly slammed him to the ground. He gave a second cop a thrust too, sending him onto his ass. The cops' colleagues tried to hold back the raging crowd. Meanwhile the cordon of riot police slowly but surely started toward us. Taking advantage of the chaos, the guy who'd thrown the fireworks sprang to his feet and vanished into the crowd. The hooded man followed closed behind. The crowd closed up behind him, everyone raving. But the approaching column of shield-toting riot police was menacing enough so no one felt all that brave. That is when I saw Nizar in the police cordon. It seemed they'd called on the police academy students too. No one else noticed, and I didn't tell anyone he was there.

Adnan was taken away one day later from the training room. He'd been followed all the way home by surveillance cameras, so he didn't have even a chance to get away. He was charged with assaulting an officer of the law. He got six years, but thanks to his good behavior he spent just four years in what was reputedly one of the toughest prisons around. By the time he got out, he was a new man. This was clear from his shaved moustache and thick beard. Of course his cousins continued to be involved with drugs, which was haram. However, Adnan's new benefactor, Sheik Taymullah, was a patient man who figured that sinners mustn't be cast away but, rather, helped so they can see the true path. Accepting this principle, Adnan thus did not break relations with his family but instead looked the other way when it came to those affairs of theirs that Allah did not approve of.

Thus it was that Adnan became a key local figure in the da'wah. He continued doing what he'd been good at even before his prison years. With

Taymullah's help he opened a training room where he held free classes for kids. This was no longer simple boxing, but general self-defense. A Muslim take on Krav Maga, or "*Halal* boxing," as Rami once observed in jest. Under its rules the body was an open target, but it was forbidden to hit the head with force, for the Prophet Muhammad had forbidden brothers from hitting each other's faces. Adnan knew how to talk to kids. Boys aged eight to fourteen adored him, and not even their parents had anything against someone working off their superfluous energy or, at least, wrenching them away from being spellbound by game rooms and smartphones. His ads were posted even on school message boards.

When it came down to it, both Nizar and Adnan were good guys. They might even have been friends, had fate not set them on different paths.

Night was falling fast. I headed home.

2 A misbaha. That's all that was left of my grandfather—with just thirty-one instead of thirty-three worn, amber-hued beads. The silver coins dangling from the end had long been lost, and only a bit of cord was left where the silver chain had once been. But the cord was practically new; it hadn't had the time to fade. Just a week before his death my grandfather had had it sewn on after the beads had gone rolling in thirty-one directions for the umpteenth time.

Grandmother hated this misbaha. Not only because Grandfather was always looking for it on her when he left it somewhere about the flat, but also because before the neighbors she held it unworthy of him, the most respected Abu Hassan. The bottom drawer of the dresser under the TV was strewn with a dozen or more misbahas, one lovelier and more ornamental than the other, that friends and relatives had given to Grandfather for various occasions. But in vain they waited to see if it would be their gift that would take the place of the overused one. Abu Hassan held stubbornly to the weather-beaten string of beads he was used to. He'd gotten it from his brother-in-law one time when he'd traveled home. They'd never been on especially good terms. Mustafa's nature was altogether too fiery for my Grandfather's taste. Why he then insisted on that particular gift, no one knew. He never did talk about it, and when I asked him, he cut me short. There was perhaps some unresolved conflict between the two of them, I think, one that on account of the thousands of kilometers separating them remained unresolved forever. Maybe Grandfather sought absolution in that string of beads.

Alongside the misbaha I inherited two things from Grandfather. One was my name. Though my father was never into traditions, it was for some reason natural to him that his first-born son should bear the name of his own father. This wasn't so important to my uncle, but it's not as if anyone expected it of him anyway. Of course, aside from the old folks no one called my father Abu Nasim, Father of Nasim, as they would have in the

11

old country. If someone among the younger generation called him that all the same, it was seen as affected, as merely cautious bantering directed at the older ones. "Abu Nasim"—which in classical Arabic means "father of breeze," would not have faithfully lived up to the tempestuous nature of the name.

The third thing I inherited from Grandfather was my thin, slightly crooked nose. When I went boxing as a kid, it caused me much annoyance. Even moderate blows made it bleed, and it's a miracle it never broke. Our coach, Master Thomas, was patient, going all out to instill in me at least a basic level of technical knowledge. I left it all behind anyway. Now, looking back, it gives me a good feeling that by giving up boxing I was not copping out of life—as my father then berated me about left and right—but, if I really think of it, I was protecting what I'd inherited from Grandfather.

Grandfather's dad had been born back in the old country, in a small village of olive growers. As the seventh of eight sons he had not had even a chance of buying his own house, which he could really have used, given that he would soon be a father himself. The only prospect for him was Europe—Europa or, as he pronounced it to the end of his life, *Oroba*—whose gates just then had opened wide. As in the case of many thousands of others in the same lot, his family threw together the money for the plane ticket. My great-great-grandmother even sold a bit of the gold jewelry she'd gotten as a dowry so as to give her son a head start in life.

Al-ghurba kurba, being far from home is a torment." So said the village elders. So my great-grandfather did everything in his power to present his emigration back home as a success story. Whenever he could, he sent money home. When he visited home in spring, his bags were always packed full of gifts.

Like most of his compatriots, he began his European career as a construction worker. With six companions he lived for five years in a two-room rented flat, skimping to get by. His sole hobby was going to the movies, once a week when possible. Naturally his favorite actor, by far, was the Egyptian star Omar Sharif, at whose feet not only all the East bowed but, by then, all the West too. The most beautiful women swooned in the actor's arms, and his effortless elegance was imitated by tens of thousands of men across the world, my great-grandfather among them. Though he was never as tall and devastatingly handsome as the star, with his lean frame, thick black hair, and his Omar Sharif–like mustache he bore a vague resemblance to him all the same. He could spew out all the dialogue of *Doctor Zhivago*, though he didn't care as much for *Funny Girl*—not because he had a problem with the film per se, but because afterward he always desired beef and potatoes, which in decent restaurants cost an arm and a leg, and in the flat he rented with the others preparing such fare was a challenge: if someone was cooking at home, he was obliged to offer some to the rest, so in the end, the chef often had little left for himself. Despite all this, my great-grandfather had seen *Funny Girl* at least ten times.

Of course, movie tickets weren't free. Standing in line at the box office, he kept reassuring himself that this was in fact an investment, for by perfecting his language skills he'd eventually get better work too. He wasn't mistaken. He really did learn the language fast, and his bosses asked him more and more often to interpret between them and more recently arrived workers, or those not blessed with such language skills. A year later he became a foreman, which earned him not only more respect but more weekly pay.

The construction industry was booming. A couple of years later my great-grandfather's boss called him into his office and told him he'd like to expand the business and wanted him to take on the task of managing the workers from then on. Thus it was that what was only a dream for most of his colleagues became a reality for my great-grandfather. He rented his own flat in the city's blue-collar neighborhood, and on the fifth anniversary of his arrival in Europe he had his wife and three children join him: Uncle Abdelkader, my grandfather, and Aunt Amal. My grandfather was then three years old.

Things went well for my great-grandfather. With the money he'd saved up, some eleven years after his arrival he bought a plot of land back home at the edge of the village, and he began building. Since it was his brother who supervised the workers, the project was accompanied by plenty of family drama, arguments, accusations, and reconciliations. Finally the house—or, as my great-grandfather called it, the mansion—was done. An imposing, four-bedroom home. With ashlar fence, white walls, and thick wooden doors, it was a beacon from far away amid the flat-roofed hovels of the neighboring olive groves. Its roof was ornamented with tiles—back then, the only such house in the village. This was in part so he could show off, and in part so my great-grandfather, when glancing upon them, could wax nostalgic about his years in Europe.

The house was now done, but my great-grandfather still wasn't in a rush to move home, for there was yet something missing for happiness: a Mercedes.

"There are two types of Arabs," he often said, "those who have a Mercedes and those who will have one." This was back then the dream of every Arab in Europe. Back home, at first only government ministers and mayors had such cars, while everyday folk looked upon those wondrous vehicles kicking up the dust on the roads with a mix of amazement and respect. When his wife was nagging him or he had to work overtime, my great-grandfather closed his eyes for a moment and imagined what it would be like to roll down the driveway of his mansion, drive down the main street of his village, and, lowering the window, receive the greetings of acquaintances and strangers alike. Not condescendingly, and not with his nose turned up, but in a friendly way, with all due dignity as befits a venerable gentleman of means.

The dream finally did come true. Four years after acquiring that plot of land, not long before his forty-eighth birthday, my great-grandfather parted ways with his worn Renault and surprised himself with a lovely black incarnation of the queen of cars. His happiness was unbounded. He saw a divine hand at work in the fact that the car rolled off the assembly line precisely in the year he arrived in Europe. "Thanks to Allah, time has not gotten the best of either one of us!" he said proudly to relatives back home.

My great-grandmother was completely beside herself. Thinking of their children, who would soon be of marriageable age, she shouted that instead of the car they could have bought at least two more plots of land back home. But once the congratulations of not only their neighbors but family back home reached her too, she reconciled herself to the fact.

My great-grandfather always left early for work and mostly got home late. Grandfather's fate was that of a neglected middle child. It was above all thanks to his calm demeanor and his primary school teacher, Mr. Bob, that he didn't lose his way and come to hate learning. He went to a school in the district, and there were only a couple of foreigners in his class. He had no common ground with the white kids, and yet he didn't find his place among the rowdy foreign boys either. That he wasn't bothered was thanks to his older brother, Abdelkader, and Abdelkader's friends, who from time to time stepped in to set the smart alecks straight.

The newly founded mosque represented Grandfather's sole island of peace. Every Saturday afternoon my great-grandfather took his sons to Koran classes with Sheik Saleh, who'd just arrived from the old country. There, among the other kids, in straight rows on the rug, they repeated the Koranic verses after the sheik. Abdelkader sat through this obligatory weekend program only on account of the sheik's cane and his father's sternness. By contrast, my grandfather took pleasure in memorizing the shorter surahs, or chapters, of the Koran, which then my great-grandfather, his chest swelling with pride, had him recite before the neighbors.

In the course of visits home every summer my great-grandfather took pains to project the image of the model family. The relatives and villagers followed with watchful eyes to see if he was raising his children to be good Muslims in Europe, with its loose morals as movies made clear. But my grandfather's knowledge of the Koran cast aside all doubts. His cousins were of course jealous. While they were seemingly kind to him, only on adult commands did they invite him to play. Not only in Europe did Grandfather remain a stranger, but in the land of his birth as well.

My great-grandfather was among the very few who finally did move home. At the age of fifty-five he resigned from the company. He sat his wife, his daughter, Amal, and his youngest son, Ahmed, who had been born in Europe and was by then thirteen, on a plane. He packed his Mercedes onto a boat, and he waved good-bye to Europe. He'd prepared to draw on his experiences and the money he'd saved to open a modern construction company with his brother, one in which his sons too could then take part. This of course took time. My grandfather and Abdelkader did not go along with them. My grandfather was twenty-two; his older brother was twenty-four. Soon it would be time for them to get married, to redeem girls from their parents at the village's good households for expensive gifts and dowries. My great-grandparents felt it would be better for everyone if their sons earned for themselves the costs of their weddings. Borrowing money from relatives would, after all, have been unworthy of the proud owner of a Mercedes.

It was my great-grandmother who assumed direction of the process. She carefully put aside the money her sons sent home from month to month, and a couple of years later she had my great-grandfather buy a large, subdividable plot of land with a two-bedroom, one-story house. It wasn't too big or too lovely, but just enough so the parents of the village's eligible young daughters would see that the family was doing well.

As the older son, Abdelkader was the first in line. No sooner had his parents purchased the land and house than his peace ended. My great-grandmother initiated an all-out assault. Not a single phone call unfolded without the subject of marriage coming up. She was constantly giving him reports on the most beautiful eligible girls from the village's very best families, girls whose parents would give their daughters' hand in marriage to posh young men the likes of Abdelkader, men with exceptional prospects, which in Abdelkader's case was thanks to the fact that my great-grandfather's company had in the meantime begun operations.

To my great-grandmother's and the family's great dismay, however, Abdelkader was indifferent to thoughts of marriage. But of course my great-grandfather, who for his part was familiar the lives of single men in Europe, knew the cause of this indifference. "God knows," my great-grandmother would say, shaking her head, "I don't understand the boy. Europe has made him batty." At such times my great-grandfather just hemmed and hawed.

By the time Abdelkader turned twenty-eight, my great-grandmother was fuming. She tried persuading the boy by turns through rational arguments and blackmail. At other times she pretended to have given in, only to then carry out yet another frontal assault with renewed vigor. In vain. Finally it wasn't rare for her to stage an asthma attack during the usual weekly phone conversations: "*Wallahi ana mesh radyana annak!*"—God knows I'm not satisfied with you—she gasped in a trailing voice on such occasions. Abdelkader said he was sorry about it. He looked for excuses and made promises, but finally everything stayed the same.

"*Wallahi bighdob aleek*"—God knows I'll get angry with you—my great-grandmother would finally say to Abdelkader. The threat was her trump card. But the promised anger never did come to pass. As impetuous as she could be, she was a smart woman. She knew that parental anger was a two-edged sword. When a parent back home in the village got openly angry, that had serious consequences for the life of the son or daughter. In small part because in Islam, unconditional obedience to one's parents was a divine law, and in large part because that's what society thought too. A father's or mother's anger was in fact a curse. No one trusted a person who turned against even his own parents. At such times relatives, neighbors, and friends would step forward as peacemakers, seeking to bring the child to his senses and rein him in. The parents almost always won. But parental anger did not extend to Europe. My great-grandmother instinctively knew that putting her foot down once and for all could easily mean losing her firstborn son.

And so she finally turned to outside help. She kept at my great-grandfather until one day he picked up the phone and called the imam of the mosque in Europe. Sheik Saleh listened to his complaint. He reassured my great-grandfather and then sent Abu Barhum, the stocky, seriously balding mosque attendant, on his way to invite my grandfather and Abdelkader for tea.

They had no idea what to make of the unusual gesture. Since the invitation was for the sheik's office after Friday prayer, Abdelkader had no choice but to sit through the *khutba* too. "Your heaven lies under the feet of your mother," Sheik Saleh began, quoting the Prophet. He bided his time pronouncing the last word, and then stroked his graying beard and passed his eyes over the congregation. Abdelkader squirmed in his seat. His discomfort grew. This khutba was about mothers, about the respect and the love they are due, and children's obligations toward them. With *ahadith*, Koranic passages, and the arguments of great religious scholars Sheik Saleh proved that on Judgment Day Allah would call everyone to account for their behavior toward their mothers.

Not long afterward my grandfather and Abdelkader were in the sheik's office. Several armchairs were arranged in an oval, and Saleh occupied the one positioned to be the main one. To his right, as the older brother, sat

Abdelkader, and beside him was my grandfather. To the sheik's left was an apprentice with a mealymouthed smile. Abu Barhum walked round with a tray full of tea, while Saleh, not sparing on formal decorum, extended them awkwardly drawn-out greetings. Finally he got down to the subject at hand. His eyes half-closed, referring again and again to his khutba, at length he quoted the Koran's commands to children. "Do you understand what Allah says about mothers?" he finally asked, turning to Abdelkader. He understood full well but was not about to give in. One word led to another until finally, to the bewilderment of my grandfather, the sheik, and the still-smiling apprentice, Abdelkader announced that if this were to continue he would get on a bus and not get off until London. Neither his mother nor the sheik would see him any longer, and he, Abdelkader, would talk things over himself with Allah. Seeing that the situation was unsalvageable, Saleh gave a big sigh of retreat and sent them on their way. Abdelkader was sulking all the way home.

Not even three days had passed when Abu Barhum looked up my grandfather at his workplace.

"Sheik Saleh wants to speak to you again."

"It is Allah who sees Abdelkader's soul," my grandfather began by way of excuse, but the mosque attendant waved a hand and said, "Just with you this time."

Grandfather was not enthused at the invitation. He too had had quite enough of my great-grandmother's incessant badgering. His mother was, after all, a stubborn woman for whom *inshallah* was not enough. With the close of each weekly phone conversation it invariably took Grandfather some time to calm down. At such times he tried to forget about the promise he'd made a couple of minutes earlier that, yes, he would naturally speak with his older brother. The last thing he desired was to have the sheik, too, use him as a stick.

The following Friday my grandfather headed off glumly to the mosque. He found that his legs did not carry him across the park, as usual, but took the longer route, toward the row of shops. Once at the mosque he could hardly pay attention to the khutba.

Soon Grandfather was sitting to the right of the sheik and across from that apprentice with his imbecilic smile. Soon Abu Barhum arrived too, carrying a round tray with three cups of steaming hot tea. The usual, drawn-out greetings over, Saleh finally got down to the matter at hand.

"Allah has hardened your older brother's heart, my son," he said in a woeful voice. "Your mother's heart will break. Your father's face will blacken before the relatives and the village."

"Your older brother is walking a false path," he went on, shaking his head. "May Allah strengthen his faith." After pausing for a couple of seconds, he continued with sudden cheer: "But your heart, *Subhan Allah*, is gentle and pure. And the merciful Allah rewards the pure-hearted"— again he paused for effect before resuming with an even more festive tone. "So I have good news for you. The religion does not prohibit the younger son from being the first to marry."

Grandfather nearly choked on his tea. The sheik paused for him to finish coughing then, not even waiting for his reply, went on.

"The key to your own and your family's future is in your hands. And Allah loves and rewards obedient children. Your parents will choose the most wonderful girl for you; an obedient, God-fearing girl who will be your faithful pillar, and with whom, if Allah wants that as well, you will be in heaven too."

In his shock Grandfather couldn't even reply.

"But I don't want to move home yet!" Grandfather finally burst out. But Sheik Saleh had been anticipating this excuse.

"Why would the two of you need to move home right away, my son?" he asked, emphasizing the plural as he opened his arms wide. "Does not a good wife follow her husband to the ends of the earth?"

To this Grandfather did not know how to respond. He had not yet given thought to marriage, but neither would he have done everything in his power, like Abdelkader, to avoid it. And since Grandfather was not much of a womanizer, marriage would bring him concrete advantages. Moreover, it would also give him an excuse to move from the flat he rented jointly with his older brother.

As a prudent man, he asked for time to think about it. That was his mistake. The genie got out of the bottle, and the forces whirling around it proved unstoppable. To himself, Sheik Saleh regarded the conversation as a success, and in sending Grandfather on his way he said that with Allah's help he would notify the parents, too, that nothing stood in the way of a younger son marrying first.

Grandfather got home to find that Abdelkader, quite unlike him, was already there. No sooner had Grandfather opened the door to the flat than his older brother's head popped out of the kitchen. After a suspiciously sweet greeting to his younger brother, Abdelkader led Grandfather into the kitchen, sat him down at the table, and had him tell what happened. Only the suppressed smile faintly visible at the corners of his mouth betrayed the superhuman effort with which Abdelkader sought to conceal the happiness that threatened to erupt from him at any instant. When Grandfather got round to the sheik's proposal, Abdelkader could resist no longer. He sprang up, hugged his younger brother, and showered him with kisses before knocking over a pot he'd left at the edge of the sink, then whirled round with him in a dance. From then on he only called Grandfather 'aris, or "groom."

Of course, Sheik Saleh's mission did not end with that. He had yet to sell his client on the compromise. After brooding for a while he decided that instead of trying to persuade my great-grandfather as his wife shrieked away in the background, he would call the imam in their village and ask him to take matters in hand.

The imam paid a personal visit to the family. For the esteemed guest's arrival my great-grandmother had her daughter and grand-nieces scour the guest room floor and dust off the gold-armed armchairs, and she sent off her youngest son, Ahmed, to the market for fresh fruit. My great-grandfather, his older brothers, and one of their uncles were all waiting at the mansion at the agreed-upon time. In honor of the occasion the family members wore festive *jellabiyas*, while my great-grandfather—faithful to the fashion of *Oroba*, the Europe where he had once lived—wore immaculately ironed, pleated pants, suspenders, a dress shirt, and a sport coat. The sheik arrived precisely on time, accompanied by his apprentice. The relatives awaited him by the front gate. While shaking and kissing hands they all entered the guest room, whose wall my great-grandmother had had Ahmed hang the house's loveliest Koranic tapestry.

My great-grandmother knocked on the double door that opened to the rest of the home to signal that the refreshments were ready. Ahmed went round serving black coffee, and then brought in top-heavy trays that had been placed by the door and were full of fruits and roast nuts. The family members greeted the sheik with drawn-out, circuitous courtesies, which he bore with dignified calmness. The formalities out of the way, the sheik now looked upon my great-grandfather and set out on a lengthy presentation about how the Koran and the Sunnah bid not only children to obedience but also parents toward their children. The circle of men's faces nodded enthusiastically. After acknowledging the agreement, the sheik took a small turn to point out that while a good parent can advise a child he cannot force him to do anything. Especially not to get married. The double door shook. As if not even noticing, the sheik went on. Weaving in further religious references, he went on to argue that not a single servant of Allah is obliged to obey a command or constraint from another son of man that contradicts the will of Allah. And a child who wishes not to marry is not obliged to marry on parental command. Knitting his brows, my great-grandfather fidgeted with his teacup.

"But I have good news, Abu Abdelkader," said the sheik, turning to my great-grandfather. "Religion does not mandate that it is the oldest son who must marry first. "Especially not"—and here he raised an index finger toward the sky—"if in waiting to do so he would delay the marriage of his own younger brother, who, to the utmost satisfaction of Allah and his parents, can hardly wait to tie his life with a good Muslim woman."

The male coterie nodded yet again. My great-grandfather just stared into space. After thoroughly grounding the subject in religious law, the sheik slurped his tea. Then he proceeded to approach the matter from a practical perspective by detailing the wonderful things he'd heard about my grandfather. He took pains to emphasize what a transgression it would be to sentence such an exceptional boy to waiting. And considering that Abdelkader faced great prospects in London, prospects that promised even more money but whose realization were yet uncertain, it was particularly justified that the younger boy should marry first.

"Would it not be difficult for the young spouse if Abdelkader took her to a place where neither relatives nor friends could help her in raising the children she would bear?" So came the sheik's rhetorical question, to which the men nodded in unison.

The matter was settled. My great-grandfather had no choice as head of the family but to pronounce the last word. This was not easy, however. His wife fought him for two nights straight. On the third day the phone rang. It was Abdelkader. He spoke for a long time with his father, and then asked for his mother. In a teary voice he begged for forgiveness, and then explained just how excited my grandfather was to be waiting for them to find him a wife. He promised that he would indeed really be the next, and at the same time he offered to gift to my grandfather the house and the entire plot of land they had bought with both their money. Moved by the generous offer, my great-grandmother accepted his apology. She did not realize that Abdelkader had killed three birds with one stone: as a generous brother he had reinforced his reputation in the village, he had weaseled his way out of having to pay yet more gifts, and finally—his foremost achievement—since he now had nothing left to his name in the village, he'd pushed off his own marriage to an imponderable future.

The sheik also had a personal interest in the wedding happening sooner, for he had a widowed younger sister whose daughter had just stepped in line as the next to be married off. As for my great-grandfather, thanks to his nascent company and of course his Mercedes, by then he counted among the village's most distinguished men. The girl's late father had been the son of the village's famous mukhtar, who had carved out his reputation for generations to come back in the days of the fight for independence. Binding the two young people together would thus yield an alliance of the old and new elite; it would be a marriage of prestige and capital. And not even my great-grandmother could object to that.

Her struggle had not ended, however. The night before the wedding she had my grandfather agree to move home before long. "Inshallah," he replied, passing the buck to the Almighty.

Abdelkader never did marry. Nor did Grandfather ever say whether his brother had had a girlfriend. Not long afterward Abdelkader moved to another city, and from then on they met only rarely. Grandfather always changed the subject when I asked him about it.

After the wedding my great-grandmother's weekly phone calls re-
verted to being the familiar psychological warfare. In contrast with her,
however, Allah must not have wanted my grandfather to move back home.
The marriage had indeed brought him luck. To marry the grandchild of
a mukhtar counted as special not only back home but also in the Muslim community in Europe. Meanwhile, thanks to President Strauss, he
got citizenship too. My grandfather, Abu Hassan, became a distinguished
man, and work as a trucker now seemed unworthy of him. My great-
grandfather telephoned his old acquaintance Abu Radwan, with whom
he'd arrived in Europe on the same plane so many years before. Abu Radwan was the district's leading grocery wholesaler. He'd been the first to
recognize that workers missed not only their parents, their families, and
the air of home, but also the flavors of their native lands. This recognition
had made him a wealthy man. In the course of his trips home, at first he
brought back spices, bulgur, and pepper paste only for his friends. At that
time he gave it so little thought, he took orders and brought back a whole
shipping container full of goods. Soon he rented a warehouse, and then he
opened a store, and twenty years later he had a whole chain of stores—and
restaurants as well.

Abu Radwan, then, offered my grandfather a job: deputy manager of
his newly opened market. For the sake of family peace, the top manager
was his own younger brother. Grandfather was tasked with carrying out
responsibilities instead of the half-wit little brother: maintaining contact
with city hall and overseeing the rental of spaces to vendors. They rented
the market space itself from the municipal government, and the vendors'
main supplier was, of course, Abu Radwan.

Before long the market ballooned into a veritable constant fair, where
alongside fruits and vegetables you could buy clothes, household supplies,
and even antiques. Grandfather's standing grew along with the market's.
He did favors and managed various affairs, and the vendors did their utmost to be on Abu Hassan's good side. This was his domain.

But the flat he rented not too far from the district's center, where he
lived in with his family, was not. His marriage to my grandmother was a
real tragedy. Summer, when Grandmother passed a portion of her days in

the park and in front of the building with other housewives, was almost peaceful. But when the cold set in, Grandmother became unbearable too. Nothing was good enough for her.

Evenings were calmer when my grandfather came home with all sorts of gifts from the market vendors. With pleasure Grandmother received the objects, which she then used to build up her own domain. She had a natural talent for that. As a child she had seen her grandmother, as the mukhtar's wife, manage the lives of the village housewives. And so my grandmother was a clever steward of the various objects: she gave the pair of child's shoes to Umm Ahmed, the manicure kit to Umm Bilal, and the artificial flowers to Sulafa. Of course, she set aside the loveliest, most valuable gifts and now and then sent them home to my great-grandmother, who could thus raise her favorite son and daughter-in-law to the heights of storybook heroes, who were thinking of the family from afar and would soon return home. Because return home, they would, inshallah.

Grandfather concluded that perhaps he could better his wife's mood if she had a loved one nearby, whether a sibling or some other relative. Fortunately there were plenty of options to choose from back home. The most promising candidate was her youngest little brother, the twenty-year-old Mustafa, who was old enough to travel—and motivated enough, for he was facing the prospect of marriage himself and needed money. Grandfather stoked his contacts and sent an invitation letter, and before long Mustafa could indeed board a plane. Grandmother was happy for a couple of weeks, then her hard nature got the better of her short-lived peace of mind.

Grandfather found work for Mustafa in a used clothing distribution center. His task was to sort out incoming donations. Well-to-do citizens left clothes they'd grown tired of at collection centers, and in doing so they supported the work of the SACHIA (Struggle against Children's Hunger in Africa) Foundation. The clothes arrived in big green sacks the workers opened and sorted through. First women's, men's, and children's clothing had to be separated, and then came sorting by quality. Most of the clothes were in excellent condition. Respectable citizens of the West did not give rags for the cause of starving children. Mustafa was responsible for the first phase of sorting. Standing by that table on which the sacks arrived was for him like panning for gold. A year later his residence permit expired. Mustafa traveled home with four huge sacks of clothes, and Grandfather sent the other five after him later on. Out of gratitude Mustafa sang the praises of Abu Hassan and his wondrous European career throughout the village.

Grandmother was left alone once again, and if possible, she was even more unbearable. Her hard nature was understandable. She'd always had big ambitions relative to the other women of the village. As a young girl her model was her uncle, who had studied to be a doctor and thus became one of the village's most respected men. Grandmother, who also wanted to be a doctor, was furious to have belonged to the poor side of the family, and that while her male cousins, whom she'd never regarded as great minds, had been able to go to college, and her brothers had learned trades, while she, being a girl, had been taken out of school after finishing four grades. After her wedding she, too, arrived in Europe full of dreams, but she soon came face to face with reality. She spoke no language other than Arabic and had no employment skills, so she didn't stand a chance of finding a job. While my grandfather became an esteemed member of the community, practically speaking, she spent her life between the walls of their flat and within the insular, villagelike community of the tower blocks, left only to bask in her husband's glory. Nothing could abate her frustration.

It was into this world that my father and his older brother were born.

As with my grandfather, so too my father was the second child. They might even have understood each other, but life did not let their relationship be cloudless. My father really did grow up like a weed. Grandfather woke at the crack of dawn, prayed, went to work, and came home only late at night. Grandmother meanwhile, as a housewife, could not really offer him useful advice about life. And yet Grandfather got word of every instance of his younger son's roughhousing. At first he heard about his dubious goings-on from teachers, and later often from the chief of police, with whom, as the market manager, he was on good terms. His favorite was his firstborn son, Hassan, who in contrast with his younger brother walked the appointed path: he graduated from a technical college and found work in the auto industry.

Father stood his ground in school and on the streets. Unlike his big brother, who was of a calmer nature, he was constantly getting into fights and often played hooky. It was around then that our district came to be known as the Zone, not least on account of troublemakers like my father. Supposedly the not-too-imaginative name stemmed from an occasion on which someone heard a police officer say into his crackling radio, "I am in the Zone." The fact that other, worse districts were to later rise up out of the earth no longer helped restore our district's reputation. All told, the Zone was not as menacing a place as reports made it out to be. As in other residential districts, human beings lived here—full citizens of the Pan-European Federation who worked, went to school, got sick, got better, had fun, and sat about in cafés. And, yes, sometimes they also went to the mosque.

Grandfather was angry with my father for not finishing college. Father figured that the numbers were on his side. Grandfather jointly ran several businesses and other concerns with his boss's nephew, who later became well known as Abu Sa'id. Naturally Grandfather, too, eventually got a Mercedes.

No matter how big a guy my father was on the street, before Grandfather he hid his tail between his legs and silently bore his father's outbursts. Though he smoked his first cigarette at fourteen and was a chain smoker by his twenties, he never lit up in front of his parents. When he was sitting with his friends on benches and he noticed my grandfather approaching, with a guilty conscience he flung away the butt. During big family lunches in his youth, he and his big brother would steal away to the stairwell for a smoke. This is how things remained even once I was born and he himself had become the head of a household. As for the frustrations he'd inherited from his father, he successfully passed them down to his own son.

My grandfather's and father's problematical relationship was an open secret. Still, no one forced Grandfather to face up to this, neither in the mosque nor in his favorite café, where aging gentlemen would watch the TV news coming to them via the satellite dish. They thoroughly discussed wars, business and economic news, elections, and coups. Friendships were born and died, and then they were born again on account of such important world affairs. But they never spoke of their personal crises. They all walked in the same shoes in any case. They'd gotten from life what they'd always yearned for: money, a flat, a car, and the illusion of respect from those back home, but they'd lost that which, as they grew older, they were coming to regard as more important than anything else: their own children.

I was Grandfather's favorite. He always took me everywhere and was never angry with me. Maybe he wanted to restore through me all that had gone off track with his own younger son. It seems that my father didn't mind this. Similar to Grandfather, he could reason it away to himself, seeking absolution through his only son for his disobedience toward his own father.

Grandfather's plans to move back home finally went to shreds with the death of my great-grandmother. His nephew and his family moved into the house Grandfather had there. Though they'd always insisted that they were just taking care of the place, on his visits home Grandfather felt more and more like a guest who was being put up with. His cousins, who still meant something to him, died one after another. As for the young people, he told us that they were no longer any different from those in Europe. The world, which in truth had never been his, now turned forever foreign to him. And yet he finally did move home. Like everyone, he too wanted to have his final resting place in the earth of his bygone home. I was fourteen when he died. I was in bed with the flu, which was why I couldn't go to his funeral. What hurt much more than my having to miss the ceremony, however, was that in the year or two before his death, we'd grown distant from each other. It was my fault, but a teenage boy is more interested in everything than spending his afternoons with his grandfather. He often phoned me, asking if I'd go along with him to the lookout tower. By way of excuse I always came up with some terribly important business I couldn't put off, promising that I'd go up there with him next time, inshallah. Then this next time never came to pass. I know he wasn't angry with me for not going along, but I could never forgive myself.

A couple of years later Grandmother followed him in moving home. We stayed here.

3

The concrete was still pouring out heat. No longer was the sun beating down though, and the breeze from the forested slopes had begun sweeping away the sweltering air that had been suffocating the settlement. On scorching hot, late August days it was around this time that the locals would venture out of the coolness of their homes, cafés, and the plaza. Old Ashraf and his assistant closed up the large sun umbrellas with their Coca-Cola logos that they'd earlier set up on the square in front of their kebab stand, and the benches in the adjacent park began filling with people. Women in hijabs pushed strollers, families were picnicking on the grass, and old men were playing backgammon on the benches in front of tea shops in the row of shops beside the park.

We were sixteen years old then. Rami and I were in the habit of meeting in front of our tower block, walking from there down the length of the row of shops, and then across the park to the playground, well away from the picnickers and the young men who were busy working out. A firewall ran along two opposite sides of the playground, while the two other facing sides had fencing along them; the gate to the park had long before been torn from the once-green fence, which was as tall as a person. By then the smaller kids had completely dropped away, so kids our ages took complete control of the territory. We couldn't have found a better hangout if we'd tried. Not only did the overgrown bushes along the fence provide exceptional opportunities for pissing all over them, but their leaves hid from the eyes of the uninitiated all that unfolded on the playground.

Rami and I zigzagged between the empty sandbox and the metal jungle gyms with peeling paint as we approached the benches, where the others were waiting for us. It might have been an average Friday evening. But it was *tour day*. One of those special occasions on which we ventured out of the Zone's familiar sense of security. This time a concert was the excuse. No need to imagine some big, thunderous affair: a couple of local guys had organized a rap party in a warehouse rented for the occasion. Though the music didn't particularly interest me, the tours promised

28

excitement of a sort that was invariably a subject of conversation even months later.

Five guys were waiting for us on two benches that had been turned around. Snatches of Marwan's voice filtered through the speaker in bellowing bass tones.

"I'll bet you ten to one he's talking about some woman," said Rami, giving me a nudge.

I would have been crazy to bet on this. It was completely obvious that Marwan would have been going on to the others about only that. Two days earlier, with emojis aplenty, he'd posted on his profile, "Mission accomplished." If that hadn't been enough, his lascivious expression, his exaggerated gestures, and the others' incredulous and yet curious glances left not a shred of doubt that he was bragging to the guys about his latest episode of whoring about or, as he put it, his "project." At most, a bet might have ridden on the chick's age or color, and of course on how much she'd cost. As for her being a hooker, of that there was no doubt. It was common knowledge that Marwan's wooing technique was insufficiently refined for him to pick up a more normal girl. His method generally reached its limits with him either wolf whistling from the window of his tower block or else giving compliments to gals walking by the open window of his uncle's kebab restaurant, while taking breaks with the excuse of sharpening the large knife he used to slice meat off the rotisserie.

He couldn't keep it up for long though, because old Ashraf quickly realized that it did good neither for his business nor for his good relations with the neighbors if his cretin of a nephew was showering compliments on the local young ladies from under his business sign. After all, those ladies had fathers and, mostly, older brothers too. One of them, in fact— precisely four days after Marwan began his job—called Ashraf's attention to the fact that Marwan, were he not Ashraf's nephew, would already be lying in the sludge along the riverbank with his very own cock in his mouth. Amid profuse apologies, Ashraf thanked the visitor for the friendly warning. That night, having entrusted his business partner to lock up the place, and with a big portion of kebab, flatbread, salad, falafel, and a cup of *ayran* in hand, he paid a visit to his older sister, Marwan's mother. Firing a family member was a rather awkward matter. Especially if the mother of that family member was called Umm Marwan, who always had been known as a tempestuous woman. After her husband's untimely death saw her saddled with the job of raising two unbridled boys, her demeanor became decidedly masculine. Ashraf's anguish finally proved unnecessary. Thoroughly appreciating the problem, Umm Marwan not only did not get angry with Ashraf, but she bombarded him with apologies while shouting her son's head off with choice curses as he arrived home for having swept his blessed good uncle into such an unpleasant situation. As an example she cited Marwan's dad, who'd worked hard all his life, never so much as looked at women—other than Umm Marwan, of course—and was now no doubt spitting a big one from heaven down onto the son of a dog. Marwan sneaked into his room with his tail between his legs. When it came down to it, he wasn't sorry that this was how things unfolded. It's not as if it was that much to his taste in any case, sweating away in the sweltering summer heat amid the greasy steam emanating from the rotisserie. Moreover, to ensure unmitigated peace, Ashraf handed him an envelope containing a full month's pay for four days of work. Marwan took hold of the money, and when, after a quick count, it hit him that it was enough for no less than five full extra "missions"—moreover, with mid- to high-level girls with their own pads—an ethereal bliss shot through his soul and, of course, his body.

Marwan invariably had two moments of pleasure: when the thing happened and later, when he gave an account of it among a big circle of friends. So expressively did he reconstruct all that fucking, so elaborately did he choose his words, his metaphors, that every fiber of his being exuded this: that he was reliving an idealized version of each and every one. Though the stories varied in their details, each ended the same way. Marwan came, saw, and then conquered as befits a superhero before finally, transfigured, taking his leave from the girl, with her trembling legs and her grateful expression.

When Rami and I arrived, Marwan happened to be giving a play-by-play of the hours he'd spent with a Ukrainian girl he'd even posted on his profile, as it turned out. He didn't even flinch on our arrival. As we quietly exchanged high fives with the others, not for a moment did our eyes slip off Marwan, who, with weird wriggling and even weirder sounds, was busy demonstrating how he'd finally given the girl one hell of an orgasm.

"I swear that even her voice was like that politician cunt's."

"Sandra Bollen?" I asked, suddenly looking up.

"That blond, conservative cunt," he added. I too had been thinking of her. Not that I'd ever liked blondes, but Bollen was my fetish. Her black-framed glasses provided a titillating counterbalance to her lush lips and crooked, impish smile. I would turn rock-hard just watching her speeches.

"She moaned just the same for the client before you and after you," said Husam with a laugh. "Even louder for anyone who shells out an extra ten euros!"

Marwan was offended to the bone. "Don't believe it, do you, *dickwad*? Why then, be amazed, disbeliever!" With a wide grin he pulled his cell phone from a pocket. "Every minute is worth gold."

Amid ardent murmuring the group looked on as Marwan fiddled about a bit and then started the video.

"The picture wasn't too clear, but it would have cost an extra twenty euros for her to her let herself be filmed," he said indignantly. "So instead I carefully folded my pants on the armchair, and the top of my phone was just sticking out of its pocket, so I could record the whole thing. For free!" He grinned triumphantly.

All six of us huddled together to better see the screen. We were disappointed. The recording was worth just as much as it had cost. Sixteen megapixels, sure, but all that could be seen of it was some grayish black blob that, even with Marwan's expressive narration, did not reveal who was doing what, and how.

"Bollen my ass," said Husam, breaking out in laughter. "For thirty-five euros all you got was a sack of coal in a burka!" With a dismissive wave of the hand, Marwan then slipped the phone back in his pocket, as if certain that his audience was not up to the standards of the performance

The concert began at 10 PM. We would have had plenty of time to spare, but the point was not the concert but the trip there. We were getting ready to leave. A guy in his early twenties, Riad, who was among the organizers, whistled out a call to depart, and the rest of us scrambled to our feet and headed off in a noisy group across the park toward the metro station.

There were eighteen of us in all. Rowdiness was guaranteed. Though we called such outings beyond the Zone tours, in fact we had more in common with swarming bees. We headed toward the city in packs to show the world how tough we were. The disorientation that such trips meant always turned into aggression sooner or later. Not that we ever planned anything particular, but in the security of the crowd even the more peaceful among us easily went wild.

Of course, I'd be lying if I claimed that only in packs of twenty or so did we all get up our courage. Some tough dudes among us stood their ground even if they were on their own when trouble struck. True, this would happen only within the Zone, where they were known as men of action. How they behaved when on their own outside of the Zone, who was to say? There were some who, I could well imagine, would charge right into a concrete wall.

One thing is certain though: no matter how tough he may be, a fellow is not inclined to make trouble on his own. If he winds up in some humiliating situation and no one he knows is there to see it, he'd rather slink away as if nothing happened at all. At most, maybe he'll work off the frustration bottled up inside him by lashing out at someone else later. The situation is no better in pairs. Not enough gravitational force drawing you in. The more aggressive of the two is held back by the more cautious. Even if conflict does start unfolding, two people can interpret a situation in two different ways, and before you know it, the rowdier one hesitates. In short, the more aggressive dude often lets himself be talked out of making trouble. Since there is someone on hand to hold him back, and his self-respect comes through without a scratch, he settles for just squabbling. When there are three, things hang in the balance. At such times it's always the makeup of the group that decides things. If there are two alphas who are subconsciously rivals, anything can happen. Not that a threesome counts for much. In Arabic we have the dual, a grammatical form for two, just an ending you add to the noun in order to double it. If it's more than two, you have to use the plural, which is pretty ambiguous. For my part, I always felt that the plural shouldn't start until five, or at least no less than four.

It's not as if most of the guys were aggressive in their everyday lives. I never did understand what Husam, a good student, was doing among us.

Even Rami was a decidedly peaceful sort. Six feet tall and weighing in at some two hundred pounds, with a stocky, muscular frame, he was among the biggest, thanks to which he commanded respect even while rarely raising his voice, and even more rarely resorting to physical violence. When he happened to be there, the smaller guys, knowing they had a certain backup, charged bravely at foes larger than they were. Hence Rami was more of a "psychological accomplice," as a prosecutor was to put so nicely some time later. Of course, even he sometimes struck out too.

"I only beat the weak," Rami once revealed to me with a self-satisfied smile. "Even I give respect to the stronger ones. The smaller guys should respect me too, if they don't want a beating!"

Before the others, even Rami attended painstakingly to his own image. But he had no secrets before me. When we were touring with the other guys, the two of us often felt the whole thing was awkward. When some grass-, alcohol-, or adrenaline-dazed kid did something crazy—pissed all over the side of a bus stop or picked on a pedestrian, we stole a glance at each other, signaling our mutual opinion by burning our eyes skyward amid quiet sighs. At other times we walked among the others, hooded and staring at the ground, trying to be invisible that way. After a while Husam drifted to us too. Why were we there with the others anyway? We didn't always know for sure. Maybe because it was good. And maybe because we needed it.

One thing was certain: when it came down to it, no one liked to venture out of the Zone on his own. The river—even if it was only about four yards wide—separated our home from the outside world like a national border. Anyone who wanted to could live out his life without ever venturing out into other parts of the city. Those who could got work inside the Zone, and if that didn't pan out, they commuted between the Zone and their workplace, cutting their route to the shortest distance and shortest time possible.

Things were relatively in order until we reached Station 34. But as soon as we left the residential zone, we entered another world. There were more and more smug-looking characters in suits or ironed, checkered shirts. They didn't say a word to us or give us a second look. A few of our guys swore up and down that they were scared of us and hated us. Such sentiments fanned the flames of the rage. Though at such times I always nodded in agreement, in fact I figured that some of those mean mugs simply couldn't care less about us, while others among them really did despise us. No matter what the truth was, my gait, which back at home in the Zone I'd honed to radiate virtually unadulterated confidence, all but collapsed out there. I didn't even dare to fling away a cigarette butt, and in stores I stood in line either at the self-service checkouts or at registers where the cashier had skin similar to mine or darker.

We reached the subway in no time. After a few final drags of our reefers, one after another we jumped over the turnstile. Not bothering one bit with the "Please stand to the right" announcement, we crowded onto the escalator, noisily blocking the way down. Only a couple of folks were moving upward opposite us. Even I was almost caught up in the mood. But then my eyes froze. From down below an old Turk donning a flat cap was approaching with his husky, white-veiled wife. The woman was staring angrily at our group. Not moving her head one bit, she began to pass her eyes over us contemptuously at the speed of the escalator. The other guys evidently didn't bother with her at all. My armor was not thick enough though. When her eyes had reached Samer, who was a couple of steps below me, suddenly I turned toward Rami and, not that I recall any longer what I said, but I tried asking him some utterly nonsensical question. In vain. The woman's gaze burned right into my back. Thanks to the grass, this couple of awkward moments felt like long minutes, but finally the solution arrived. Some fifteen steps below the Turkish couple, the Boufikara brothers were approaching.

"Are they handing out free pussy or what?" they laughed.

"And nothing will be left for you, *Habibi!*" someone among us called back. That was quite enough for them. The older brother reached over to our handrail, and in a single bound leapt over to our side. The tunnel resounded with laughter and cheers. His little brother proved clumsier. He slipped just enough so his half-baked jump ended with him on his belly on the metal surface between the handrails. A minor tumult erupted on our side of the escalator as a forest of hands reached out toward him.

"If you rip it, you'll pay cash for a new one!" he growled while smoothing out his jacket as a series of friendly slaps rained down on his curly black hair.

The subway train was just pulling into the station. The doors opened and we poured in, practically filling up the middle part of the car. A large black man with a shaved head and a neatly trimmed beard stepped in at the end of the car. He sat down and began typing on his phone.

"He knows he can be pretty here, but not strong," one of the guys whispered to me.

I smiled at him. I myself wasn't so sure about this. My doubts were reinforced not only by the black man's six-foot-plus frame and the visibly taut shoulders and biceps lurking under his thin leather jacket, but also by the restrained tone of voice with which Bassam delivered his own scornful remark, in contrast to our group's general zeal. As if he were deliberately taking care that the muscular colossus should not hear it. Our experience on the streets of the city outskirts suggested that there was little that was breakable on the faces of blacks. What's more, their arms were long relative to their bodies, so even a shorter fellow could cause an unpleasant surprise. It wasn't by chance that in boxing clubs they were the coaches' favorites, and they were the ones who then became professionals. Twenty of us could no doubt have floored him, but I don't think any of us would have taken it upon himself to pay him our respects with the first smack. Besides, a premature clash carried the risk of shattering our group morale before the real fun even began.

The black dude got off at 34th. Aside from a few insignificant characters, we were the only ones left in the subway car. Though we were increasingly loud, I had the feeling that the volume was nothing but an attempt to counter our growing tension. The industrial park station was next. This was foreign territory. The train came to a screeching halt. The doors opened, whereupon we were met with the stares of homeward-bound commuters on the platform. Fifteen or twenty of them stepped inside as if we weren't even there. But a few middle-aged women opted to get into another car.

"Whatsa matter?" Marwan howled after them. "Do we stink, you whores?"

Our new fellow commuters didn't give him even a passing glance. But Marwan wasn't giving up. He set his sights on a man wearing a checkered shirt and carrying a shoulder bag. A spectacled egghead between thirty and forty. He was standing to the left of our group, his left hand gripping the handhold as he stared out at the dark tunnel.

"You think we stink, bro?" asked Marwan, stepping over to him. The man pretended not to notice.

"Do we stink?" he asked even louder. Again in vain—the man didn't even bat an eye at him. "I think he doesn't understand. He must speak only Arabic." Marwan grinned our way, and then turned back to the man. "*Nihna qabha?*"

A few of us couldn't help but smile at his Arabic: Marwan had mixed up the words for "stink" and "ugly." Not as if it mattered, of course. But Marwan was not giving up.

"If he's not Arab, he's got to be deaf," he reasoned. "Are you deaf?" he asked, now inches from the Egghead's ear. And yet his victim just kept staring out the window. The other passengers didn't rush to help him, and as the man's white face began turning red, strangely enough I felt sorry for him.

The next station came. The Egghead didn't stir. Maybe he was in shock, or maybe he hoped that someone getting on would come to his aid. If the latter, he was to be disappointed.

"Seems he really is deaf," Marwan said to us with a shrug, "But I'll cure him." Turning back to the Egghead, he bellowed into his face, "At-tennntion!" like American drill sergeants do in war movies. It was as if the man didn't even notice. "That's a real soldier for you," Marwan declared. Slipping between the man and the window, he let out a gorilla call while beating his own chest.

"This is just the sort of perverse fucker that screws children at home!" "Or his mother!" quipped someone in the back. "What do you want, you kid-fucker?" asked Marwan, "For me to sing to you?" And since once more no answer came, he really did strike up a tune.

What Marwan performed could hardly have been called a song. He bellowed out the lyrics of a rap song a couple of years old about how knives end up in the chests of those who get in the way of the singer. The man's lips began quivering, but he just went on staring out the window as if his life depended on it.

Meanwhile the train once again jolted to a halt. The Egghead stared straight ahead. He evidently did not see a possibility of escape, or if he did, fear nailed his feet to the floor. His opportunity evaporated, like that. The bell flashed and buzzed as the door of his jail cell closed on him once more. By then Marwan had finished the song. He held a short creative break, trying to think up a number even more effective than the previous one.

The spark soon popped out of his head. Clearing his throat, he again leaned close to the Egghead's ear and struck up his newest tune:

"*Allahu Akbar*, *Allaaahu Akbar*," he blared like a muezzin calling the passengers in the car to prayer. "*Ashadu an la ilaha illa-llah.*"[1] His inflections were quite off the mark, and he had an accent, too. "*Ashadu anna Muhammadan Rasululu'llah. . . .*"[2]

The air froze. The passengers turned to stone as the Egghead melted away, staring convulsively out the window. His face was burning, beads of sweat covering his forehead.

"*Haya ala al Salah. . . .*"[3] With ever greater piety Marwan called the other passengers to prayer. Like a veritable sheik, with his thumb he pressed his right ear closed and tried to inflect his voice with evident diligence while, from under his half-closed eyelids, he watched his victim's reaction.

"*Haya ala al Falah. . . .*"[4]

Suddenly our group found itself in an odd fix. The guffawing we'd been engaged in until that moment automatically stopped at the sound of Allah's name being pronounced. Moreover, the situation—more precisely, Marwan's horrible yowling—was comical on top of that.

"Ya Allah," a couple of guys in our group called out, praising the performance, their pious voices betraying a bit of mockery, too. Sensing his success, Marwan tried his hand at even more complex inflections, but in

---

1. I testify that there is no god but God (*Ashhadu anna lâ ilâha illa-l-llâh*).

2. I testify that Muhammad is the Prophet of God (*Ashhadu anna Muḥammadan rasûlu-l-llâh*), with an erroneous additional syllable.

3. Come to prayer (*Ḥayya 'ala-ṣ-ṣalât*).

4. Come to salvation (*Ḥayya 'ala-l-falâḥ*).

vain. While yowling away Marwan didn't even notice the lights of the next station as the train again came to a halt. We'd arrived at Martyrs' Square. That's where we had to transfer. Egghead had gotten off scot-free. Bored with his victim, Marwan bounded out of the car, and the rest of us poured out after him. As the doors closed and the train pulled away, I glanced back and saw that the man was still staring straight ahead with those glassy eyes of his.

4   I awoke well-rested. I'd slept through the night on my belly without stirring, from the moment I'd landed in bed after midnight. It had been a hard night. By the time I stepped into my room the adrenaline rush was over, and my limbs felt as heavy as lead. I could hardly drag myself up the stairs. With my left hand I held the railing, and I swung my weight into each turn. By the time Rami and I had said good night out in front of the building, both of us were moving with difficulty. We'd taken the long way back, after all, through the park and then along the canal so the surveillance cameras could not track us. My legs were not used to running for hours. It had been a rough night indeed, even for an eighteen-year-old at the top of his strength.

Sleep brought me back to life. All that remained of the exhaustion was a tingling in my muscles. Lazily I let my right arm slip off the side of the bed, and with it I poked about on the floor for my phone.

"Fuck it," I growled. Of course it was still in my pocket. Somewhere in the bottom of the heap of clothes on the floor at the foot of the bed. Gathering up my will power—best to get such things over with quickly— I sprang up, leaned over to the end of the bed, pulled the phone from the pocket of my jeans, and then in the same motion flopped down onto my back and pulled the blanket over me. The battery was at a 14 percent charge. Good enough for half an hour in bed.

It was almost noon. The first post on the news feed was a picture. The photographer had caught a guy from behind as he raised both his fists skyward. The contours of his black figure were sharply delineated against the light of the burning car behind him. Everything in the news feed was about the previous evening. A mass of shares, links, pictures, articles, commentaries, and announcements. No one was crazy enough to post a picture of his own. Indeed, ever since the police had been able to look inside cell phones during random ID checks, the guys didn't take pictures at the evening disturbances. When a situation began getting hot, we turned off our phones, and the more careful among us even took out their batteries so the cops couldn't turn on the phones and figure out where we'd been in the course of the evening. So instead of selfies made by fellows beside burning cars and smashed-in display windows we were compelled to look at the pictures taken by news agencies and professional photographers.

The street riots had been under way for five days already. That was big news. In the past they'd invariably lasted for three days. We'd get bored and simply gone home. This was different. Everyone in the country had their eyes on the Zone and other such suburbs. Just what had started the troubles didn't matter. Maybe the police had beaten some young guy. Or the government had reduced welfare payments. Or something else.

The combination of adrenaline, energy drinks, and grass has the singular effect of limiting one's memory of events to disconnected splotches. I was able to conjure up the previous day's events in the form of GIFs and frozen images. All I knew for sure was that we'd all met up in Rafiq's billiard hall at 6 PM and waited there for darkness to set in.

Rafiq, the manager, was a popular character. He must have been thirty or so, but he'd already set his reputation in stone by fourteen. He was a good, friendly, big guy with a tiger tattoo on his lower arm. He received guests with custom-made jokes, and everyone concurred that it wouldn't be good to have their face at the receiving end of his hand. He took over the place after the police sent the former managers to jail. The members of the Boufikara family had spread their influence with remarkable speed considering that they were new to the Zone. Their secret was in being unscrupulous and disregarding the community's unwritten code of honor. Word had it that that they had spelled trouble for the cops back home too, cops who helped them—if only so they would leave the country. Together with another couple of families, they held many in fear in the Zone. Their glory was short-lived, however, for in short order they wound up in a cross fire with the authorities. They weren't citizens, so extradition awaited them after incarceration. After that, practically every business of theirs would wind up under the jurisdiction of Abu Sa'id. By then those Boufikaras who were still free, and those families tied to them knew their place. Peace was restored. After all, folks liked Abu Sa'id, who, as a son of the Zone himself, regarded the fate of those here as a personal matter.

Finally darkness came and we left. Not one of us was concerned about the demonstration set to take place by the mutilated statue of Martin Strauss. Besides, fall was in the air, and we were in no mood to hang out for long in the cold. We went out to the square through the park, each group of three or four straggling a bit behind the next so as to avoid raising attention. Rafiq did not tolerate drugs or smoking, so Marwan and a couple of other guys, using the darkness that had descended on the park to their advantage, puffed away or imbibed in something harder. I stuck with grass. I never used synthetic stuff, for who was to say what the Vietnamese concocted in their rat-shit-littered laboratories. A drawn-out streak of faint smoke marked our path.

At the playground Husam stepped over to the bushes. He pulled out a black plastic bag, looked around, and opened it up.

"There will be fireworks too," he said with a knowing grin.

Taking out a Roman candle, I pulled up my sweater, loosened my belt, and hid the firework by my cock. A thorough frisking would have been my undoing, but at least I gave myself a fighting chance. The prospect of being ID'd in the park was low anyway, since the police focused on the roads leading to the square. Before we reached the illuminated square, we all carefully pulled our hoods up over our faces.

The statue was already surrounded by a crowd of at least three hundred. Guys our age—Arabs, Turks, Africans, Kosovars, and Serbs—from every corner of the Zone. The demonstrators protesting the New Loyalist Act had trickled home by then.

The police lined up on the far side of the square. The wind swept tear gas our way, but we were undeterred. The air was filled with shouting.

"We inform you that your presence here is a violation of the law," crackled the police megaphone. "We call on you to leave the square!"

Marwan stepped forward and did some pelvic thrusting in the direction of the police cordon. Over time we had learned that we needn't fear riot police. Only on command could they move to break us up, and until that was heard they just stood there, frozen still, as objects and curses flew their way. Trouble would come only if they ran toward us, batons in hand. Then it really was best to flee.

"We inform you that your presence here is a violation of the law. We call on you to leave the square!"

I took out the Roman candle, held it toward the police, and lit the fuse. I fired it too horizontally. Burning purple, it crackled along the concrete and, fizzling away, stopped in front of the police cordon.

"Final warning! We inform you that your presence here is a violation of the law. We call on you to leave the square!"

Round plastic projectiles the size of tennis balls struck the ground around our feet. The night had begun. Broken glass crackled under the soles of our shoes. The air turned hot. This is why we'd come. Finally we mattered.

Politicians were up in arms. The minister of internal affairs held a joint press conference with the chief of police, Omer Sakman, who'd taken his post a day earlier, vowing to restore order within days. Standing there in his dark-gray suit and service cap, Sakman promised to quell the troubles by calling in the locals. The scumbag Turk had been appointed only a couple of weeks earlier, but everyone in the Zone hated him already. It was obvious that his being Muslim was the only reason he was in the post. Just as they added some dark-skinned faces to the ranks of the riot police.

The president of the conservatives' youth division, Sandra Bollen, also issued a public announcement. She denounced the events, and—in the company of the younger members of the conservatives' Muslim division, as well as an assortment of dandies in suits—took a pedestrian tour of the scene of the street battles. The images showed her speaking to locals, and she made as if she was concerned to hear the lamentations of the old shopkeepers and their kerchief-bedecked wives.

In a proclamation titled "Run Out," the Patriotic Front praised the police and lamented that liberal laws did not authorize them to take "more determined measures against the rabble." From my perspective, I don't know what more determined measures they would have wanted. Clearly not one of them had been struck on the temple with a baton or right where the kidneys were. Sure, I hadn't, either. Up till then my survival had always told me when to retreat. Tear gas? I'd already gotten my share of that. Moreover, the police used stronger and stronger stuff every year. The previous year's had only irritated my eyes, while this year's compressed my pharynx so much that it made me retch. Everyone already knew that they mustn't try washing off tear gas with bottles of water; for if the spray of water wasn't wide enough, the toxic liquid on your face could easily flow right into your eyes, which would start burning anew.

The grand mufti of the newly established Ministry of Religious Affairs issued a public statement too. He called on the public to partake in a national silent demonstration called Muslims for Peace, to be held after Friday prayers the next day. He also publicly called on the imams to spread the message of peace in their khutbas, or sermons. I couldn't help chuckling as I read this. The mufti probably didn't suspect that those involved did not go to the mosque.

My phone began losing steam, what with all the videos. I had to rise up out of bed and get the charger. After plugging it all in, I took a look at my clothes. Grabbing my hooded sweatshirt by the sleeve, I pulled it out of the heap on the floor by the bed and held it to my nose. It was still giving off the stinging scent of tear gas. It had been on me for the third time the previous day; for I'd quickly realized that it wasn't worth putting a clean one on every night. So I now took out a not exactly new, dark blue sweatshirt, one whose hood would stay on me even amid the fastest running, and that became my work uniform.

The day passed slowly. I should have been studying for the graduation exam, but instead I just sat on my bed, leaning my back against the wall, pressing away at my phone. I was calm. Husam wrote that he would soon get the answers from a friend, so we wouldn't even need to write cheat sheets; no, it would be enough to upload the answers to our smartwatches or make tiny printouts of them. We weren't worried about being caught. It was an open secret that it was not in the interest of the school administration to flunk its students. Not only because they were happy to be free all the sooner of the eighteen-year-old, testosterone-fueled, uncontrollable youth, but also because poor academic performance could see the school bid farewell to a good bit of its government subsidies.

One look at my grades told me I didn't stand a chance of higher education. I planned to complete some vocational course and then get to making money as soon as possible. That was my only chance of getting away from home. Not that I had it so bad. Compared to lots of kids my age, I was downright lucky when it came to my family. Neither my father nor my mother was all that religious, I had my own room, and I couldn't even say I'd ever been in want of anything at all. That being said, my father didn't take it well at all that, by his own standards, I had no ambition. He'd chew me out regularly, saying that my grandfather, who'd always considered me his most talented grandchild, would turn over in his grave if he saw what a good-for-nothing I'd become. And in his harangues—for our arguments were pretty one-sided—he then always got round to saying that when he'd been my age, he had been full of ambition.

My mind always drifted in the course of his endless monologues, and it jolted me back into the here and now only when a shift in his tone of voice turned on an automatic sensor within me that then forwarded the signal to my nerve endings telling me that a question was coming. Since my father's questions where rhetorical, I automatically shot back with the expected "no," "yes," or "of course," and I was already flying back into my thoughts. Not that I would have stood a chance, but out of a son's defer-ence I never argued with him. And yet my father's memory was rather selective. Over time he brought up the example of his own exceptional relationship with his own father so many times that by then perhaps even he believed it. Had I reminded him that my grandfather had considered him to be just as much of a good-for-nothing as he did me, he surely would have thought me crazy for misremembering.

The worst, however, was that there was a grain of truth in what he said. Who was I, after all? The blood-kin of the village mukhtar, the great-grandchild of the Mercedes owner who'd been to Europe and back, the grandchild of the well-respected deputy manager of the market, the son of the Zone's chief onetime hell-raiser. But aside from that? Deep down I still wanted to be a journalist. While the other guys were watching fictional drama series, I gobbled up the news. There was a lot at stake when it came to all that—real wars, secret meetings, theatrical announcements, new alliances and betrayals. In the real world there were neither clichés nor happy endings. Indeed, there were no endings at all, so I never had to be concerned that my favorite soap operas would come to a close. Moreover, on reading more about things, I was invariably struck by just how complex the world really was. I would have happily cried out my discoveries right then and there for all the world to hear. My father, though, considered my dream foolish. Journalism wasn't work, as he saw it, besides which, he said, working wasn't necessary, only making money was. On a couple of occasions I surreptitiously sent short writings of mine to web portals. They didn't even respond. And so instead of shouting out my opinions and discoveries for all the world to hear, mostly I shared them with Husam alone; and by the time the graduation exam came along, I'd given up all hope of ever becoming a journalist.

Sometimes, however, alongside my flare-ups of self-flagellation, my ego slowly but surely spread its wings. And my nascent ego was finding it harder and harder to endure sitting around at home and the restrictions of family life. Among us, after all, alongside rigid parent-child relationships, roles wove their way through everything. We followed the ideal images passed down from generation to generation of the good son, the good husband, the good wife, the good father, the good mother, the good big brother, the good little sister. Fitfully we insisted on customs and models of behavior whose roots had ossified way back in the chalky soil of the old country. The "real man," the "respectable woman," the "family reputation." Not even to ourselves did we admit that we were nothing but wild shoots of an old tree. We enjoyed the rain and the balmy breeze, but in vain did we reach for the sky, for we couldn't free ourselves from the shadow of the ancient trunk. From it we came to be, and we could grow only as tall as it let us. Deep down I held the utmost respect for my grandfather's older brother, Abdelkader, who, leaving everything behind, took his fate into his own hands. I figured that if finally I could earn money, I too would step onto my own path. But at the moment there was a more pressing matter. I had to prepare for the evening melee.

Around six I met up with Rami, and we ate at old Ashraf's. The meeting that day, too, was at Rafiq's place. After exchanging high-fives with everyone, we showed each other videos on our phones. We waited for it to get dark and to charge into the night as warriors yet again.

The door opened. Five strapping men came in.

"Fuck, it's the police," I said, giving Rami a nudge, whereupon he quickly quit the game on his phone so he could sign out of his profile. The others noticed too. Since there was nowhere to escape, we could do but one thing: make as if we—respectable citizens just having some fun—were not bothered in the least by the sudden appearance of the authorities. Not everyone was a good actor. Husam, ending the conversation he was having, fixed his eyes on the floor. I was certain that he was trying to replay last night's clash in his head to determine whether his hood might have slipped back in the chaos or if he'd turned off his cell phone in time to avoid revealing his location to the police.

They weren't police after all. They went over to the counter and gave Rafiq high-fives. I glanced out the window. Two dark BMWs were parked out front. Police didn't drive cars like those. The sense of relief inside was palpable. That's when it hit me that I recognized two of the faces. The men stood at the entrance to one of Abu Sa'id's dance clubs every Saturday night. I'd never seen the others, but they too looked rather like bouncers.

"You've got to get all paranoid when there's no trouble at all?" Rami growled at me. I nodded in relief as Rafiq turned down the music. Everyone stared toward the counter.

"Who's the boss here?" said a bald guy in a black leather jacket, stepping forward. The other four formed a semicircle behind him. The air froze. There were no takers. The bald guy passed his eyes contemptuously over everyone. His eyes locked on me.

"Aren't you Semir's son?" he asked, pointing at me menacingly. "Your dad will not be happy to hear that we met here!"

To my great relief, he did not press the issue. Back home I'd lied that I was off to do some PlayStation gaming with Rami. The bald guy next locked his eyes on Marwan.

"I know you too. You're a relative of old Ashraf. Get yourself over here!"

Marwan reluctantly stepped forward.

"Is there a problem, Jalal?" he asked in a strained, backslapping tone of voice. He spread out his arms, palms turned upward.

"There will be, if you all keep this up," said the bald guy in the leather jacket, raising his voice. "Enough of this shit. You guys are not going anywhere tonight. Or tomorrow. You'll all sit tight on your asses."

"But Jalal," Marwan tried again.

"Don't you understand what I'm saying, dickhead?" Jalal said, grabbing the front of Marwan's sweatshirt. "What the fuck do you think this is?" he screamed into Marwan's face from less than a foot away. "Be glad I won't be stomping out your guts, and that goes for everyone here! Everyone has had enough of this shit!" He shoved the frightened Marwan backward and then paused for a couple of seconds. Dead silence. "You know whose car you set on fire, you dickheads? Old Hajji Ahmed's. That's what he took his sick wife to the doctor in."

We stared at the floor.

"You know what's going to happen now?" said Jalal, walking about among us like a guard among the condemned. "You will be charitable fellows. You'll all write a letter to old Hajji Ahmed." Jalal put a hand on Marwan's shoulder. "You know how to write, huh?"

Jalal held out his upturned open palm toward the counter, whereupon Rafiq handed him a pen and paper. Grabbing Marwan by the scruff of the neck, Jalal led him to a chair behind the desk, onto which he slammed down the paper and flung down the pen.

"I'll dictate: 'Dear Hajji Ahmed. We were sorry to hear what happened with your car. We deeply condemn everything that happened. It came as a shock to us that not even such an honorable man . . .' *Honorable* is one word, not *honor able*, shithead." Marwan's face began turning red.

"So then," Jalal continued. "'It came as a shock to us that not even such an honorable man as you are spared the wrath of a rampaging mob on the streets. Please accept our sincere sympathies.'" Marwan's face was beet red by now, and the bouncers could hardly mask how much fun they were having.

"And that will do, Habibi," said Jalal, punctuating his words with a slap.

"And now everyone will be so kind as to sign it. Let Hajji Ahmed be happy that so many were thinking of him."

We stood in line. I just scrawled something illegible. The last thing I needed was for anyone, much less my father, to know I'd been there.

Rami and I exchanged a wink. Jalal caught us in the act.

"You guys didn't imagine that this was it, did you?" he asked, pointing to the younger Boufikara kid. "Let's have your cap," he said to him, whereupon the Boufikara kid, like a good little soldier, immediately took his red baseball cap off his head. Jalal took it away and put it on the billiard table upside down.

"Empty your pockets. Let Hajji Ahmed feel that the young people bear his lot in their hearts."

We looked at each other.

"What the fuck are you waiting for? Empty your pockets! What money you have on you, I want to see it in the cap. If you screw around, then old Hajji Ahmed will get your phones. I assume you don't want that respectable old fellow to have to bother with trudging all that shit to a pawn shop?"

We had no choice. We gave what we had on us. I threw eleven euros into the cap.

"Let's see how generous you all were," said Jalal, shaking the cap.

"Eighty-seven," he said, shaking his head after a quick count.

"If any of you do anything stupid, you'd do best not to go home ever again." Raising his index finger, he added, by way of warning, "We know where each one of you lives."

"Hey, but I'm not gonna be a scumbag. So you don't get bored, tonight each one of you can play billiards for free. It's on me." Rafiq nodded from behind the counter.

They left just as quickly as they'd come. Cold air whooshed in the swaying door. It was still silent in the room.

"Do you know who that Hajji Ahmed is?" I whispered to Rami. He shook his head.

"You all heard what he said," said Rafiq, breaking the silence. And he threw a handful of tokens on the counter.

"It's cold out there, anyway," said Marwan. "Who the fuck wants to catch a cold?"

He took a token and headed toward the cue rack. "Who'll be up against me?"

In a couple of hours I looked at the message board. That day there was no riot. When Rami and I walked home around 10 PM, the streets were just as empty as on any weeknight.

5 The Prophet was a cat person. I'm sure as hell that it was in the interest of his favorites that Muhammad—peace be upon him—qualified dogs as unclean. With that, after all, dogs were banned from Muslim cities, and cats got a heaven on earth. In the Zone, though, this maneuver did not bear fruit. The guys would go crazy over fighting dogs, clean or not. Some pampered them as they might have done to children, and they even let slobbering pit bulls and other terriers into their beds. The puppies with their wrinkled mugs and big paws soon grew up though, and the ideal ended, like that. The pit bulls proved stubborn, their owners impatient, and the apartments too small. The net was full of ads for year-and-a-half- to two-year-old dogs that, for lack of interested parties, regularly ended up at shelters.

For a while even Rami had a sandy-hued male pit bull terrier. As sweet as it was, like others in its breed, it was an ill-mannered beast, with a broad chest and a massive jaw. After buying it, Rami deliberated at length over its name. His first idea was Hamzah. Not the most well-advised choice, though Rami couldn't have known, for in contrast with me, he had never visited sheiks, so he was bereft of thorough religious knowledge. I was the one who had to caution him that Hamzah ibn 'Abdul-Muttalib was the Prophet's uncle, and so the name Hamzah didn't exactly suit a dog, which might be lovely, smart, and brave, but will nonetheless remain an unclean beast. Rami fell to thought again, then suggested Saladin.

"This is a fighting dog," he added, "not some fairy Pekingese."

Though this was a tad better, I was still compelled to argue against it. While Salah al-Din, Saladin, the first sultan of Egypt and Syria, was not a member of either the Ahl al-Bayt or the Sahaba, all of whom were close to the Prophet Muhammad, as a great Muslim leader he surely would not have been enthused to learn that a slobbering dog, one that sometimes sticks its nose into the asses of other slobbering dogs, bore his name. A series of names followed.

50

"Hannibal?" Rami finally offered. This time I didn't resist. After all, the person behind the name was a great warrior and not Muslim. I felt that my mission was fulfilled.

I'll admit that by then I found dogs revolting. But when was a kid of six or seven, I too had wanted one. Surreptitiously browsing ads on the net, I had downloaded images of dogs and marked must-have offers. Of course, nothing came of it all. If there was one thing my father and mother agreed on completely it was that animals do not belong in a flat, at least not in theirs; besides which, they already had two kids to deal with.

As time passed, I realized that I myself was disgusted by dogs. Whenever I found myself playing fetch with some guy's dog in the park, and it stuck its snout too close to me, my instinct was to pull away to keep its mouth, foaming with white drool, from touching the legs of my pants. Those blockheaded beasts of course generally did not get the hint. Thinking I wanted to play, they climbed up on me, panting away. I bore it bravely. No one could tell I abhorred them. Gathering my strength, I would pet around the base of their ears. But after I realized that this meant that a sweetish, nauseating, dog-scented layer of felt would adhere irrevocably to my palms and that there was no way of scratching it off, I got out of the petting habit too. One time a while back, while browsing the web page of a pit bull kennel, an Islamist popup virus notified me that I was on an unclean site, and that the Koran writes—or the Prophet said (how am I supposed to remember?)—that a person must wash his hands with earth seven times after touching a dog. I understand this too. I would rather my hand be muddy than smell that stomach-churning odor. My relationship with dogs ended once and for all when someone called my attention to the association between two facts: first, that dogs' asses are never shitty; second, that they can wipe them only with their tongues.

"Saliva keeps changing," Rami explained when I told him this. Hannibal must have been about five months old then. "He doesn't lick you with the same surface he licks his ass with." He didn't manage to convince me.

Not long after, Rami sold Hannibal.

For many, keeping dogs was more than just a hobby. Serious sums were in play and changed hands at illegal dogfights. According to those who attended, not only the arenas were bloody at such weekend events held in abandoned warehouses. Owners and betters dissatisfied with the results sometimes sought to fight it out in place of their dogs. After a while the organizers hired bouncers to keep knives and clubs from slipping inside.

Amr, however, was different than the other dog owners. He had not a pit bull or an AmStaff, but a fox terrier. A thin, tiny little hound with cowlike spots. Amr insisted that this sort of terrier was related to fighting dogs. I wasn't so sure. In contrast with doltish terriers though, Amr's dog could give a paw and fetch. It could catch a tennis ball thrown its way at five feet high, and it was motionless as it carefully kept watch on a treat placed on its nose until Amr gave it permission to take it in its mouth. I have to admit that it was a smart animal. Which didn't keep me from hating it, too.

It was a balmy, early spring evening; the sky at the horizon was pink. The riots that had begun so promisingly the previous fall had soon ended thanks to the intervention of Abu Sa'id. So too, the unusually cold and long winter helped bring order to the Zone. Along with Amr, Rami, and Husam we sat about on the edge of the park beside Strauss Square. Lately we hadn't been hanging out as much with Marwan and his crew, so we had bowed out of the riots.

Husam was still one of the coolest dudes around. It was possible to talk with him about weightier matters too. But that's not the only reason I got on well with him. His little sister, Latifa, was four years younger than us. She was from a good, respectable family. The sort of girl you think seriously about. Husam didn't know it, but even from the age of nineteen I regarded him as my future brother-in-law.

We weren't alone in being psyched up because the weather was finally getting better. Najib and his buddies were two benches away smoking grass. The fox terrier was playing with Najib's pit bull by the base of the statue. The stocky, silver-gray bitch was doing circles with the abandon of a pup. The fox terrier, which reached only her shoulder, was yapping away as he jumped about around the pit bull. All was calm. We were listening intently to Husam, who happened to be in the middle of some story of his when all of a sudden we heard a deep rattling sound, and then a drawn-out, awful yowling. Turning our heads, we looked on in total shock as the pit bull, holding the fox terrier up high by the scruff of its neck, began shaking it like a rag doll. Amr's presence of mind did not abandon him when it mattered. Swinging open his butterfly knife, he was by the dogs in one leap, and brought that knife down dead-on between the pit bull's eyes. Despite the adrenalin rush to his brain—or maybe thanks to that—the blow was precise. The dog collapsed at once. To the fox terrier's good fortune, the pit bull's jaws had not yet locked, so it escaped from the grip of the needle-sharp teeth.

Stoned as he was, it took Najib at least ten seconds to come to from the initial shock. Out of his mind, he dashed over to his dog. The puddle of blood grew quickly around the pit bull, its silver fur turning black in increasingly larger splotches. By then we all stood there. Having dropped to his knees, Najib embraced the thick, blood-soaked neck, trying to revive his dog, whose left hind leg was jerking as if it were trying to run. In vain. The knife had found its mark. Najib quickly came to his senses.

"Pharaohhhh . . . ," he growled under tear-drenched eyes. His voice at first turned into a rattle similar to a dog's growling, and then came out-and-out screaming. The patrons sitting at old Ashraf's place were all staring at us. From some twenty feet away Amr was intensely examining his fox terrier's wounds. He didn't notice as Najib now picked up the butterfly knife lying on the pavement beside the pit bull and headed his way, his eyes glazed over, his steps quickening their pace. By the time he did realize what was happening, Najib was just a couple of steps away from him. To Amr's good fortune, the others were ready.

"I'll tear your guts out, you fag!" Najib foamed as his pals held him back and twisted the knife from his hands. The patrons at the café across the way craned their necks. Amr picked up his wounded fox terrier. We left the scene together, running. We sped across the square and, having left the rows of shops behind, turned toward the tower blocks. Najib's bellowing could still be heard even after we'd turned the corner.

Everyone knew that this sort of offense could not go without retribution—especially because, as someone told us, that pit bull was no cheap bitch out of a breeding kennel but an award-winning gladiator. The beast had earned its owner serious sums as a favorite in illegal dogfights, and for everyone who'd bet on her. Her market value was well over ten thousand euros. Indeed, lots of folks made offers for her, but no matter how much they were ready to shell out, Najib wouldn't have parted with her for anything. He was in love with the dog. Revenge was inevitable.

For the next few days Amr didn't set foot outside of home. Of course, he couldn't keep that up for long; he had to work, after all, and the fox terrier's wounds weren't so severe that it didn't need walking. We weren't chums who would leave him high and dry. From then on we didn't let him go anywhere alone.

A week and a half after the incident, Rami and I were walking Amr home along the lamplit path that ran between the tower blocks. We'd just reached a crosswalk when two cars screeched to a halt beside us. As their doors opened, we were overwhelmed by fear. It was Najib and six of his pals. I'll admit that it wasn't bravery but shock that kept me from hightailing it out of there.

"What is this, fags, six against three?" said Rami, assuming a fighting pose and raising his fists. I stood beside him.

"You stay out of this," said Najib, pointing an index finger at me as his left hand raised his sweater from his side. A pistol was underneath. At least that's how it looked there, under the lamplight. All three of us were petrified. My father's reputation guaranteed that I'd be spared a beating. Rami, too, decided that it would be better to be weak for a long time rather than strong one time. He raised his hands at once.

But Amr didn't stand a chance. Not only did he suffer a torn eyelid but, as it later turned out, he even broke two ribs. The story might have ended there, for the revenge had been accomplished. But this wasn't enough for Najib. After giving Amr, who was sprawled on the ground, one last farewell kick, he commanded that in compensation Amr was to pay him twenty thousand euros within two weeks.

"What the fuck now?" Amr asked us on the front steps of one of the tower blocks as I pressed a tissue on his eyelid.

"You need to go to the hospital," said Rami. "We'll say you fell off your motorbike."

"That's not what I asked," Amr mumbled.

We knew that much. Amr was in deep shit. Not even by selling both his kidneys would he have 20,000 euros. And yet giving Najib the finger was inadvisable. His family had influence: everyone in the Zone knew his older cousin's name, and what's more, they belonged to Abu Sa'id's broader circle. Turning to the police was not at all an option for Amr. Not only because the patrolmen knew his name too, on account of minor doings of his, but also because you simply don't do that sort of thing if you want to look the others in the eye ever again.

"Maybe your dad . . . ," said Rami, casting me a glance, but on seeing my expression he swallowed the rest of his words, like that.

I was not on such terms with my father that I could have gotten him involved in this sort of affair. If by chance he had helped, he would then have expected me to crawl before him in gratitude for the rest of my days. And yet my father really could have helped. He'd practically grown up with Abu Sa'id, the younger cousin of that Abu Radwan who had once made my grandfather deputy manager of the market. As a teenager my father, who must have been about five years older than him, had been a deft boxer, and Abu Sa'id, as one hell-raiser of a kid, needed his protection. Later on the opposite was true. Abu Sa'id became a big man, and yet his respect for my father remained intact. It was thanks to this fact that when I turned eight we could move from our previous rental into a more spacious apartment, and that when it came down to it, we were never in want of anything.

Abu Sa'id was a veritable *zaim*. At first he was called just Rashid, but among his contemporaries he perhaps enjoyed the sole distinction of having earned the title Abu from the community. His business interests gave permanent employment to at least 150 people and temporary work to even more. He had a knack for choosing his people from among those families through which he could then extend his influence to other families too. Besides, as a onetime member, he also contributed generously to the Golden Glove boxing club. His sports foundation—in which he was humbly content with a simple chairmanship—also established a scholarship program to support young talents. Grateful for the help, the beneficiaries, once their boxing careers came to a close, provided the muscle for the protection of Abu Sa'id's business interests.

A zaim and a respectable citizen. Abu Sa'id was often at Al-Nour on Fridays to hobnob after prayers with the elders and of course with local council representatives. In times of need he was known far and wide as the Zone's most effective fixer. He mediated quickly and justly in disputes. Besides that, he was a banker of favors and a redistributor whom everyone owed something to, and who collected debts in the interest of those who turned to him again and again, creating yet newer debts in the process.

Abu Sa'id, then, might have solved Amr's problem. And yet I couldn't ask my father for a recommendation, and you couldn't just drop in off the street. Especially not Amr, whose family was poor and, when it came down to it, didn't count for shit. His dad worked as a plain old forklift driver, his connections mostly limited to other laborers. It simply would not have been in Abu Sa'id's interest to offer protection to a guy like Amr over his own people.

"*Abdelghani!* That's it!" Amr exclaimed. Rami and I looked at each other. There was something to that. He might even help.

Amr's older cousin, Abdelghani, was a hajji, after all. The guy must have been twenty-eight when, in the slammer for pretrial detention, he discovered Allah's proper path. After being freed with a suspended sentence, he left behind his buddies who were involved with drugs and similar matters and began hanging out with the Tawhidis. He grew a beard, shaved his moustache, and from then on wore only pants that hung above his ankles. He changed his name to Abu Bilal, and word had it that he'd become an influential figure among the Tawhidis. He belonged to the inner circle of Sheik Taymullah, and at the age of twenty-eight he even took the pilgrimage to Mecca, thus earning the title of hajji.

By the time the strife between Amr and Najib erupted, the Tawhidis already commanded general respect in the Zone. Just how many of them there were, no one knew could say, but not just a few, that much was certain. Young men resembling Abu Bilal were now a constant presence on the streets, not to mention woman donning black niqabs and covering themselves from head to toe. Arabs, Africans, and even converted whites reinforced their ranks. Of course, most younger guys in the Zone would not even have considered joining up. After all, everything a regular guy's life revolved around was haram to the Tawhidis—alcohol, grass, girls, Internet games, rap music, and dogs. As more and more tough dudes joined up with them, however, they became an unavoidable factor to contend with. Their standing on the street really shot up when Adnan got out of prison and joined them too.

Taymullah was a believer in peaceful coexistence. In contrast with his predecessor, he did not criticize Al-Nour or other mosques the Zone's residents attended. When the Patriot Act went into force, he declared that politics and Islam were incompatible anyway, and so his followers avoided politics like the plague, even boycotting the elections. Under his leadership the Tawhidis abandoned participation in pointless street demonstrations meant as shows of strength. He ceased sharia patrols, strictly forbidding his followers to intervene in people's everyday affairs. They left at home any Arab garb they used to wear. No longer did they keep da'wah on the streets. It was unnecessary. Still, when the hajjis appeared someplace, young folks would toss away their joints and hide their beer cans. Taymullah's public profile had several thousand followers. I among them. Not that his stuff particularly interested me. His followers' remarks were entertaining though. "May Allah bless you for your wise words, sheik of sheiks!" "The light of your face shines upon the city, oh sheik!" These and a bunch of similar tacky felicitations and excessively flowery turns of phrase. The funniest words came from the mouths of those who, the previous night, had lurched out of their whores' places of business with pot-dazed eyes or else didn't even dare step out onto the street since they were in debt to half the Zone on account of their gambling addictions.

Taymullah was an affable sort and, most important, available to all. Anyone could pose him questions on religious matters on the Internet or ask for guidance, and he replied in short order. Even those who attended Al-Nour on Fridays asked him for advice. The sheik there made as if Taymullah didn't exist. His pay did not depend on how many people listened to his khutba. He saw to his business, chatted with the older folks and the local council representatives, and then got into his Mercedes.

Taymullah became a central figure in the Zone. Locals sought him out ever more often as an arbiter in disputes. He was famous for never showing bias toward anyone but always making his decisions in accord with the *sunna*. The parties invariably departed in satisfaction, spreading his good name.

As time passed there were more and more people who visited the Tawhidis' mosque for Friday prayers or followed them online, and even paid their zakat to them. The money wound up in the most suitable place; of that no one had even a doubt. The Tawhidis didn't spend much on themselves. They considered it self-evident that gold was haram. They didn't buy expensive cars, and yet they donated generously and expediently. They ran a soup kitchen for those in need; when someone died, they assisted their families with the burial or with the transport of the body back home; and they found lawyers for young people in trouble with the law. Indeed, thanks to them many avoided prison, and as for those they couldn't save from being locked up, they ensured them protection on the inside. On account of their charitable work and their constantly expanding connections, they turned into an invisible and yet omnipresent authority not only in the Zone but also in other areas inhabited by Muslims.

Abu Bilal was among them. Weighing his words carefully, Amr wrote to his cousin. Writing much was inadvisable. Everyone knew that all Tawhidis were under surveillance.

"Salam!" Amr typed into his phone. "Can we meet? It's urgent."

"*Wa alaykum as-salam wa rahmatullah wa barakatu,*" came the reply hardly five minutes later, "After the *Isha* prayer by the mosque entrance."

That night Rami and Husam and I waited for Amr at Rafiq's billiard club. The usual rap was playing. Only a couple of other guys were lolling about. We weren't in the mood to play. We were sitting at a table clicking away at our phones. Back then I was all agog about Wartribe. It was a serious game, and everyone was playing it. The guys in the Zone formed a digital clan, and we competed at least four times a week with clans from all over the world, and in chats we often coordinated when and where to meet up. My name was Conqueror, and I was the clan's coleader, which meant I could accept and also kick out members. More than ten hours were left until the next war, which was why I happened to be engaged in a one-man battle.

Amr had promised to come join us right after the meeting. The mosque was a ten-minute walk away. He should have arrived long before. The Isha had ended two hours earlier. Of course, it was not out of the question that Abu Bilal might refuse to help, in which case Amr would have turned instead in the direction of the train station or, worse, the bridge.

The door creaked open. It was Amr. He was grinning like a Cheshire cat. Fortunately, the war had just ended. Some Chinese dude had clobbered me.

"He says 'inshallah,'" Amr proclaimed with an unearthly, blissful expression. Inshallah. We looked at him in shock.

"Then why the fuck are you so happy?" I asked. To cite Allah's will was not a promise but the passing off of responsibility.

But Amr did not stop grinning. "A Tawhidi inshallah is different.'

He proved right. The next day he proudly stuck his phone under our noses with Abu Bilal's message:

"Inshallah, everything will be all right." The Tawhidi network had kicked into action. And that, at least temporarily, meant protection for Amr. His fox terrier could once again go on regular walks.

"Only say good things about the Tawhidis," said my father, raising his index finger by way of warning. As the red light turned green, he pressed the gas pedal. Three days had passed, and we were on our way to Abu Sa'id's office. Smiling spontaneously, I quickly turned my head, as if just staring at the store windows flitting by. It was funny to hear this sort of thing from the mouth of someone who, deep down, held all Tawhidis to be good-for-nothing ex–drug addicts, as kids who, not being tough enough to stand their ground on the street, flee instead into religious zeal. My father kept voicing this conviction of his all the way up until Abu Sa'id's younger cousin joined their ranks. A worthless kid, he was, but Abu Sa'id was fond of him.

We'd been summoned to Abu Sa'id's place to testify about the dog case. Amr had been questioned earlier. Abu Sa'id's office would not have been far even by foot, and we still went by car. It would have been unworthy of such an important meeting to go any other way. From the outside the building did not differ much from the others along the row of shops. With its display window, shutter rolled up above it, and with its sign out front, its gold lettering on a black background, the place gave the impression of being a respectable business. Indeed, as far as I knew, Abu Sa'id earned his money legally.

We parked the car in the makeshift parking lot fashioned out of the empty lot opposite.

"When he speaks to you, look him in the eye," said my father, giving me his final instructions before we got out of the car. "No foolishness," he warned. "Don't you bring shame on me."

The lot attendant didn't ask for money. He knew my father. Abu Sa'id's black BMW SUV stood in front of the office. Even one of its rims cost more than two months of the attendant's wages. Father led the way. As the door opened, the doorman sprang up from behind his desk, paid us his respects, and offered us seats in the black leather armchairs. Newspapers lay on a glass table with mahogany legs. Father took a copy of the *Independent News*. The lead article on the front page concerned the terrorist attack the week before against police headquarters. Encouraged by the New Patriot Act, the government had put forward to Parliament a tightening of the surveillance law. Father turned to the sports section. After quickly flipping through the selection of papers on the table, I pulled out my phone instead. Not that I had the time to start a war on Wartribe, but I did have time to check on my upgrades.

"This way, please. Abu Sa'id is waiting for you." So the doorman said, stepping before us to show the way. Father went behind him, and I went last.

The doorman knocked on the thick oak door, then opened it, and we stepped into the office, which was bathed in late-afternoon sunlight. Seated on one side of a large conference table was Najib's cousin and one of his pals who'd been present at the initial melee and later at the beating too. On the other side were Abu Bilal and another Tawhidi. Minutes passed before I recognized the latter as Adnan. Since I'd seen him last, his beard had grown even longer, and it seemed that his face had even rounded out a bit. As we stepped in, Abu Sa'id stood up from the head of the table. In his early forties, he sported a Newgate fringe under his chin and jaw, and the sun streaming in the room through the window behind him sparkled on his shaven head.

"Semir, brother! Welcome!" He greeted my father with a peck on each cheek and a hug. He had a good build and was just a hair shorter than Father. His black tennis shirt was tight against his chest. He genially shook both my hands, signaling to all that we were honored guests.

On the wall was a row of pictures in identical golden frames in which Abu Saʿid stood strutting his stuff with various characters. One showed him in the company of the police chief, another with the mayor, yet another with the famous actor Ammar Hakim, whose comedies were rather popular in those days. In one picture Abu Saʿid was handing out chocolate to children; in another, in his younger days but with just as little hair, he stood in ready position, with three sinewy boxers on each side of him. A glass cabinet in the room held various trophies and memorabilia. As for the trophies, I had no idea where he'd gotten them, since I was unaware of him having been a serious fighter in his day.

Abu Saʿid took his seat in the black leather revolving chair at the head of the table. Father and I sat at the other end of the table.

"Will you have coffee or tea, brother?" he asked Father with a smile.

"Your cardamom coffee is unequalled," said Father by way of flattery. I asked for a cola.

"Do you know why I asked you to come?" he asked, turning to me.

"Because of the pit bull case?"

"No. Because you are the grandson of Abu Hassan and the son of Semir. Your father and I boxed together when we were your age. No one had a right hook like his, isn't that right, brother?" So he said, blinking at Father, who for his part giggled with an almost feminine bashfulness.

"But don't you get overconfident now, Semir," he said, casting Father a jovial smile. "The truly tough guy was your father, God rest his soul."

"Your grandfather was truly one fine Muslim man," he said, looking at me, waving a finger to the sky. The Tawhidis sitting at the table stared straight ahead with expressionless faces.

"I know the apple never falls far from its tree. Only honorable men can be raised in such a family. Help us see clearly. Your friend's fate is important to our hajji brothers."

"Brother Sa'id," Adnan corrected him, "for us the fate of every Muslim is important."

"May Allah reward you all, Adnan," said Abu Sa'id.

Meanwhile the doorman knocked and brought in the coffee and the cola.

"Tell us what happened on Strauss Square," said Abu Sa'id, glancing at me.

I told the story. Beforehand I'd coordinated with Amr about what I would say. All in all, I didn't have to lie. In this story Amr wasn't the one at fault.

"Do you have any questions for him?" asked Abu Sa'id of those sitting on each side of the table.

"Was Amr sober when he killed Najib's dog, brother?" asked Abu Bilal in a slow and measured voice. Radiating from him was the pedantry characteristic of Tawhidis. Suddenly I wasn't sure what the proper answer was. Grass could generally be an excuse too if someone did something foolish. But the Tawhidis looked askance at every mind-altering substance.

"Completely," I replied with an expressionless face.

"And was Najib sober when he attacked Amr, brother?" Abu Bilal posed the second question in the same halting tone of voice. I had to follow through on the line I'd begun to draw. But carefully, of course, since Najib's cousins were sitting there too. Besides, I could not know whom they'd questioned before me and what they'd said.

"I can't answer that for certain," I said. "Only us and them were on the square. Beforehand I'd noticed the smell of pot, but I would not dare declare that it came from them." I'd nearly said, "I don't know where it came from," but at the last moment I sensed that the subtle distinction could be a clincher.

"You said Najib didn't smoke a thing?" Abu Sa'id asked Najib's pal. So before I'd arrived they had questioned him too, and he had followed the same logic as I had.

"Not a single drag!" he firmly replied, squinting at me.

"I smelled pot," I said, raising a hand in the air, "but like I said, it could be that only the breeze had brought it from somewhere."

"So we can then determine that there is no proof that at the time of the incidents in the park anyone acted under the influence," Abu Sa'id summed it up.

"Would you turn now to that evening," said Abu Bilal, turning to me, "when you accompanied Amr home?" I broke out in a sweat at his stilted tone of voice.

"That was a beating pure and simple. If his pals hadn't dragged him away, Najib might even have killed Amr."

"Don't exaggerate!" Najib's pal shot back. "We just wanted to warn Amr."

"He broke two ribs, and he was soaked in blood afterward!" I said, locking eyes with him.

"It's a lie!" he shouted.

"You guys then sped off in a car. You say I'm lying?" I said, raising my voice. I couldn't cower in front of my father.

"This is not the place for a brawl!" Abu Sa'id roared at us. He thanked us for coming by, and after a few pleasantries he said my father and I could go.

On the way out, we saw Amr and Najib waiting in the lobby. Both were keying away at their phones in leather armchairs as far from each other as possible. Amr and I nodded at each other. Najib made as if he hadn't even noticed us.

My phone pinged two hours later. "Fuck every one of them," read Amr's to-the-point message. I expected the worst. "An hour from now, at Rafiq's?" I asked. He answered with two thumbs up.

Rami and Husam and I got there at practically the same time. Amr's dour expression did not suggest much cause for optimism.

"So, what happened?" asked Rami.

"The fucking Tawhidis left me high and dry," Amr replied, burying his face in his palms.

"Don't make us beg! What happened?" I asked, a bit impatient.

"By the time Najib and I went in, I think they'd decided everything already. Even Abu Sa'id welcoming me in such a smarmy way was suspicious. After all, who the hell am I to him? All of them can go fuck themselves! 'We've deliberated long and hard,' he said, 'and we have a pro-posal.' He then let Adnan speak. He then began quoting some tradition of the Prophet or what the fuck do I know what. He asked idiotic questions, like had I been hunting with the dog, did the dog protect my home, and did it watch over a herd. A herd, for fuck's sake! Here, in the Zone! I kept racking my brains over what he was getting to with all this." Amr's voice was trembling.

"He then began explaining that on account of my dog I'd lost the *hasanat* for two good deeds a day, but now Allah was offering me an op-portunity. He can go stick his hasanat up his ass!"

As Amr told his story, it quickly became clear to me that Abu Sa'id and the Tawhidis had settled matters cleverly. Since dog fighting was gam-bling, making it haram, Allah did not approve of keeping a dog, so Najib was not due compensation for the lost benefit brought by Pharaoh's death. On the other hand, the dog's value was demonstrably ten thousand euros, which Amr had to pay. But subtracted from that was the recompense due him for his wounds, which Najib owed him. They'd calculated four thou-sand euros per rib, so Amr owed Najib two thousand euros.

Of course not even with that was Amr much better off. That's where Abu Sa'id came into the picture, offering to assume the debt, which Amr could work off in his employ. To Najib he proposed that he would intro-duce him to an old friend of his who, it so happened, was a dog breeder, and he could choose a pup from a new litter.

"As soon as I'm back in shape, I'm starting to work as a messenger," said Amr.

"Hey, but that's fucking great!" Rami whooped. "From now on you're Abu Sa'id's man. No one can fuck with you ever again."

The new perspective perked up Amr. But the arrangement also had a painful side. For the peace to be complete, Amr had to give his fox terrier to Najib.

"I'll say he got lost," he declared.

We looked at him as if he'd gone mad. That would have been the worst idea of all, with which he would have earned the wrath not only of Abu Sa'id but also of the Tawhidis. If he did that, from then on he'd be free prey.

There was nothing to do. Two days later, in the presence of one of Abu Sa'id's men and a Tawhidi, with a bleeding heart he handed over his fox terrier to Najib.

"The matter has come to an end," declared Abu Sa'id's man.

Had he not had to keep up appearances, Amr would no doubt have burst out in tears as Najib, with his fox terrier in his arm, got into his car with a self-satisfied grin. One week later Amr got an email from an anonymous address. The attached pictures showed the bloody corpse of a dog hanging from a branch.

When, one year later, Najib was shot in the chest, he happened to be walking the dog he'd gotten from the friend of Abu Sa'id, a sand-hued pit bull bitch. The bullet struck his heart. He died on the spot. The police rounded up everyone who might have had any motive for the murder. Amr was held for seventy-two hours but then released for lack of evidence. Amr's alibi was an Albanian prostitute whose hospitality he happened to be partaking of when the incident occurred. To head off strife, both Amr and his parents appeared at Najib's burial. The murder weapon—a serious, scope-equipped hunting rifle—was found the following spring during a search of premises. It turned out to have been used for a total of seven murders in various parts of the region. The victims were all young Muslim men. The perpetrator was a man in his late thirties who lived alone. He'd been an active anti-Muslim commentator on the Internet for years, but his activities on that front had ended abruptly. The murders began six months later. His first two victims were sixteen and eighteen.

When the police released his photo, the blood froze in my veins, and if I hadn't been reading it while lying in bed I would surely have collapsed. A disconcerted stare, a checkered shirt, short hair, glasses. It was Egghead!

Rami said I was crazy, for one freak of a loser was just like the other. With all my might I wanted to believe him.

6 All my strength proved insufficient to reverse reality: the more photos and other information came to light about the murder, the more certain we were that Egghead was the perpetrator. His name was Thomas J.—no last name given, under the law, as he was formally but a suspect—and earlier he'd been a member of the Patriotic Front. The Front, of course, washed its hands of him. In an official statement distancing itself from the murders, it claimed that the man had been a member for only seven months and had left three years ago.

While searching the premises, the police seized homemade weapons and live cartridges. The press also learned that the thirty-eight-year-old Thomas J. had worked as an administrator at a freight company. According to an unnamed coworker, he was a polite but fundamentally reserved individual who did his work as expected but otherwise avoided all group events. Never had he expressed anti-Muslim sentiments. His neighbors, who likewise knew him to be a quiet, solitary man, said the same thing. An older woman recounted that Thomas J. had once even helped her carry heavy bags up the stairs. The most shocking statement was that of the Muslim family that lived in the same building. Only their names suggested their religion, since the young woman speaking on behalf of the family did not wear a hijab. She said that when she'd crossed paths with Thomas J. by the front door of their apartment building, he had been the first to offer a greeting and had even smiled at their two little kids. No one would have thought him capable of such a thing. As I read the accounts, a cold shiver passed down my back. Impossible, I fumed to myself. It wasn't true that no one had noticed a thing.

Then I remembered Abu Hurayra. Maybe it wasn't so impossible, after all. Abu Hurayra's original name was Philon. He was raised a Christian who had nothing to do with Islam. He had been my classmate in high school. I learned he was a Christian because one day the police showed up at the school to interrogate the whole class—but not Philon because he didn't really have anything to do with the other students. He was a quiet, withdrawn kid. The sort others don't even bother picking fights with because he causes so few ripples to begin with. Then one day this gray little mouse got up and boarded the metro, and when the train he was on had rolled past Station 34, he pulled two hatchets out of his bag and struck out at everyone he could reach. His bad luck was to have gotten onto a car in which one of his fellow passengers happened to be a security guard in civilian clothing, and that man shot him down before he was able to fatally injure anyone.

Those who knew him did not believe Philon was capable of such an act. Not until they visited his profile and saw that shortly before the attack he'd uploaded a short video in which, raising an index finger to the sky in Islamic mode, he had pledged loyalty to the Caliphate. Of course rumor quickly spread that the intelligence service had recruited Philon. Indeed, in school it was whispered that his mother was in fact Jewish, and only to deceive others did he wear a cross around his neck. One thing was certain: if the idiot had wanted to win recognition with his act, he utterly missed the mark. Later I heard that he was buried in the Greek Orthodox tradition. According to the patriarch, Philon had been possessed by the Devil. Aside from the press and his family, no one went to his funeral.

I had to admit the possibility that perhaps no one had suspected a thing about Thomas J. He'd lived with his elderly mother, who had died exactly four years prior to his arrest. A quick mental calculation told me that that is about when the subway incident must have happened too. Thomas J. had boarded the train after work, and then at home, alone, had washed Marwan's spit off his face.

The story didn't let me rest. The news let it be known that Thomas J. had been an active anti-Muslim commentator at one time. So I too began searching the Internet. It didn't take long to figure out that his online name had been J. Jacobs. And I found an ancient forum where, under his own name, he'd sold and traded American film posters. That had been his hobby. All sorts of old odds and ends, but above all, film posters from the 1960s and 1970s. An email address popped up when I clicked "contact": ActForbidden14@skymail.com. A strange name. The search engine turned up all sorts of alternatives. But scrolling down, I found a couple of specific hits. ActForbidden. That happened to be the name of a commentator on a far-right portal. He was active indeed, with 3,429 comments to his credit. The last was from four years earlier, which must have been more or less at the same time as the death of Jacobs's mother and—by my calculations—as the subway incident. The first murder happened six months later. I began browsing his comments. Up until then I'd known that there were lots of folks who didn't like Muslims. The posters and proclamations of the Patriotic Front left no doubt that many would have preferred to pack the lot of them onto ships. Through ActForbidden, however, I stepped into a world so dark that I would never have imagined it existed.

I'd already determined that the Patriotic Front did not lie. If ActForbidden really was Jacobs, then their paths really did diverge.

> I too supported the PF, but my eyes have since opened. This self-professed "patriotic" community is no different than any other political party. Zero principles and zero willingness to accept responsibility. They do nothing but suck up to the liberals. Rutter even boasts that his wife is Muslim.

A quick search revealed that the president of one of the states, Robert Rutter, was in fact Muslim. A second-generation Indonesian immigrant. In everyday speech, *Muslim* was usually a synonym for Arabs, Turks, and Africans. Southeast Asians seemed to constitute a separate caste. In the Zone, at least, they did not attend the mosque. While most Arab and Turkish women did not marry non-Muslim men, this had not been a cause for concern for the Asians.

At the start of his posting on the forum, ActForbidden had shared his thoughts on world affairs only in brief. "It's shameful how the police look on helplessly at ravaging by Muslims," he wrote under one video in which hooded youth smashed in a store window. It was impossible to make out what they were saying; nor were their faces visible. But to ActForbidden and the other commentators, their religion was obvious. I sneered at the thought. After all, in the Zone, Christian African guys were just as apt to go on the rampage as anyone else. Indeed, since they drank more alcohol and did so more often, they alone were the truly brutal.

Naturally, ActForbidden was not fond of refugees, either. More precisely, he didn't regard those who fled from wars, bombings, and terrorism as refugees.

"These are not refugees but continent-occupying warriors," he commented on a news story accompanied by an image of a group of Afghans marching across a Ukrainian steppe. He went on: "The Islamist occupiers arrive as 'refugees.' Then those who get deportation orders simply vanish. The other Islamist Muslims hide them. Those providing them 'legal aid' are none other than the Islamists' collaborators. Supporters of the terrorists."

In ActForbidden's world, all was black and white. "It's obvious that oil billionaires are supporting them financially. How else would they have money for the journey here?" Hadn't he heard that refugees sell everything they own, that their families throw together every last cent so a young man capable of working can travel away?

"Muslim families average six children apiece. Soon they will be the majority." Jacobs had no children. But when it came down to it, he nonetheless did his part to ensure that the relative proportion of Muslims and non-Muslims changed in favor of the latter.

"Even among Muslims bred in European no-go zones, female circumcision is the norm. The police of course don't dare intervene, fearing that an uprising will erupt." So he reacted to a commentary under yet another news item, about a Kurdish man who'd killed his unmarried younger sister after she fell pregnant. What that had to do with female circumcision, I didn't get.

He clearly had a firm conception of Muslims' treatment of women: "To Muslims," he explained, "gang rapes of women in conquered territories is a sport. It even has a name: *taharrush*." I started getting wound up. The word in Arabic means "harassment." Never had I heard anyone say it in my presence, and I couldn't even remember anyone I knew—with the exception of that asshole Marwan—harassing women on the street.

What I'd earlier suspected later became clear: ActForbidden had evidently been quite the self-taught student of Islam.

I agree with Phill Bronner, the chemist and prominent authority on Islam: there is neither moderate nor radical Islam. There is only Islam.

> There are people who call themselves Muslim who do not follow the text
> of the Koran literally, but they are in fact bad Muslims. The true Muslim
> acts in all matters as written in the Koran and as Mohammed acted.

I had to read this twice. Had he not simply referred to Mohammed as
he had, but added, "Peace be upon him," this text might even have been
voiced in some propaganda video of the Caliphate. I did a quick search for
this Phill Bronner. It turned out he was an American professor of chemistry who'd written some eight books analyzing the Koran. The balding,
bow-tie-adorned character was a real star among Jacobs and his ilk.

Agitated though I was, I read on. It was none too easy to navigate the
page, but I kept looking for ActForbidden's comments.

> Islam is a virus that forever remains in the body of its carrier. Even if a
> Muslim is temporarily symptom-free, the virus still lurks within, wait-
> ing to weaken the body of its host. Muslims are raised from childhood
> on to fear hell. And those who do not achieve the sixth pillar, the obliga-
> tion for jihad, go to hell. So the beast can erupt at any time from those
> born to Muslim families.

He even linked to an article at jihad-watch.com whose author likewise as-
serted that those Muslims who fail to achieve the pillars of Islam, including jihad, can, according to the Koran, be fated to hell. The Koranic quotes
were arranged randomly.

I began trembling with rage. But ActForbidden's next comment
calmed my nerves.

> We Europeans are individualists. It doesn't matter to us what color
> someone is, what God they worship, or how they behave at home. All
> that's important to us is how the other relates to other members of
> society and how he does his work. We condemn crime and ostracize
> criminals from our midst. Muslims do not think like this. If a Muslim
> commits a crime, those who share his faith stand by him unthinkingly
> against those they see as heathens. If a European sees ten white men
> kicking a Muslim, he goes over to stop them. But if a Muslim sees the

same thing in reverse, he will sooner stand in as the eleventh. For them, the *ummah* is most important of all.

He posted this comment three months before the subway incident. Could it be that he'd had similar experiences earlier too? Or had he witnessed something of the sort? That would perhaps forever remain a mystery. But one thing was certain: not even we belied his notions.

ActForbidden was not one to bear a grudge, however. In his later posts, at least, he insisted that he harbored no ill feelings toward Muslims.

> I read my comrades' comments and writings with shock. I get the sense that lots of folks are proud of their hatred for Muslims. Not only is hatred unworthy of the European ideal, though, but it's also dangerous: it fogs our vision and good judgment. We must remain composed and focus on the goal. That is what our forebears taught us, those who once beat back the hordes of darkness. In contrast with our enemies, we are not creatures of instinct. We believe in the laws of logic and nature. Let us accept that the world comprises living creatures that, from threadworms to rats to Muslims, behave as their core being dictates. We don't hate rats either. It's not their fault that they make our homes filthy and infect us. It's our transgression, ours alone, to let them.

As time passed, ActForbidden became ever more fanatical.

> European laws cannot apply to Muslims. The question is: Is it expedient to individually punish those who commit their crimes collectively? Should those who would destroy the culture that protects them be included in the protective embrace of European values and laws? I say: collective punishment alone can be the solution to collectively committed crimes. As I've often written: there is neither radical Islam nor moderate Islam, only Islam.

"There is neither radical Islam nor moderate Islam, only Islam." The recognition that he was talking about me, too, hit me in the gut. To him it didn't matter one bit what sort of person I was. What could be done with people like this? Were I to give him a good smack in the face, he'd smile with smug satisfaction that the Muslim in me had emerged.

Would things have turned out differently had I stopped Marwan that day on the subway? I could have somehow gotten a word in, called him aside as if wanting to say something important—or, I don't know, I could have retched right then and there. At least before getting off I could have trailed behind long enough to whisper an apology into his ear instead of that prick Marwan. Would it have mattered? Perhaps.

As I read more of his comments, I was increasingly troubled at the thought that Marwan's crap and our complicit laughter had been a nail in the coffin of Jacobs's victims. Then it hit me.

> Should those who would destroy the culture that protects them enjoy the security of European values and laws? I say: collective punishment alone can be the solution to collectively committed crimes.

That was an older comment of his. By the time Marwan had humiliated him, Jacobs had been ready for murder. When my friends complained that folks hated them, often I only smiled at their whining. But ActForbidden's comments revealed a world darker than I could have imagined. Who, after all, would have thought that Jacobs might in fact be ActForbidden? What if the handsome HR person who had so gently broken the news to Rami the other day that the driver's job he wanted had been filled had in fact been Martell88, TemplarKnight, or PhoenixRising?

Were those idiotic jihadists right? Was a war really close at hand? And what, in fact, would the greater catastrophe be: if the world rising out of the ashes would be that of the jihadists or that of the Patriotic Front and people like ActForbidden? As far I was concerned, the former would at least ask me if I'd side with them. For the first time in my life, I felt Muslim, though I had no brothers. I shut off my machine and went to the kitchen for a glass of water.

7   From week to week, more and more news appeared on my timeline of Islamist terror attacks, peace demonstrations, attacks on mosques, and assaults against Muslims on the street. More than once I planned to block such shares, but then I figured that it was better not to flee reality. Not that that would have been easy to begin with. In the meantime, an election campaign got underway, and the Patriotic Front's anti-Muslim and anti-immigrant rhetoric spewed out of every tap. The stakes were high. The Front and the Conservatives were neck and neck. After the Conservatives eked out a victory, their leader, the aging Martin Alfonz, was able to take the office of prime minister with the support of the other parties. In the Zone we all breathed sighs of relief.

Then the *mim* began popping up. At first I didn't attach much significance to the fact that the Arabic letter *m*—م, starting out as a hook and ending as a tail hanging down—was to be seen here and there. Initially I noticed them on the wall of Husam's apartment block, and soon enough street signs farther and farther from the center of the Zone were spray-painted. That the symbol was not some everyday tag became clear when early one morning a circled م loomed on the facade of Al-Nour mosque, which was among those few buildings the local graffiti artists always spared. Soon it turned out that the م was the reply of some anti-Muslim group to the *noon*, the Arabic letter *n*, that is, or the first letter of the Arabic word *Nasrani*, Nazarene, meaning "Christian." It was the letter with which, long ago, Islamists in the Middle East, Africa, and Asia had marked the homes of Christians, who could then choose between escape, conversion to Islam, payment of *jizya*, or death. Some time ago the noon, ن, had become the symbol of solidarity worldwide for persecuted Christians. Politicians, musicians, actors, and everyday people made it their profile picture after this or that atrocity. And then the tables turned, and there came those who figured the time had come to turn from being the persecuted to being the persecutors. Of course a bit of graffiti did not suddenly transform the Pan-European Federation into a lawless world racked by civil war. The Zone's residents washed off or sprayed over the graffiti.

While the world around me kept changing, my life kept trickling along in the same old rut. My hopes of maybe finding some work after graduation and moving away from home were slowly dashed. At first I'd enthusiastically embarked on efforts to realize the plan. To my great disappointment, in browsing the list of state-funded professional training programs I found not a single one in journalism. So instead I enrolled in a course that earned me a certificate as a "foreign-language client relations specialist administrator." Why "foreign-language"? Because on the application form I'd lied that I am a native speaker of Arabic, and when it came to the examiner tasked with verifying this, well, it turned out that he was even further from native fluency than I was, so we mutually concluded that it would be best for neither one of us to spill the beans about the other. The course itself had lasted just six months, which predetermined the value of the certificate; my résumé was rejected left and right, everywhere I applied.

So in the years to come, instead of carving out my niche as a foreign-language client relations specialist administrator, I lived off of all sorts of work that came my way. Then Rami and I rented a truck to offer moving and other freight services. We didn't form a company. Since we acquired clients by way of our circle of acquaintances, we didn't have to worry about the tax agency. And then when I threw my back out for the third time, I got out of the business altogether. I took on all sorts of paperwork and sometimes did courier work, while in my free time I went to the fitness club, where, on the advice of my doctor, alongside the usual bench presses, curls, and deadlifts I carefully began building up my lower back muscles as well.

The seventh anniversary of my high school graduation was drawing near, and I still wasn't earning enough to move away from home. At least that's the lie I told myself and everyone who asked. Though rents were in fact going up all the time, had I really wanted to, I could have easily gotten a two-bedroom flat in the tower blocks with some buddy of mine. The truth was, moving did not seem as urgent as it had way back when. The routine of life at home had undermined my earlier determination, from my mother's constant dissatisfaction and my father's cynical nitpicking to the usual arguments with my little sister—in short, the sometimes stifling but, on the whole, comforting role of the good son and good big brother.

Only pot rekindled in me from time to time the desire to move. Every night, after locking the door to my room, I would rest my elbows on the windowsill and light up. Staring at the red lights of that lookout tower in the distance, I would then sometimes resolve that, come hell or high water, I would find a place the very next day. At such times by turns I texted Rami or Husam that we should rent a flat together. At first they took me seriously, but after a while they only replied with funny gifs in which there was invariably some reference to grass. When it came down to it, they were right. By morning, once the effects of the THC had passed, my desire to move away went with them. Lying in bed, I would reassure myself that my grandfather's big brother, Abdelkader, had had it easy in his day, for back then there had been as much work as anyone could want, and rents were low too. But these days, with the country chock full of refugees who worked for a dime and with Eastern Europeans, it was no longer so easy for my sort to start a new life for himself.

By then, of course, hardly any refugees had arrived for some years who might have threatened my prospects on the labor market. The new Alfonz government had, in its first year in power, seen to that by bringing final order to the situation in the Mediterranean. A year of negotiations, high-profile diplomatic visits, and drawn-out conciliation resulted in the signing of agreements. Ever since, the Arabic governments along the southern coast had gone all-out to secure both their sea borders and those stretches of border in deserts through which caravans of refugees had earlier reached them,

The surge of those wanting to live was, of course, like the swell of groundwater after a flood. Whenever the road was blocked in one place, the surge erupted elsewhere, always turning toward the path of least resistance. That path meant, more and more, the war zones of the North African Union, where rival militias lived in undisturbed symbiosis with the networks of human traffickers.

The Pan-European Federation, however, had asked for almost none of the fresh arrivals in years. Its satellite offices in Africa and the Middle East were charged with adjudicating locally over asylum applications. They had lately granted entry visas to no more than about one in a hundred applicants. Even those were almost exclusively young women, single mothers, and transsexuals. At first homosexuals had been admitted too, but after half the male applicants had, unsurprisingly, turned gay from one week to the next, they too were quickly dropped from the list of favored applicants. The gates closed.

The Pan-European Federation's flotilla thus did what it was well-practiced at doing: it imposed a naval blockade along the coast of the North African Union. To be sure, the Alfonz government announced that human traffickers would now be subject to laws similar to those addressing terrorism so that, if necessary, live rounds could be fired at them. The political parties all figured that a big ruckus in the middle of the Mediterranean was better than a smaller one in the heart of some city in the Federation. Thanks to this recognition, the rising popularity of the Patriotic Front began to wane, and then seemed to stop in its tracks.

Rights groups of course continued to protest the deportation of refugees. But only a few thousand people showed up for the In Solidarity with Refugees demonstration in front of the parliament building—mostly Rastafarian hippies and black-clad anarchists. And the organizers had deliberately timed the event for a Friday afternoon, hoping that those praying in the mosques would also join in.

"Why? Would they stand up for us if they were in our place?" Rami shot back at me one day at the gym when I suggested that we go take a look at the protest, He didn't let me reply.

"You think if we put your passport on the table with a knife next to it, and told any refugee that by driving that knife into you they could get the passport, they'd think even for a minute?"

"What sort of fucking example is this?"

"It's true," he said. "If I needed to stick the knife into any of them to keep my passport, I'd do it without thinking," he huffed. "Besides, what good does it do anyone if more of them come here? Why, they can't even eat normally with forks and knives."

For a couple of seconds we locked eyes.

"Oh, sure," he finally said with a wave of the hand. "These fuckers straight out of the Middle Ages hate dogs just as much as you do. Of course, you have a thing for them."

It wasn't worth continuing the argument. I resolved to go take a look at the demonstrators sometime on my own. But then somehow I never got around to it after all.

A couple of years passed. Since far fewer new refugees were arriving, the Conservatives hoped they could finally get back in shape with the coming elections. But the Patriotic Front didn't even allow them time to catch a breath. After Martin Alfonz was diagnosed with cancer and announced he would not be running again, it took aim at the new candidate for prime minister, who was then the interior minister, Sandra Bollen.

Public opinion polls had the Front and the Conservatives still running neck and neck, while the Socialists could not manage to scrape themselves back together after their recent defeat, and the Liberals and the Greens just barely made it into Parliament. Every terrorist attack, and indeed every bit of news equating the word *Muslim, immigrant, migrant, Middle Eastern*, or *African* with the word perpetrator served to expand the Patriotic Front's base of support.

"If people can't see the problem, then there is none," reasoned the interior minister. And yet escaping the refugee problem was not so simple. The mass deportation of refugees would have required international treaties and a ton of money. Moreover, the Obligatory Work Program—despite the Patriotic Front's assertions to the contrary—worked quite well. Decked out in blue-yellow coveralls, the refugees did a fine job of keeping public squares clean, and the news portals wrote that they had completely replaced Eastern Europeans in the unskilled labor force and as seasonal agricultural workers. But the terrorist attacks and the economic crisis had their effect. The Patriotic Front kept gathering strength.

And so Bollen decided to make the refugees invisible. There was only one way to do it. There were accommodations that had been built in those well-traveled areas of cities where the voters of the Patriotic Front and, more important, her own party lived. The plan would be to move them to other, preferably less expensive urban areas inhabited by Muslims and Africans. The Zone was just such a place.

8   The first buses arrived on a Monday in April. The renovation of the empty tower blocks in the northern reaches of the Zone had been completed a week earlier, so as the din of construction faded away the refugees began occupying the flats allotted to them. Arabs, Afghans, Africans, and Bangladeshis found themselves living alongside each other. Families and single women were placed in the blocks to the east; single men in those to the west, on the other side of the park.

Of course there was a political scandal all the same. With the opening of the newly renovated tower blocks slated for the refugees, the Zone's finances became political fodder. The most strident voice in this debate was naturally the Patriotic Front. Its representatives charged Bollen with sweeping problems under the rug and said it was unacceptable that the government should be throwing money into a district that—so they claimed—fell outside the supervision of the authorities and was under the control of criminal gangs and Islamist groups.

Our streets were flooded with news photographers and TV crews. They came, they captured what they wanted, and they left. They stayed not a minute longer than necessary. From the way they moved and behaved, and from what they pointed their cameras at, it was evident even from afar what sort of picture they sought to paint of our home. They went about unabashedly sticking their microphones under people's noses and fixing their cameras on the faces of women in hijabs. Rumor had it that some crews had offered young people money to hurl projectiles their way. Some residents of the Zone just snapped. A ZEF1 news summary once showed old Ashraf's son, Basim, chasing away a news crew while shouting uncouth words. Though his face had been obscured, anyone who knew him immediately recognized the voice as his. Moreover, Basim had not bothered to put down the knife he'd been using at work to slice the meat he'd been roasting on the rotisserie to make kebabs—which made it seem as if he'd been out to cut down the reporters. The poor kid never had been a genius.

The new arrivals had been fond of the Zone earlier. Rents were less than in other parts of the city, and it was easier to find work there without language skills. Abu Sa'id employed quite a few. Never had such a surge of people arrived before. The scene on the street in the Zone changed in the bat of an eye. Strauss Square was overrun with loitering Arabs, Afghans, and blacks, and the sight of all those young men with unfamiliar faces filled many longtime residents with unease. Mothers were less and less apt to take their kids to their playground in the park, and rumor had it that it was no longer safe for women to walk the empty streets after dark. From then on my brother-in-law always sat around in the hospital lobby waiting for my little sister so after work she wouldn't have to go home on her own. Khalil—to my utmost satisfaction, I might add—was jealously protective of her.

Husam got anxious too. He had three little sisters, not one of whom wore the hijab. And some of the new arrivals were not really in tune with the behavioral norms hereabouts. Some of them were real assholes.

"We've become strangers in our own city," Rami used to say. He used to send pictures when he saw Africans sitting in the park where we used to play.

Most conspicuous of all was the change to the fitness club. The weekends now saw the weight machines swarming with scrawny local guys who until then had been in the habit of lifting only their phones. Deep down perhaps they figured that by expanding their body mass they could come to look daunting enough so they wouldn't have to prove their strength in practice too.

But not everyone was bothered by the refugees. Those northern apartment blocks were barely a fifteen-minute walk from the Tawhidi mosque. Sheik Taymullah and his men believed that the time had come for da'wah. They organized free-clothing distribution, held religious instruction for children and teens, and after Friday prayer lured in people with soup kitchens. At such times the line in front of the army tent set up on the inner courtyard of the building was so long it often wound its way right out to the street.

Security checks were meanwhile tightened at junctures leading out of the Zone. We were often ID'd as it was on our way to the city center, but from then on, if I had to be there by a certain time I always had to add ten minutes to avoid being late. Not that I had any reason to complain. The officers on patrol and the machine-gun-toting, black-uniformed soldiers of the Anti-Terror Office were more or less civilized. Sure, at first they invariably made some crude remark to get my attention, but then, on realizing that I was responding with all due respect and, moreover, in their native language, they immediately let down their guard and turned polite. They took a quick look at my ID, sometimes posing a few routine questions, meanwhile observing how my pupils expanded, whereupon they wished me a good day and let me on my way. Later they installed cameras with facial recognition. That saved us some time. As for the streets in the Zone, the police patrolled those even more often than they used to, which, oddly enough, even those chums with whom I used to run from the cops on those tear-gas-filled nights were glad about. No matter. We'd grown older.

Husam and I were sitting about at old Ashraf's. We were waiting for Rami. He was talking about the office while I kept wondering how I could turn the conversation to Latifa without him getting suspicious. I'd liked her ever since I was a kid. She was majoring in sociology and had only one semester to go before graduating. We were in touch about once a week, actually. I wasn't pushing it; mostly we just exchanged films and music. Earlier we'd both been fond of the more lyrical variations of rap, but more recently she'd begun taking a turn to jazz, which I, despite my utmost efforts, just didn't know what to make of. Since she would soon be a college graduate, I figured the time had come for me to signal my interest a bit more seriously.

While Husam was talking away, I had one eye on the screen: a new documentary about the lives of border guard units. The episode happened to be about the work of the Federal Coast Guard. The aerial film was edited to good effect, with close-up shots showing coast guard motorboats towing a dinghy to a ferry. From the whites of the eyes flashing from out of the black faces it was hard to tell whether the boat's passengers were in awe, afraid, or angry. The background music, in any case, suggested dramatic tension. Machine-gun-toting soldiers looked on from a tower aboard the ferry as officials in red jackets handed out packages to the refugees, and then led the families, after separating them from the single men, into designated areas. The narrator explained that sometimes the ferry loitered on open water for days before heading back to reception centers established on the territory of partner nations. Years earlier the governments of the Pan-European Federation had lauded the centers' creation as a huge success story. It had taken decades of negotiations, diplomatic pressure, and, not least, loads of money to persuade African governments that the Federation could deport refugees to their territories.

Husam had turned his attention to describing the ass of some Indian lady colleague of his, distracting me from the narrator, who happened to be singing the praises of the Federal Coast Guard's humanity and perseverance. But with the next clip, Husam again lost my attention, for next on was my favorite program host, Jolanar Mahdavi. She was interviewing the officer in command of the operation, who, standing beside a long metal table, was pointing out various objects seized from the migrants. Mahdavi's cascade of black curly hair was tied above her head with a band that made her look like quite the wild gal, and the camera had zoomed in on her mouth, adorned with dull lipstick, and her snow-white teeth. The plastic bags on the table, each bearing a number, contained money, phones, knives, scissors, and other things that could only spell trouble on the ferry. At the far end of the table were rectangular brown packages. The thickset officer kept replying to Mahdavi's questions from below his brush cut with the incomparable, robotlike voice of those in positions of authority, but written all over him was what he would really have preferred to do: sweep all that shit off the table and fuck Mahdavi on it right then and there. I didn't blame him for an instant.

"The lab testing has yet to be done, but based on prior experience there is every reason to suspect that the packages contain a prohibited narcotic substance," said the officer.

"So if the boat had reached its destination, the coast, the drug would already have been on the streets of Europe," Mahdavi concluded, giving her lower lip a sexy bite on finishing the sentence, whereupon the commanding officer concurred with a smile.

Three refugees at the table next to ours were also staring at the screen. From their accents I guessed they had arrived from the Middle East. Their clothes, which were practically like those of any local, suggested they had been here for a good while already. They didn't bother me in particular, and since they comprised two aging, fortyish men and a scrawny young guy, Husam didn't get anxious on account of them either. He happened to be looking at some job search link. He'd been after me for a good while to find some office job for myself. He said I could do better than being a gopher at a real estate agency. I had to agree. Not that I'd ever held a high opinion of myself, but I knew I had it in me to do more with my life than waste it standing in lines in government offices and being a courier. My father, too, made remarks all the time letting me know just how dissatisfied he was with me. He kept saying that it would take only a word from me, and he'd put in a good word on my behalf to Abu Sa'id, from whom I'd surely get some job more worthy of me. No doubt that's just what would have happened too, but it was the last thing I wanted. For the rest of my life my father would have kept haranguing me every time we'd get into an argument about how, if it hadn't been for him, I'd still be lolling about in office lines.

"Here we are," said Husam, sticking his phone under my nose. H&H had a bunch of open positions. Just when I was about to look them over, I noticed that those sitting at the table next to ours had fallen silent and were looking at us. I returned the stares.

"Don't mind me, my friend," said one of the fortyish men, a mustachioed, balding fellow. "May I ask a question?"

"Sure," I replied.

"What mosque do you pray in?"

Now I wasn't in the habit of praying in any mosque, but a fellow doesn't go about admitting that sort of thing. Especially not to a stranger.

"In Al-Nour," I shot back after a couple seconds of thought. That was the closest to the truth, for Al-Nour was the only mosque I'd been to at all. Up until I was six my grandfather had often taken me to Friday prayers there. The whole thing lasted barely an hour, and yet to me it seemed an eternity. To make time go by faster I kept picking at the thick threads of the burgundy patterned rug. Grandfather was proud of me all the same for sitting through it all in silence. On the way out he would always show me off to all the other old men, and afterward he'd take me to the sweets shop too. Then, encouraged by what he saw as my great patience relative to my young age, he told my father that he'd enroll me for lessons at the sheik's during one summer vacation. Father didn't resist. The classes were taught by a young sheik's apprentice. There were eight of us kids there from the whole Zone. At first I wasn't really in the mood for it all, but the apprentice sheik was a good guy. We played all sorts of games and watched cartoons about the lives of the prophets. What I know about religion, I know from there. *I was last at Friday prayer thirteen years ago*, I now thought. If there's a God, and he really is as strict as some folks say, no doubt I'll burn in hell for eternity.

"Ah, Al-Nour. Yes. We've heard of it, but up till now we've just gone to the Dar al-Sunna." On pronouncing the name of the Tawhidi mosque, his tone of voice turned a bit grudging, which piqued my curiosity.

"Didn't you like the Dal al-Sunna?" I asked.

The other man shook his head.

But it was the mustachioed fellow who began: "It's an odd place to be sure. When we first stepped in, everyone looked at me as if I wasn't wearing pants. After the khutba this guy with a beard and wearing a white jellabiya came over. 'Assalamu alaykum,' he said. 'Wa alaykum as-salam wa rahmatullah wa barakatu,' I replied. 'I welcome you to the mosque, my brother. How do you feel?' he asked cordially. We chatted a little, and then he blurted out what he wanted. 'Do you know that the Prophet, peace be with him, shaved his moustache, and we, followers of the Sunna, must proceed in all matters according to the Prophet's example?'"

While telling this story the man guardedly stroked the length of his moustache. It must have taken years of work. He was clearly proud of it.

"Tell the other part, too, Dad," the younger fellow, apparently his son, ⸺d him.

⸺ even had it in them to tell me what to think about prayer too," ⸺ustachioed man. "And they made a fuss about me holding my ⸺ the *Qiyam* lower than, according to them, is appropriate. ⸺ing for forty-two years, *alhamdulillah*, and no one has said ⸺g to me before. If I'd wanted to live among folks like that, I wouldn't have come to Europe. I would have moved to the territory of the Caliphate."

Husam was meanwhile conspicuously immersed in his phone.

"You won't have any such problem at Al-Nour," I said, slurping from my coffee. "But I'd recommend going there only if your papers are in order."

I wasn't making this up. It had been happening more and more often that plainclothes cops were stopping cars on the roads leading to the mosques and rounding up everyone who didn't have a valid ID or residence permit. But even the staff at government-owned mosques bent over backward to uphold the laws. Rumors were abuzz that after Friday prayers the staff called aside people who looked like refugees and asked them if their papers were in order. If the answer was no, they politely asked that next time they not cause a problem for the congregation. After a while the refugees stopped attending mosques.

"Everything's in order," replied the mustachioed man. "*Alhamdulillah.*"

"Then there won't be a problem," I said. "I can tell you speak the language well. That's good. At Al-Nour there is no Arabic khutba."

I opted not to let him in on the fact that not only the pious attended Al-Nour. Even back when I was a kid it was public knowledge that among those praying were undercover agents there to observe groups of people who drew aside from the others, as well as the people's reactions, and that they recorded the khutbas with devices in their pockets. Since then technology had improved a lot, so not a word that passed in the mosque stayed secret, that was for sure. Besides, the sheiks at the mosques allowed the men from the various secret services to come and go. Everyone knew that the repair workers who looked like Arabs, wandering about in the vicinity of the mosques, were in fact intelligence agents. It was also an open secret that the sheiks often voluntarily reported on those who began voicing overly radical opinions.

"What is your line of work, my friend?" asked the mustachi

Here we go, I thought. The next question would be abou
knew about some work that paid better than the work doled o
ernment. I didn't, and I was in no mood to embark on a long

"I just happen to be looking for work, and I'm talking with my friend," I said. "It's been a while since we last met. Excuse me, my friend." And, with that, I turned back to Husam. That day I could no longer quiz him about Latifa. Moreover, thanks to the guy with the moustache, I even had a guilty conscience. *Maybe Allah, if he exists, is now angry with me.* After pondering this for a while I shrugged my shoulders. After all, I figured, if those guys take my advice and go to Al-Nour, everyone will be better for it, with me having gotten a few hasanats from Allah.

9

"Are you kidding me? This is no hate crime. Obviously it's just Muslim criminals murdering each other."

"Most of the victims don't have criminal records, Sandra."

"If you're trying to say that the police aren't doing such a great job, unfortunately I've got to agree. Criminals ought to be in the database."

"Public opinion is on edge."

"You know better than anyone what battles I wage for resources. Every damn center. The police [indecipherable words] deserve more. I'm the interior minister, but for what? My hands are tied. The very reason we drafted the New Loyalist Act was so we could get right down to work after the elections and put things in order."

"The victims include women."

"That's really awful, Robert. But you know perfectly well what top experts on the advisory boards say, that women's status in Muslim communities isn't much. Often enough a woman's murder isn't much more than a warning signal directed at another clan. I'm sure the authorities will find the murderers. But now the priority is protecting respectable citizens. That's the public opinion. And they happen to be in the grip of fear, fear of Islamic terrorists."

The leaked recording first emerged on a blog and then spread like wildfire on the net. Everyone waited for the government to call the recording a cheap fake. But they didn't even try to deny that on it were Sandra Bollen and her deputy, Robert Schwarz.

The left wing press was fuming:

Bollen denies the racist motivation behind the murders

A woman's life has no value for Muslims, says Bollen

Do the lives of Muslim citizens not matter?

A total offensive ensued against the Conservatives' nominee for prime minister.

For its part, the Patriotic Front must have been concerned that, with the recording's anti-Islamic invectives, sympathy for Bollen could rise precisely in the ranks of its own voters. Which is why they called the leak staged, alleging that it was a deliberate media ploy on the part of the Conservatives. They kept saying that Bollen had been a failure at her job as interior minister, and by misleading Conservative voters of good faith she was now seeking to convince them that as the new head of government she'd be capable of making order. They spoke from fear. Though some opinion polls had the Front three or four percentage points ahead of the Conservatives, ever since Alfonz, the incumbent prime minister, had announced that he would pass on the nomination to Bollen, the gap was closing.

The right-wing media, meanwhile, defended the interior minister out of habit. As always, its commentators blamed the left for everything. They pointed out that the political correctness of former socialist governments had allowed matters to reach the point they had. That the Conservatives had already been in power for four years, well, they were generously silent about that. And yet they published long analyses arguing that Bollen's New Loyalist Act could mean new hope for the restoration of order and public trust.

Muslim organizations from across the spectrum unanimously and stridently condemned the phone conversation.

"It's me that can be heard on the recording," Bollen finally announced flat out. For the extraordinary press conference—which I watched on my tablet while jolting along on the subway—she'd put on a tight burgundy costume dress that, together with her thick, black-framed eyeglasses, imparted her a foxy look indeed. Though the things she said and her views about Muslims sent a cold shiver down my spine, thanks to her exterior I overlooked a lot of it.

"I take responsibility for my words. If you were to hear the recording in full, it would be clear to all of you that Mr. Robert Schwarz and I happened to be talking about the increasingly untenable security situation in certain parts of the country."

She looked about the room before continuing.

"I never made it a secret that I stand on the side of order. As interior minister, even at the cost of serious conflicts I struggled to secure the resources needed. We increased the budget of the police and the intelligence services by close to twenty percent, thanks to which our homeland is today more secure than four years earlier."

Following this she spoke for many minutes about how, if elected, she would extend the New Loyalist Act, with which she would secure an alliance—without regard to religion—with every citizen loyal to the homeland, and with zero tolerance toward all forms of radicalism. While listening, I had the distinct impression that she was holding not a press conference but a campaign speech.

"Minister," came the first question. "On the recording you say Muslims don't regard women as human beings. Would you explain that?"

"What I said was this: the status of women is low. And I did not come up with this idea myself. This is a well-known fact that our country's most prestigious research institutes and their staff, including the State Migration and Integration Office, have also confirmed. You can find the relevant research on their Internet pages. But I'd suggest we talk of the main subject at hand. Among the Muslims living in our homeland are some who do not regard European norms as applying to them. And this is untenable, for it is detrimental not only to society in general but also those of our Muslim compatriots who live in harmony with the majority population."

"Don't you feel, Ms. Bollen, that the words voiced on the recording have Islamophobic overtones?"

"That assumption is not only unfounded but also offensive. I call your attention to the fact that in implementing the New Loyalist Act we have regarded as key partners both our party's and our allies' Muslim wings and the Central Fatwa Council."

A few days later in the Zone you could hardly find a Bollen or Conservative Party poster in one piece. From then on Bollen smiled down upon us only from giant posters glued high up on billboards and the walls of buildings. And of course from aggressive online ads extolling a supporting cast of Conservatives of all colors and religions; promising economic growth, security, and social harmony; or conjuring up alarm with the bogeyman of a Patriotic Front government.

The Socialists fell to action. Knocking on every door, they sought to position themselves as the last hope. Soon enough the Conservatives'

Muslim wing also found their steam. Activists in hijabs handed out fly-
ers on Strauss Square, seeking to persuade the locals that if Bollen was
not given the chance to restore peace, then the Front would come with a
Muslim Holocaust.

From one day to the next all my friends became political experts. Most
began regarding Bollen's possible victory as the lesser evil and agreed that
the greatest danger was the Patriotic Front, which some pollsters already
had ahead by as much as five percent. They didn't convince me, and Latifa's activism had a lot to do with that.

"No one should be fooled by Bollen's siren song!" Latifa posted. "The
New Loyalist Act is in every respect just what the Patriotic Front wants
too. Indeed, it's even more dangerous. The Nazis are dumb, but Bollen is
smart enough to do the same thing in a legally and constitutionally unas-
sailable manner."

Latifa believed this very seriously. Every day she shared a whole series of secret amendments to Bollen's Islamophobic New Loyalist Act, like
the Trust Score. I always appreciated those posts, and sometimes I shared
them.

Moreover, I resolved to go vote for the first time in my life. No one
in our family had been into politics. As with Latifa, my grandfather, had
been a big fan of that bygone Socialist prime minister, Strauss, whom he
could thank for his citizenship and the fact that his wife had been able to
join him here. My grandfather—who perhaps never connected the dots
enough to blame that prime minister for his unhappy marriage—had remained grateful all his life, and he voted for the Socialists to the day he
died. I had nothing against the party either. I decided that out of nostalgia
for Grandfather I too would give them my vote.

The polling place was fashioned out of the old post office building. I
arrived late in the afternoon. Only two people were ahead of me: an elderly Turkish man using a cane and the young woman who held him up.
I couldn't determine whether everyone had already voted or no one was
interested in the whole thing. I stepped over to the counter. The polling
clerk—a fortyish woman with her brown hair in a bun—smiled as she took
my ID and held it under a scanner. The machine beeped, and she shook
her head.

"I'm sorry, but the records indicate that you are prohibited from participating in civic affairs."

I looked at her in shock.

"You are banned from public affairs," she repeated as if thinking I hadn't understood her the first time. "Unfortunately you can't vote." She glanced at the monitor. "According to the records, almost four years ago you . . . yes, to be precise, on May 16 you were formally banned from participating in civic affairs."

That's when it came back to me. It had happened toward the end of my days with Rami working in freight. At the end of a tiring day we sat down in the park to smoke a joint.

The smoke quickly caught the attention of two plainclothes cops. After checking our IDs they informed us that according to the latest amendment to the relevant law, any form of public consumption of marijuana was illegal. It then began to dawn on me. Earlier several people had posted the news, but because I couldn't even imagine that anyone in the Zone would give a shit, I didn't give it a second thought. In scanning our IDs they did a background check and determined that since we'd not committed our violation as previous offenders, they would not take us in. We'd probably receive only a reprimand and be banned from participation in civic affairs. They said we could find precise information about the ban on the police website. Two weeks later we received formal notification from the prosecutor's office, saying we had eight days to appeal. We didn't bother.

Banning offenders from public affairs was among the first measures implemented by Bollen as interior minister. The gist of it was that if someone was caught doing something stupid and illegal, the authorities would start with a digital reprimand and then prohibit them from participating in elections or referendums until a date stipulated in the law. Most guys in the Zone, like Rami and me, were not bothered by this. Of course all sorts of civic organizations were up in arms, and maybe there were some demonstrations. I don't remember exactly. Back then people took to the streets over every little thing.

"But that happened four years ago," I said to the woman. "My prohibition was for a year."

"The prohibition does not end on its own, sir," she explained. "The individual concerned must initiate the restoration of his rights."

"Then I am doing so now. Please restore my rights."

"I'm sorry, but you would have had to apply no later than fourteen days before the election, on March 5, at the Citizenship Office based on your registered address of residence."

"You're being serious? I would have had to have go there in person and stand in line?"

"If you request a number online you won't have to wait in line," she replied mechanically. "Besides, you can request the restoration online too, if you are registered in the Digital Citizenship Gateway. And your Trust Score is 70 percent." Naturally I wasn't registered.

"Let's just forget it, dammit," I said and turned around.

The Conservatives won the election. Everyone was surprised that they got 41 percent of the vote. The Patriotic Front captured 32 percent, and the Socialists, 15 percent. At least my vote wouldn't have made a difference. So Bollen had a towering victory. After that I was no longer even in the mood to jack off to her image.

10

Since after earning my certificate I didn't get a job anywhere that might have set me on the path to a career, for a while I gave up hope of ever going to work for a multinational. But Husam, who was luckier than me, told lots of stories about the office he worked in, and finally I found myself psyched up yet again to give it another try. Just what he actually did there, I'm not sure. He told me in detail when he got the job, but I lost track after just ten seconds. All I remembered was that he made lots of phone calls and that his group included a foxy Indian gal. And so I submitted my application for the position of "corporate data phone researcher" at H&H.

Husam helped me fill out the online registration form. With a last name like Nasim, applying would normally have been a thorny affair, but since the Zone qualified as a "socially disadvantaged" district, and under a new law companies could reap a tax advantage by employing those living in such districts, my prospects were greater. For now, then, it seemed that Bollen would not usher in the end of the world after all. Of course the tax break alone would not have been enough to get me a job. Everyone in the Zone knew full well that "Muhammads" were not exactly welcome at better workplaces. But Husam saw this differently too, as he did everything. He figured it wasn't that Muhammads were not welcome at better workplaces but precisely that most Muhammads were incapable of working at the better places.

"Seriously now. Who do you think would let the guys anywhere near a serious client?" he asked, and I had to agree with him. Going through the list of our onetime friends, it was easy to see that eight of ten of them would have no business in an office. To raise my chances, Husam told one of the HR people at his workplace over lunch one day that he'd known me since I was young and that he considered me a reliable fellow.

Finally I got through the first round of applications and was called in for an interview. When I reached the home stretch, my anxiety was every bit as intense as had been my initial resistance to the very idea of vying for such serious work. I was past twenty-eight, and at home I was badgered more and more about marriage. After my little sister got hitched, not a single dinner at home passed without the subject coming up, if in no other way then in bantering. There were two ways of changing the increasingly untenable situation. One was to move away from home. I could have easily scraped together enough to rent myself a decent room. The money I pulled in at the real estate agency was just enough to share a flat with some buddy of mine. But I figured that if I was to move away, I wanted to be my own man. The other option was, of course, marriage, which did not seem as simple as my parents and folks their age imagined. The only candidate I could imagine was Husam's sister. I had to admit, however, that at the moment I wasn't exactly a good catch for a beautiful Muslim girl who, moreover, had a college degree. For some reason I felt that if I got the job and it worked out, that would get me on the fast track to Latifa. Then, at least, her family wouldn't resist the idea.

Once I learned the date of my job interview, for several nights straight I woke up in alarm, gasping for air. Fortunately Husam was there for me to lean on. He tried cheering me up, describing his own interview in detail and devoting hours to reviewing the possible questions with me. Beyond that, I watched some twenty videos from on the net about the secrets of successful job interviews and got myself a nice, new, light blue dress shirt. Later it turned out that my anxiety was pointless. The interview was merely a formality. On the way out of the office afterward, the HR person reassured me, saying I shouldn't worry, that even a moderately skilled chimpanzee could do the work.

My job was to be on the phone all day long calling all sorts of small and midsize businesses in Europe and the Middle East, and if the person I was supposed to reach had the time—usually he didn't—I would, referring to a list in front of me, question them about the company's circumstances, and then enter the data into the records. The workday was eight hours, with a lunch break. Twenty-eight of us sat in front of our computers in a large, fifth-floor office whose glass walls afforded an imposing view of the other office buildings around it. But we mostly just stared at our monitors. I didn't have much contact with my colleagues. Only when waiting at the same time by the coffeemaker, in the kitchen, did we say a few words to each other. That left me feeling a bit tense during my first few days on the job, but then I quickly got used to the office culture. "How are you this morning, Wladek?" "Everything OK, Petra?" "It's raining cats and dogs, Tokumbo—I hope you didn't get soaked." At other times I was more apt to be immersed in my phone, as if I had some pressing matter to tend to. Lots of complete strangers locked up in a small space. The only thing we had in common was that all of us spent a third of our day in the same aquarium.

Judith alone piqued my curiosity. Sitting two desks away from me, she was a short, vivacious girl with a sweet round face and a short, plucky bob of hair. When she smiled, her dimples appeared and her bunnylike longer front teeth flashed.

For weeks I toyed with the thought of asking her out. Then when I finally noticed her profile name, I quickly scrapped the idea. Her hobbies were bicycling and wall climbing. While that explained her tight thighs and incredibly shapely ass, it also dashed my hopes. In most of her pictures she was in the company of likewise sports-minded male friends, every last one of them of the broad-shouldered or at least sinewy sort. I had to accept that we were not made for each other. Outside of the gym I didn't move a whole lot, and as for bikes, I'd hated them since childhood. They simply hadn't been invented for my legs. Their narrow saddles broke in my ass, pounded away at my balls, and sent pins and needles through my prick. I shuddered at the thought that after a bike ride together I might not even have anything left to screw Judith with. Even as my interest in her quickly waned, I still found her alluring. She was a veritable bundle of energy, her aura brightening my mood on those humdrum days at work. I sought out her company. As an alibi over lunch I even asked her advice on running shoes, for naturally enough she was a runner too. She went on at length about how to choose the ideal pair, and she even sent me a link afterward. I didn't open it.

The recipe for survival was the same for each of us: getting to work on time in the morning, communicating as little as possible with the others, and shutting off our machines at 4:57 PM. The remaining three minutes were just enough to get back downstairs from the fifth floor, so at 5:00, or at most two minutes later, we could swipe our cards to sign out.

Since the subject of marriage now came up even more often at family dinners, and finally my pay seemed plausible enough, I decided to move away from home. It took only five minutes of browsing to find a simply furnished flat on the top floor of a five-story, somewhat renovated apartment building with a red-brick veneer at the edge of the tower blocks in the southern part of the Zone. The water heater was on its last legs, so by the time the hot water flowed out of the shower head, at least ten liters had to flow. At the same time, I was happy: besides the living room that opened to a French balcony there was a separate bedroom, and I didn't have to spend on furniture either. Most important though, finally I was free.

Father was not enthused about my new work. He said I could earn this much money in a manner "more worthy of" me, and offered to ask around among his acquaintances. I said thanks but no thanks, explaining that I wanted to prove to myself that I could stand on my own two feet. He called me an idiot but didn't push it. Mother let on that deep down he was happy that I was giving it a go on my own in the world.

With the job, a new world opened up before me in many respects. Among other things, I soon realized with dismay that police ID checks and strangers' suspicious glances were directed neither at me as an individual nor at my face, but mainly at my wardrobe. This hit me one morning on the way to work.

The day began as per my new routine. The subway train pulled into the station, and on getting aboard I plopped down on a seat and pulled out my phone. I was just about to start scrolling down the news when my eyes fixed on the girl sitting across from me. As the train started off, she loosened her hijab. She pulled out the needle that held it together and put it between her lush lips while first drawing the beige hijab backward and then, in a well-practiced move, winding it round her neck like a shawl. Pulling a little cosmetics case from her handbag, she put the needle inside before then opening up a little folding mirror to check her makeup and hairdo. Her series of movements were routine: under the New Loyalist Act religious symbols could now be worn only in residential districts. Judging from her elegant attire, I figured that she, too, worked in some office. Catching my gaze, she seemed to smile at me momentarily before her eyes flitted away. The smile—or at least what I perceived as a smile—filled me with happiness. Such a girl previously wouldn't have even noticed me, or if she had, even in the best-case scenario her eyes would have radiated only pity.

I made as if to stare into the depths of my phone, but just before doing so, I stole a glance all around me. The older man sitting beside me was staring straight ahead at some on-screen collecting game. Warily I opened FaceDetect and homed in on the girl's face with the camera. Though laws on the protection of personal data prohibited the use of the software, one of Marwan's cousins had a phone shop, and since he knew me, he agreed to break into my phone's operating system. FaceDetect found three profiles, on one of which I immediately recognized the girl. She was called Nora, which was probably really Noura. Her info was set as secret, so I didn't find out much about her. Just to be sure, I narrowed the personals application range to a ten-meter radius, figuring maybe she'd turn up among the search results.

At that moment my phone began beeping and flashing red, and the phones of the other passengers on train did the same. An anti-terror raid. The car arrived at a station, the doors opened, and a pleasant, mechanical female voice announced the rules for leaving the station. While being swept up the escalator with the others, I scrolled down the message the application had sent and was fuming inside over why the anti-terror signal hadn't come thirty seconds later. That is when, out of the corner of my eye, I noticed that an anti-terror commando standing by one of the exits was nodding in my direction and muttering something into his microport.

For fuck's sake, this is the last thing I need, I thought to myself. *They've picked me out, and now I'll be late to work for sure.* I was already anticipating the awkward scenario of having to report at the HR department with a police report to prove that I hadn't simply been playing hooky. Two men were approaching as the crowd I was in moved their way. The three of us formed a perfect triangle in the teeming mass. Although like most of the passengers they, too, were brown-skinned, I had no doubt that they were with the anti-terror service. Try as I did to force an indifferent expression onto my face, deep down I was preparing to be thrown to the ground or, at best, to be surrounded. The two men were by now only meters away from me. *I'll let them do what they want,* I thought. *If I don't resist, there won't be any doubt that I was surprised, so I can at least clear things up faster.*

Taking a deep breath, I let myself relax, so hopefully not a single muscle of mine would seize up if they were about to take me to the ground.

A moment later, they were nowhere to be seen. The third point of the triangle wasn't me, after all, but a guy being swept along behind me. Just before the crowd closed up behind me, I had enough time to catch a glimpse of a figure in a hoodie, white sneakers, and a baseball cap being tackled. At that moment it struck me that I—the office worker, Nasim— was invisible to the police. An ironed shirt coupled with a V-neck sweater had transformed me from being a grimy resident of the Zone into a re- spectable citizen. A taxpayer beyond all suspicion, a useful member of so- ciety. This was the moment when I decided to leave behind the style of the city outskirts forever and dress just the same way even in my free time.

Later I further realized that this new way of dressing could be even more effective when combined with practical accoutrements: a workplace ID card hung around my neck and a file folder stuffed under my arm would hide me not only from the police like some magic cape but also end the suspicious glances. I could now walk the length of downtown as if I, too, belonged there, and even younger gals now sat down beside me on the subway. Why, one day a girl of about twenty, with blue eyes and light brown hair, even smiled at me before taking a seat directly across from me. Instinctively I returned the smile and caressed the ID around my neck before, embarrassed, I fell to typing away on my phone.

I was in love with my new look. Each morning before heading out, I would gaze at myself in the full-length mirror in the vestibule, and then sometimes I'd toy with the thought that if I were a terrorist I would carry out attacks only in such elegant attire. Indeed, I'd even wear a suit. With a dapper belt and, naturally, a fashionable, narrow silk necktie versus some cheap, prettied polyester fake. I'd learn to tie a real Windsor knot. If I were wearing such attire, they'd even let me into anti-terror headquarters. Of course the devil is always in the details. Moving about in a suit is at least as hard as it is to aim with a machine gun. Indeed, from afar this is ap- parent if someone is used to wearing hoodies and bomber jackets. I would naturally aim for perfection. A good posture, eyes staring straight ahead, and moving forward as naturally as can be, but meanwhile focused on the mission. At such times I was always reminded that terrorists are all fucking idiots. If they already believe so much in some nonsense to give up their lives for it, at least they could try for effectiveness. Instead—with some rare exceptions—the news was constantly full of news of low-frills attacks claiming only one or two lives. This, however, invariably led me to conclude that it was best for everyone this way.

The new fashion brought unanticipated challenges, however. One was picking out a pair of shoes. I quickly realized that my feet were just too broad for the sort of slick leather shoes that best matched linen trousers— shoes that, it seemed, had been crafted specifically with the narrow-footed in mind.

Fashion racism, I often chugged away to myself while searching through shoe stores in vain. Wide feet were perhaps useful in deserts, since their owners didn't sink quite so deep into the sand, but in the world of elegance they were decidedly a disadvantage. Finally I happened upon a pair of pointed shoes that were a suitable compromise. And I was happy with them right up until the moment when I stepped into the office the next day.

"New shoes, huh?" said Wladek with a smile as the two of us waited by the coffee machine. "You look perfect." My first impulse was to give him a smack.

"Thanks," came my somewhat forced reply. No matter what Wladek said to me, the odd peal of his tone of voice always filled me with suspicion. When it came to him and other Easterners, I always had the unpleasant sensation that they harbored some sort of poorly camouflaged superiority complex toward those with darker skin than theirs. That suit and fashionable narrow necktie helped with a lot of other things, but not with this.

11

After Husam bought a car, he took me to work every Monday, Tuesday, and Thursday. Not that it was any faster than the subway, but at least we talked along the way.

That day I could sense the tension radiating from him the moment I opened the car door.

"Is something wrong?" I asked.

He nodded his head anxiously.

"Will you tell me?"

A half-minute of silence ensued.

"But you can't tell a soul," he said.

"Latifa is in love."

I felt the world turn over with me in it as my stomach shrank to almost nothing.

"She told only me," he went on. "She didn't dare tell our folks."

"Who's the guy?" I asked, meanwhile hoping that my voice was not shaking. "Do I know him?"

He shook his head. "Someone in her class. But there's a big problem."

"What?"

"He's not Muslim. My mother will kill her."

"He's Christian?"

Husam shook his head.

"Jewish?"

"Atheist," he answered in a tone of voice even more mournful than before. I gave an understanding nod. In the depths of my soul rage was doing battle with relief. On the one hand it infuriated me that Latifa had hooked up with an atheist, and even more that she had so effortlessly admitted it to her big brother, as if she didn't care what he would feel. On the other hand, it filled me with relief that that son of a bitch was an atheist, for her parents would never approve of their relationship. And surely Latifa wouldn't give up her family for a sudden flame.

But by the time I thought it over, I wasn't so sure of this. What would happen, after all, if Latifa simply up and moved away from home? She could. She wouldn't be the first. Moreover, it was invariably those like Latifa who jumped ship—the most beautiful college-educated girls. And their families couldn't do a thing about it. The guys—including me—were ever annoyed that pretty, shapely gals were apt to be hooking up with lame white losers who were beneath them. Guys who obviously had never had a good fuck and who didn't even stand a chance of picking up even a half-way homely gal among their own kind. Of course, if I don't want to be unfair, I must admit that this was often true in reverse too. Handsome Arab and African men often picked up blubbery European women not even dogs would have needed. A big ass, blond hair, or, say, the hope of citizenship often saw the deficiencies overlooked.

"What's the guy's name?"

"Peter."

I didn't want to ask for his family name. That would have made it all too obvious that I was spying. I could hardly wait to say good-bye. The moment Husam pressed the pedal after I got out of the car, I pulled out my phone. I'd earlier figured out what name Latifa used on the profile on which she kept in contact with her college friends. By the process of exclusion I quickly found Peter among those friends. He was blond, tall, and athletic. It hurt, but I had to admit that he was handsome. Moreover, he was the exact opposite of everything and everyone Latifa could have gotten in the Zone. Including myself. His photos and shares revealed that he was soon to earn his second degree. Besides that he was a competitive rower and a jazz lover. That fucking jazz! Judging from the photos he'd uploaded, he was renting a studio apartment in some good area. Yet other photos suggested that his parents lived in the provinces. This was bad news: if things turned serious, Latifa could easily move in with the guy. But would she dare?

At first I concluded that a girl who'd passed her whole life with her family and was basically on good terms with her folks wouldn't upend all of that just because she fell in love with someone. But then I wasn't so sure. I remembered the parrot Rami had kept back when we were kids. A green-yellow bird that rattled on in an annoyingly shrill voice. Since its cage wasn't too big, Rami regularly let it out to fly around the room, and after getting some exercise it would always return to the cage. It had its boundaries but seemed happy enough. It knew it would get food there and was safe there. But there came a day when one of Rami's brothers happened to step in the flat right when the parrot was flying about the room. Well, that parrot, taking advantage of the situation, flew right out the front door. Rami ran out frantically after it into the stairwell. The parrot, which had never been outside of the flat, kept making anxious circles. When its owner tried to catch it, it must have gotten scared, since it began flitting about even faster. Then, all at once, it flew right out the open window of the stairwell. It never returned. Rami was down for weeks. I tried cheering him up by saying his bird was now no doubt happier somewhere, but even I knew that was bullshit. A tropical bird used to life in a cage could not survive for long on the streets. It would starve to death, get sick, be torn apart by gulls, or, in the best-case scenario, freeze on the first cold night. The lesson in this didn't make me one bit happier now.

In the weeks to come, Latifa occupied my every thought. Every day I looked at her, Peter's, and their mutual friends' profiles at least twenty times, hoping to come by some new crumb of information. To my great pity, however, they shared only uninteresting stuff. What films they'd seen, what was on their minds, why Bollen should go rot.

Husam, then, remained my key source of news. The matter wasn't so simple, of course, for I couldn't show more interest in his little sister than appropriate and justified for a good friend. To my good fortune he never was tight-lipped about it all. I was the only friend with whom he could talk about it freely, without shame. Of course he made me swear every time we met not to pass along the story to anyone, not even Rami. I would have been crazy to do so. Though at other times even Husam emphasized that he didn't care one bit what Marwan, Nidal, and those other idiots thought, this was vital. Husam insisted that his sister was honest with him, that she kept no secrets from him. That said, I was racked with doubt when, in cautious, flowery language, he informed me that Latifa was still a virgin. Their parents didn't suspect a thing, of course. That filled me with a sort of hope. *If things were so serious, surely they'd know by now*, I told myself.

Then the ball dropped. One week later, Husam, his face one of utter despair, told me Latifa wanted to marry Peter. As a good friend I listened with understanding, but in reality I was the one who could have used some comforting words. Marriage is serious business. From there, there is no turning back. And yet I also saw a glimmer of hope. Maybe this meant they hadn't slept with each other after all. Why else would the guy want to marry her? Latifa must have informed him that they could not have sex before marriage. A good upbringing did have something to be said for it. For a fleeting moment I was filled with pride. But then the feeling vanished, as if it had never been there. Latifa was serious about all this, for she was ready to tie her life to the guy.

Her intentions were indeed serious. She could not keep them secret from her parents for long. One week later Husam told me on the way to work that Latifa had spoken with their mother. At first she fumed, but after calming down she thought it over and decided to start lobbying her husband for their daughter's happiness.

"And what did your dad say?" I asked Husam.

"He doesn't want to hear of it."

I wanted nothing more just then than to pull the emergency brake and jump up and down on the hood of the car in delight. Of course I restrained myself, and only in spirit did I dance with joy. I'd hoped, I'd known, that this was how it would be. What Muslim wants to give his daughter's hand in marriage to an atheist, after all?!

In the weeks to come Husam found himself on the frontlines.

"Mother is constantly after me to talk to my sister," he complained. "And meanwhile I'm the poor thing's only pillar of support." I should have pitied Husam, but I was too devoted to the parents' team.

Then their father resolved to take a dramatic measure: he out and out forbade his daughter from contact with the guy, and just to be sure, he asked her for her class schedule so he'd know when she was supposed to get home. Latifa's good fortune, though, was that her father didn't know his way around the new online community applications. So he left it to Husam to check her profile, and Husam, out of brotherly loyalty, invariably told their father what he wanted to hear. All in all, things seemed to be going well. Two weeks would be enough, I figured, and Peter—rowing and jazz and all—would be history.

I figured well as regards the two weeks. It was a Monday, and Husam, as usual, hit the brakes at 8:25 AM in front of my building.

"Hop in!" he called out. From his enthusiastic greeting I sensed right away that something had happened. His expression only confirmed this. Husam was clearly chipper.

"Everything's solved!"

I had a bad feeling.

I was right.

"Peter has said the *shahada*," he announced. "Our parents have given their blessing for the wedding."

I felt as if I'd been punched in the belly. So the guy had become a Muslim. There was no turning back from there. Husam rattled buoyantly on, but I no longer heard a thing.

The lying asshole, I thought to myself while forcing a smile to my face. An atheist doesn't become pious from one day to the next, I knew. No doubt he'd lied. It was absolutely clear: Latifa had not wanted to choose between her family and her love, so she'd convinced the guy that the *shahada* didn't mean a thing. All he had to do was go to Al-Nour in the presence of Husam and her father, recite the shahada after the sheik, and meanwhile imagine that he was ordering a pepperoni pizza. Of course, beforehand he should pretend that he had read the informational materials he'd received and that he believed deeply in their truth. The asshole lied without blinking an eye. I sincerely hoped he'd burn in hell for all eternity.

The obvious lie was enough for the family. To doubt another's faith is a serious sin. Just what was really in their prospective son-in-law's heart was for Allah to judge from now on. The asshole got the top prize. From that point on he could do as he well pleased. He could drink alcohol and pig out on pork, and he didn't even need to pray. If asked, at most he would explain that he was a bad Muslim. All at once I began feeling sincere empathy for the jihadists. Such lying, fucking hypocrites surely deserved having a real Muslim behead them, for fuck's sake!

Husam went on talking, and I didn't even notice that we'd meanwhile turned into the parking lot.

"Nasim," he said, putting a hand on my shoulder just as I was turning away to get out.

"Yes?"

"I know you always had a thing for Latifa. I appreciate it that you always spoke about my little sister with respect. I thank you for having listened to this whole sordid tale. You're my best friend."

"Such is life."

"I'm sorry."

It wasn't easy for me to let go of Latifa. Maybe I never did. At night I'd often stir awake from some dream of her. A great weight pressed down on my chest, and I gasped for air while lying there in bed. At such times I always experienced the pain of loss yet again, and the awareness that the story I'd woven for myself had come to an end once and for all.

It hurt even though I knew that what had happened wasn't about me. Latifa liked blonds. Peter. The athletic but sensitive jazz lover. Who doesn't remind her in the least of those macho, futureless dickheads she'd grown up among in the Zone. She sought in him someone with whom she could hand in hand leave it all behind and live the life she'd always dreamed of. I knew for sure that this was how it was. After all, I'd sought exactly the same in Latifa.

12

I was between eight and ten years old when I saw a certain film. It was set in a world following a plague that had wiped out virtually all of humanity, and it was about the last living human—some black guy—and his dog. The story was nothing to write home about. As the last knight of humanity, the guy raced around by day in his turbo car, slaughtering mutants hiding from sunlight in abandoned houses, and barricading himself in his house at night so they wouldn't catch him. In the end, though, he happened upon a woman, and it turned out that somewhere there was a base where a hell-bent band of humans was working away to rebuild civilization. The happy end was not to be. The black guy died, but on account of his sacrifice the woman and her son got to the base. As with everything I watched back then on my tablet under my pillow, the film had a big effect on me. So much so that one night, mimicking the film's hero, I made my bed in the bathtub, and for days on end while walking the streets I avoided shadowy corners.

More than twenty years passed before the remake. *I Am a Legend*. Yes. That was the title. Pleasant nostalgia filled me. Worried that the new version would just disappoint me, I downloaded the old one instead, rolled myself a joint, prepared all sorts of food and watched it again. It transported me right back to the age of eight, and I felt this shitty movie to be a real masterpiece.

The nostalgia felt good. It yanked me out of the world all around me, which was colder and scarier by the day. Alarming news stories were mushrooming on my news page alongside the funny images, the gifs, and quotations that were thought to be stylish but were in fact clichéd and fucked-up. "New Anti-Muslim Law." "Secretive Islamophobic Attackers Keep Claiming New Victims." "Killed because of Religion." "Muslim Persecution in Europe." "A New Sign of a Coming Muslim Holocaust." No longer did I even have to directly follow IslamophobiaWatch.org, UmmaNews.info, or the other popular news portals to keep up with what was happening in the world. Friends and acquaintances shared such news as if there were no tomorrow. At first I didn't even notice, but the world became more and more suffocating all around me.

But it was clear from those news items and commentaries that appeared under sensational headlines that the end of the world had not yet come. As always, the reporters spruced up the news a bit so as to maximize the number of clicks. Even bearing that in mind, though, the world really did grow more tense. Not even those portals that stuck to more low-key headlines could deny that murders were specifically targeting Muslims and that Molotov cocktails were being lobbed at Muslim-owned stores.

I knew the stories did me no good, but I didn't block such news from my page. Indeed, at the start I read nearly every one. I continued to be of the opinion that fleeing reality did no good, that you should know what's going on all around you. But when I realized that facing up to reality in this way did no good at all to my mood, I resolved to stop reading the news. I swore repeatedly to stop it, and yet somehow I kept clicking on this or that sensational headline all the same. I'd become an addict. Whether at home, on the subway, during a walk, when with family or friends, or anytime, if I happened to be doing something that did not demand my complete attention my fingers began involuntarily groping about for my phone. With an automatic motion I scrolled down my news page, and with a shudder of excitement I shot myself up with yet another dose of news. As time passed, though, the flashes became shorter and shorter. Five minutes after reading an article, I often didn't even remember what it had been about. I needed another dose. Even while the content of the news vanished without a trace from my brain, however, ever deeper fears tore at me. My world, which until then had been relatively carefree, now filled up increasingly with shadows: my days passed in uncertainty as I was continually oppressed by what I read in the news. Not even the nights brought relief. A recurring nightmare afflicted me, one in which zombies were approaching me at dusk, zombies I struggled against in despair or else fled from over winding paths, toward what remained of the sun. Not that there really was escape.

"Sara can step out onto the street at night only with me," my brother-in-law told my parents at a family lunch one day at home. "No need for any of you to worry," he added, his tone of voice a bit too confident. "Your daughter is in safe hands."

"God watch over you for us, Khalil," my mother replied. My father said nothing as he reached for a big spoon with which to shovel out a bit more bulgur to place beside the mutton chops on his plate.

"The point is that the two of you shouldn't be walking outside the center of the Zone after dark," I chipped in. "The hijab is dangerous. You may be brave, Khalil, but you're not bulletproof."

"Khalil waits for me every day in front of the hospital," my little sister said. It was good to see that after five years of marriage they were still on such good terms. "The other day he waited for me even when I had to do overtime on account of a birth that went on longer than expected."

"A person's got to be careful these days," said Khalil.

"Why, it's as if we're living in Kabul, no?" said my father. "Militias, ethnic cleansing, and sectarian strife."

"Soon enough, yes," said my brother-in-law. He hadn't noticed the irony in my father's voice. "The persecution of Muslims is underway all over Europe."

My father's patience went up in a flash: "Just look around!" he called out, spreading out his upturned hands. "Is anyone around here being persecuted?" He was not one to be reading news on community portals. "Stupid Tawhidis and even more stupid Islamophobes are jumping about. That's it. And the government is trying to shovel the shit back into the horse."

No one was quick to take on the head of the household.

"But all the news . . . ," I ventured after a short pause.

"What counts is not what they say but who says it," he said, shaking his head. "And to think that you had wanted to be a journalist."

Despite my father's rebuke I didn't mind the argument taking this turn. At least they weren't on my case about when I'd finally get married.

"The question is always this," said my father, raising an index finger to his temple, "Whose interest is it in? Who benefits from Muslims living in fear? Think!"

"We're not afraid," Khalil ventured. "We're just cautious."

"You're not scared?"

"No."

"But you don't let your wife alone at night on the streets."

"The danger's got to be recognized. And then there are those faces in the park. . . ."

"Think!"

What my father said always did give me pause. When he voiced some criticism, I had it in me to ponder for hours whether there could be something to it. As a child this bad trait of mine caused me many sleepless nights. Not even now could I relax. OK, the news he read was different from what I read. But what if there was something to what he was saying? It was a fact that attacks on Muslims were gathering pace. But what if not everything was really what it seemed to be, and in fact the countdown had not yet begun? I wanted to believe that my father was right. My brain was already worn out from all the news I'd read, and it tried latching on to anything and everything that gave hope that our world would not soon become a slaughterhouse.

I began browsing the mastheads of the pages I followed. I would have liked to, that is. Most news sites didn't have mastheads, or else the names that appeared on them were clearly fake. So I then broadened my search to sites popular among people I knew.

"The Muslims of the Pan-European Federation are Being Incited by Fake News," came the fifth hit. I read beyond the headline:

> Fake news sites comprise part of a disinformation campaign behind which are individuals linked to the Patriotic Front. The aim of the sites, operated from Turkish and Russian servers, is no less than to shake the Muslim communities' sense of security, to inflame passions, and to have civil war break out in sensitive urban areas.

Even the lead was pretty strong stuff.

Among the sources quoted in the article was some dude who claimed to have written for UmmaNews before he got fed up for some reason. He said he'd never met with the editor-in-chief. He'd worked from home, and he was tasked with selecting the news and—as he put it—presenting it from an alternative perspective. He himself was not Muslim.

The article was supplemented by diagrams of financial transactions between the operators of such sites and all sorts of private individuals, and it also showed how various news portals, from IslamaphobiaWatch.org to UmmaNews.info, refer to each other. As a final trump card it presented an email—hacked from the account of a Patriotic Front leader—on efforts to build the fake news campaign.

The article shocked me so much that I shared it at once. To my great dismay, the others didn't react as I had. "Lies." "It's unbelievable how they try discrediting credible news pages this way." "Ex-journalist my ass. They paid him to lie." "Not a word of truth. I didn't even bother reading it all." My friends took these revelations with huge grains of salt.

But this didn't deter me. As I kept browsing I discovered a number of sites specializing in refuting the news found at IslamophobiaWatch.org and UmmaNews.info and other portals popular in our crowd. I began following a couple of them. The shadows weighing down on my soul began slowly to lift.

I felt I had to open the eyes of my friends. Whenever someone posted a news item I deemed suspicious, I checked it against the countersites and copied in their corrections as my comment on the matter.

"Three security guards accused of harassing a patron at a nightclub found not guilty by British court," read a news item ornamented underneath with angry emojis.

That's all I needed. I set to searching, and in no time I copied in this rebuttal: "Ahmed Khan, under the influence of drugs, attacked the security guards without provocation." I included a link to a CCTV recording on which, despite the pixels, Khan could be seen pulling out a knife and slashing one of the security guards, who was black. It was at that point that they tackled him and beat him to a pulp. It seemed to me that this was not an incident in some sort of religious war. This sort of thing could happen in or around the Zone too. Indeed, had Khan happened to act up in Rafiq's club, he would no doubt have been dragged away with billiard cues breaking on his back.

"Muslim women raped and murdered over their religion," came a share from Rami on my message page. The article went into quite some detail about how three men had hunted Muslim women night after night. They'd dragged them into a car, took them to a remote location, raped them, cut their throats, and threw their bodies into a river. It took police months to catch the perpetrators. A photo accompanying the article showed a corpse floating facedown in the water. Chilling news. It had appeared on CrusaderWatch.com, which tracked hate crimes against Muslims 24/7. I looked for the news item. The search engine turned up the original source: HinduTimes. For fuck's sake. In taking the news one virtually unimportant bit of information had been omitted—namely, that the incident had happened in India, not around here, as the article suggested. Moreover, one of the murderers was named Sayyid something or other. Not that I know Indians, but to my ear, that sounded very Muslim indeed.

"Total lie," I commented on the share.

"Just because it's not in the news, it's still true!"

"It happened in India."

Rami didn't reply this time. An hour later the link had vanished from his page. But three more took its place.

All the same, I felt it important to struggle against such foolishness.

"Stop sharing this crap," I wrote to Marwan in private one day when he posted news about a virus supposedly developed against Muslims.

"Everyone's shared it."

"Just because others swallow such crap doesn't mean you have to," I wrote back. "Read normal news portals if you're that interested."

"Because they of all people want us to know the truth," came the reply.

I struggled on, but in vain. The fake news just kept pouring in, and I kept looking on helplessly as all that crap buried my buddies like lava. And then it came slowly back to haunt me.

"Sew your foreskin back on and suck your heathen buddies' cocks," an anonymous user commented to one of the rebuttals I'd posted under one of Rocket's shares. I was just about to tell him to fuck off when I saw that the comment was no longer accessible.

"I deleted it," came Rocket's message to me. "Told him to go fuck off. He didn't know who you are."

"Thanks."

The incident was in any case a sound warning. I sensed that I'd do well to keep my trap shut if I didn't want to be known as a traitor. Those who were infected had flooded the airwaves anyway. I couldn't stop my friends and acquaintances from following such news. As for the fake news—which I kept reading all the same—I always let myself get riled up. Had everyone gone mad?

One day Rami and I were doing sit-ups on the benches.

"I'm not trying to fuck with you, you get it? Seriously. But why the hell are you on everyone's case?"

"Is there a problem?"

"Not yet. But more and more people have had enough of your shit." His words cut deep.

I decided to get out. UmmaNews.info and the other portals kept right on with their scaremongering. But I resolved to devote my attention to something else. To try finding a new drug. As much as I wanted to ignore the news altogether, I still wasn't into watching the latest TV series, so I decided to once again devote time to reading after a hiatus of several years. My first choice was *I Am a Legend*. The film, after all, was based on an old novel. Of course there were some differences. The original story had no zombies at all, and it was a vampire virus that ran amuck, making it logical from the outset why the infected could not venture into the sunlight. The plot was otherwise more or less the same. In the book, too, the main character, Robert Neville, tore the infected to bits all day long, struggling as a sort of last knight for a world fast running short of humanity. But the ending was different. The novel had neither a sexy woman nor a pathos-inducing hero's death. At the end of the novel the vampires catch Neville, lock him in prison, and sentence him to death. While being led to the gallows, Neville looks over the infected masses. The vampire mothers hold their vampire kids tight as he passes them by. He sees in their eyes the same mix of fear and hatred he had felt for them. At that moment he realizes that this is a new world. The world of the infected, in which he, the last human, is no longer a hero but a monster, who goes about murdering peacefully sleeping vampires.

It was in a dark mood that I put down the book. My phone was beeping. A message had come from an unfamiliar profile:

"Hey there, my friend! I've been reading your comments. Glad to see that you, at least, haven't lost your marbles. Keep it up. Nizar."

At first I was shocked to see the name of my onetime boxing chum. But something else happened too. My bad mood lifted. I was not the last man left.

13

"Wait a minute. The drumming will stop in no time." So said my father, and he squeezed his eyes shut.

Only the two of us remained in the hospital room.

He'd been in for only three days but couldn't even lift his hands anymore. The tumor was growing fast. He'd already had a life-saving operation; the wound was covered by a white bandage. The doctors said we'd come too late. What with the metastasizing, they said he had only a few days left.

The whole thing had begun with headaches a week earlier, and then came dizziness and vomiting. He did not want to go to the doctor himself. When the left edge of his mouth began to droop, however, my mother no longer accepted no for an answer. Father, too, must have sensed that something was amiss. He let my brother-in-law get him into a car and take him to the hospital. The neurological ward of Hospital 12 did a CT scan at once, but the doctor warned us at once that with his insurance, he could expect to be on a long waiting list no matter what he needed. We called Abu Sa'id, who made some calls immediately. We were received at St. Thomas Hospital the same day. That was the best place he could have wound up in. I stared out the window. The drums ceased and my father opened his eyes.

"I'd like a Muslim burial," he said. He was a realist. Before setting off on anything he always considered the prospects. This time, in the pauses between the drumming, he concluded that the drummers were up to no good.

His request took me aback. I would not have thought that he took religious matters seriously. He'd never prayed in his life; nor was alcohol his foe. His religiosity was perhaps best characterized by this image: sometimes after a long day, he'd listen to some Egyptian reciting the Koran on a CD while drinking whiskey. He said it was better that way. When I, as a child, once wanted to fast during Ramadan, he talked me out of it. He said I was a growing boy, that it wasn't worth my getting sick and missing school on account of this. When I then asked him why he didn't fast, since

113

he was neither a growing boy nor in school, he explained that Allah had said that those on a journey are exempted from the obligation to fast, and life is, after all, a big journey. Now that he knew he was nearing the end of his journey, I would gladly have asked him if he'd do differently.

"Return me to the homeland. I don't want some fag scraping out my bones. I don't even need a coffin." So he said before again closing his eyes. The EKG showed a slow, even heartbeat.

I was surprised at his request. My father had been born in Europe and had been back to the old country no more than three times in his life. Nor could he ever have been said to be religious. I didn't understand why this had become important to him. Then I told myself that it was because not even the doctors could say what was unfolding inside his skull.

"Promise me," he said, opening his eyes.

I would have tried to lighten the mood with something funny, but nothing came to mind. So instead I promised him.

"Do you have any message for your grandfather?" he asked with a smile. "You don't have much time to come up with something. He adored you no matter how dumb you were sometimes." Such theatrics were not at all his style. I stayed on until evening.

Visiting hours started at nine in the morning. I'd planned to get to the hospital by ten. The subway line between the Zone and downtown was no longer running. Not even a year had been enough for the borough government to repair the stretch of track damaged in the bombing. And that made life hard for commuters who needed to get between the Zone and downtown. Bus 411, which went to the edge of District 34, ran infrequently and slowly. Abu Sa'id, however, sensed the business opportunity in no time. He established a particular minibus route, and soon his white nine- and eleven-passenger minibuses were transporting people to the nearest downtown-bound subway line. When it became certain that our own subway line would not be repaired, he also established routes between the Zone's main junctures.

I flagged down a minibus. The seat beside the driver was occupied, so I opened the rear door. Seated in the first row was a sixty-something woman wearing a hijab. There was a seat beside her, but I plopped down instead two rows behind. Digging into my pockets for change, I pulled some out, counted out the fare, and tapped the shoulder of the guy in front of me. He glanced back indifferently, took the money, and passed it on to the driver, who dropped it into a box and, without looking back, passed back over his shoulder a preprinted receipt.

The route was at best twenty minutes longer than going by subway used to be. The minibus proceeded south through the center of the Zone. Though there was no traffic, the driver still wasn't in any hurry. At first I stared out the window in resignation, and then I turned to a bubble-popping game on my phone to distract myself from my almost-boiling brain. My patience ran out at the entrance ramp to the Liberty Bridge. The minibus was hobbling along as if taking a group of foreigners on a sight-seeing tour. Fortunately the veiled woman up front, who had been sighing disapprovingly for some minutes already, headed me off:

"Can't you speed up a bit? We've got business to get to."

The driver looked into the rear-view mirror as if he'd just been insulted.

"Inshallah, you'll get there on time," he said, shirking responsibility.

"Let's get going all the same," I said. Though offended to the core, the driver did accelerate.

Finally we rolled into the temporary station established at the edge of District 34. There we could transfer to regular buses, and the subway was running too. That older woman sitting up front loosened her hijab, took a dark blue knit hat from her bag, and in one movement pushed the hijab back off of her head and put the hat on top. The driver opened the door, and we got off.

The square was practically empty. Since nearly a century of peace had prevailed among the member states of the Pan-European Federation, this couldn't be said at all of city streets, and soldiers were stationed all about in an effort to keep order. On guard in the faded winter sunlight by the sub-way entrance, beside police in dark blue uniforms, were soldiers in camou-flage pants and bulletproof vests. They didn't even look at me as I glanced into the retina scanner at the gate and ran by them down the stairs.

By the time I reached the hospital room, my father was no longer in his bed. He hadn't waited for me to give a message to my grandfather. I was seventeen minutes late.

We could not accompany my father on his final journey. By then it was risky to travel outside the Pan-European Federation. Abu Sa'id warned us that he knew a man who'd gone abroad for some straightforward family matter, and on attempting to return was arrested at the foreign airport on suspicion of terrorism. The family back here couldn't do a thing. The Foreign Ministry didn't lift a finger to help those branded as terrorists in any corner of the world.

Since we ourselves couldn't travel, there was one solution left. We hired a burial company specializing in this sort of thing to transport my father home. Fortunately the battles had ended in the part of the country where the relatives lived, so it could be done. Of course the company, just to be sure, leveled a special risk fee.

"We're sorry, but according to the Foreign Ministry the country still doesn't qualify as safe," said the agent while filling out the contract. We met him in Abu Sa'id's office. Abu Sa'id insisted on covering the bill. He and I negotiated with the agent. My mother and little sister were too down to come along.

The agent was a thin, clean-shaven man. Dark bags were in full evidence under his eyes even behind the thick frames of his glasses. He wore a black suit, a white shirt, and a black tie. *It's got to be shit, having a job that requires you to go about all the time dressed for mourning*, I thought to myself. I could not imagine such a person putting down his work at 5 PM and going home merrily to his family.

"We're lucky, though," he explained, "that there was no autopsy, so the body only has to be x-rayed prior to shipment. Under the law this is unfortunately mandatory." On noting our curious glances, he went on: "There was a case in which plastic explosives were placed in a corpse. It was pure luck that a tragedy was averted."

Though we couldn't travel, it would have been unworthy of my father if only the burial firm's representatives abroad accompanied him on his final journey. So it was that my mother, little sister, brother-in-law, and I mutually decided to notify the relatives abroad. At least those who'd lived through the war. Reaching them wasn't hard, since we were in touch anyway on various social media. During the war this had been a key source of information, for otherwise we could not have known what had become of whom. Try as I had to filter the messages, my news wall was still flooded with comments from relatives and others putting on airs, whose convoluted words were barely comprehensible, as well as not-at-all funny Arabic memes. But now the extended family came in handy.

My first order of business was to replace my own profile picture with one of my father, along with a black ribbon. Of course only on those accounts that those abroad could see. Back during the war that's how they, too, signaled that someone had died. Messages came showering in within minutes. "May Allah let you into heaven, sweetest Abu Nasim." "You will be missed, dearest cousin." As if they'd known him.

The burial firm took care of everything. All I had to do was give them contact information for a relative in the home country. When I asked among the extended family there who could help, everyone immediately offered to do so.

The burial was on a Thursday afternoon. Abu Sa'id rented an empty warehouse for the occasion. At least two hundred people were on hand. My mother wore a white hijab. We went our separate ways at the entrance. She and my little sister went to a room reserved for the women.

Abu Sa'id had thought of everything. The metal columns had been covered in white silk and the floor with carpeting. Everyone left their shoes outside.

A huge screen on the wall broadcast the ceremony. From the looks of the place, I figured it was in the courtyard of some mosque. My father lay on a rug wrapped in white linen. Beside him, on a separate rug, stood the imam, and behind him some thirty men, in two lines. In contrast with us, they were not in black. The whole thing looked a bit as if they had just stopped in for a bit at the funeral on their way home from work.

We too stood in straight lines, shoulder to shoulder, our big toes drawing a straight line in each row. I was in the middle of the front row; to my right, Abu Sa'id; to my left, my brother-in-law. Beside and behind us were friends and distant relatives and others who respected my father. All of us stared at the monitor.

"Allahu Akbar," said the imam on the screen, raising his open palms to his ears before placing them on top of each other on his belly. We followed along. He recited a text in Arabic, followed by another "Allahu Akbar." He did this two more times.

With the end of the prayer, four men stepped forward from behind the imam. The linen-wrapped body was placed on a stretcher, which they picked up and headed off with. The crowd bellowed. The funeral firm broadcast video from two cameras and a drone. That, too, was in the contract. The camera panned the faces in the crowd several times. I recognized a few of them from their profile pictures. Up front was a wrinkled old man. Two younger men were supporting him.

"Hajji Mustafa, your grandfather's brother-in-law," said Abu Sa'id. "He has a lot to thank your grandfather for."

The cemetery could not be far, and indeed the procession soon arrived. The grave was ready. Two barefoot men with rolled-up trousers stepped down inside, and with the help of two associates standing above them, lifted the body inside. Their job wasn't easy. My father was a man of stately size. The camera gave a close-up shot of how, as per tradition, the men laid my father on his side in the deeper-cut side of the grave. One of the men stepped out, while the one still inside placed three handfuls of earth under my father's head. To the side he packed an orderly heap of wood boards—these were more expensive than the usual concrete slabs, which might have been precisely why the funeral firm's agent had suggested them—and positioned them above the body from head to toe. This man, too, now stepped out of the grave, whereupon two others began shoveling earth into it. Not long after, a yellowish red heap of packed earth stood in place of the ditch. The imam raised his hands in supplication and began the fatiha. We did the same, though I was certain that half of those present beside and behind me did not know the text.

The relatives abroad now gathered up close to the screen, looking into a camera. I was compelled to determine that standing in line was not their strong suit. The light on the camera above our own monitor turned red, signaling that we were now being broadcast too. The wall of relatives abroad now opened up, and that wrinkled old man arrived.

"*Assalamu alaykum*, Hajji Mustafa," I greeted him in my capacity as the eldest male in the family here.

"*Wa alaykum as-salam*, my dear," he replied, and I did not understand the sentences that followed. The old man's voice kept quavering.

I too was overcome with emotion. My tongue went numb, but then somehow I gathered up my strength all the same:

"Do you remember this, Hajji Mustafa?" I said, digging out of my pocket my grandfather's *misbaha*, or string of beads, which my grandfather had long ago gotten from him. The old man began to weep. His two sons caressed his shoulder in an effort to cheer him up.

"We await you all back home anytime," he said.

"Inshallah . . . ," I replied in a quavering voice. We left it at that.

I accepted condolences for nearly an hour. Nizar came too. "Accept my sympathies, my friend. Your father was a good man."

Abu Sa'id took me home himself.

"You know, Nasim, your father always praised you," he said, putting a hand on my shoulder as we said goodbye. "He used to say that you'd already outgrown the streets. That anything could become of you. He was very proud of you."

If only I could have believed him.

14

I wouldn't have thought my father's death would get to me as it did. By the time I got home from the burial, all the energy was sapped from my limbs, and my skin turned sensitive. I pulled down the shutters and lay in bed for hours. At other times I didn't give a shit that the drones could see in the window, but now I wasn't in the mood for company. Besides which, the freezing rain kept falling nonstop. Spring would never come. My little sister and brother-in-law took care of my mother. I called them every day to ask how they were, and I hoped they wouldn't pick up the phone. They always did. Then Monday came. The work week passed slowly. In the office, neither Wladek nor even the idiotic Egyptians could get me riled up at all.

It was now, at the age of thirty, that I really came face to face with death. When my grandfather died, I was yet young, and when the civil war back in the home country claimed my relatives one after another, I felt nothing. I hadn't known them, and a sense of family obligation was just not enough to open the floodgates of any grief in me. With my father, though, there had been lots of unresolved matters between us. I decided that I no longer wanted to be angry with him for anything. The burden would have been too great for me to keep carrying. As a sign of forgiveness I begged God as well to forgive him for his sins and let him into heaven. But could a man for whom religion had never meant a thing also gain entry? A man who was not on good terms with his own father? Who'd never had a guilty conscience over anything? I hoped it could be so.

When Grandfather used to take me to the mosque long ago, I often listened languidly as the imam, mimicking a lamenting tone of voice, spoke of the fires of hell, of how they burned sinners' flesh, or else as he went about mawkishly describing the beauty of heaven in all its detail—its verdant gardens and babbling brooks. Heaven, which awaits those who have lived their lives in a manner pleasing to God. Of the two, hell and heaven, perhaps it was the latter whose allure touched me less. I didn't get why the cooling green shadows of the Garden of Eden constituted such a big reward. If you get on a train, you can look out the window and see all sorts of lovely, verdant gardens. Who would be crazy enough to move out there? I could have cared less for the idea of being bored to tears for eternity in the woods by some babbling brook. Nor did heaven seem any more alluring for its gardens being chock full of fruit and wine—a fact whose sold advantage, one incomprehensible to me, was that it did not make you drunk, and so was not haram, or forbidden. I could get the real stuff in the supermarket.

As for the *houris*, or the virgins of paradise, I did not know about them back then. They were never mentioned in the mosque. The imam must have figured that the congregation, which comprised mostly folks of retirement age, would get more enthusiastic about gardens and fruit. The first time I heard about houris it was from one of the guys, maybe Marwan. We were fourteen, fifteen, or sixteen years old and happened to be sending each other porn links, when he observed that he'd want one of the girls from a video to be among his houris in the afterworld. Not wanting to seem dumb, rather than ask him what this meant I did a search instead.

In the course of my search it fast became apparent that the houris not only moved Marwan's imagination but also inspired the porn industry. Among the four- to five-minute videos that emerged when I searched for the keyword "houri" was a half-hour film that, beyond the usual came, saw, and left script also offered a genuine story. The tale began in a car. The driver, a blond guy, is loudly telling his buddy—in the passenger seat beside him, and looking rather Arab, or at least wearing an Arabic scarf on his head—how sorry he feels for Muslims for not being able to drink alcohol, for having the pray five times a day, and for having to fast one month a year. The guy in the Arabic scarf tries to explain that Islam is in fact about much more, that it gives peace to the soul. But in vain. The other guy just laughs. The car then smashes into an oncoming truck. In the next scene the two characters are in the sky. The Muslim steps into a verdant garden surrounded by a tall metal fence while the guards don't let the blond fellow in. The seventy-two virgins then arrive. Africans, Asians, blond Europeans, Arabs, and, well, girls of all sorts imaginable. While a wild orgy unfolds inside, the blond young man just does his best outside the fence to jerk off, but for all his efforts he can't get a hard-on.

Houris were very much on my mind until I turned twenty or so, as long as I kept fantasizing about the girls in school or in the neighborhood. The houris of my dream were not the out-and-out whores in porn films, but shy virgins. I was excited not only by the thought of their purity but even more so by the idea that these veiled gals from moral families would cast off their hijabs, letting their hair spread out over the bed, and, loosened up by desire, would then relinquish their virtue. I then had to realize that virginity was not so alluring after all. This happened when bad luck swept Fuad my way. I was seventeen. She was the first woman in my life. Together we lost or, more precisely, together we muddled up each other's virginity. She knew that what she was up to was forbidden, and so the experience was tense from start to finish. And the fact that she didn't enjoy the sex deflated me in no time too.

It was Basma, an Albanian prostitute, who finally undid my desire for houris. I was nineteen; she was three years older. I found her on a specialized web page. The combination of her pictures and reviews by satisfied clients persuaded me within moments that it was worth saving up the money. I wasn't to be disappointed either. She had a perfect figure and almond eyes. She treated me like a grown-up man, touching me with determination and expertise. Had she wanted to, she could have made me cum in five minutes. "To me this is not a job but a calling," she explained. Of course it is possible that she believed only in regular customers. If that had been her aim, it worked. I became a regular. After my experiences with Basma, I knew full well that I, for one, didn't need those seventy-two lame virgins.

The houris seemed to carry just a single advantage: with them, slipping on a condom was probably unnecessary. If you're circumcised, a rubber is death itself. Fortunately Basma did take me in her mouth au naturel. But if neither those verdant gardens, those babbling brooks, all that fruit, nor even the houris were alluring enough, then what was? What would motivate me to wake up on time as a good Muslim for the dawn prayer, to fast during Ramadan, or even to just give up beer and grass? I had the sense that something was amiss about all this. But then a quote from the Koran came to mind: "And we have sent it down as an Arabic Koran so you will understand." An Arabic Koran. . . . Perhaps the promise of those verdant gardens and fruit was addressed primarily to those Arabs of yore who'd lived in deserts? But then what of us?

"*Astaghfirullah*," I muttered to myself, beseeching Allah for forgiveness, as I always did when such doubts began taking root in my mind.

The answer to my question came not from Allah but from grass. On the second evening after my father's death, Rami decided to yank me out of my lethargy. I told him in advance that I didn't want to do a thing, but he stopped by all the same. He swept a place for himself on the couch, and I turned on some greenish orange mood lighting and some music, then sprawled into the squishy armchair and waited as Rami rolled a joint with expert precision. He mixed the grass with special herbs to ensure that we wouldn't cough our lungs out after the first deep hit.

"One of these days I really will get my hands on some salvia too," he quipped while taking utmost care to sprinkle just the right amount of grass into the paper.

"If you try salvia for the first time, it's best at ten times the strength," he explained with the confidence of a veteran user. "It's best smoked from a pipe. The grains are fine, so you don't stuff it right into the pipe. You first put in a little, pellet-size bit of crumpled foil to keep all the salvia from falling right into the stem of the pipe at once. Then you sit down in a comfy spot. You take two or three quick drags one after another and hold your breath until you feel as if you're ready to suffocate. Then you blow it out, and the feeling hits you right away."

After tapping the filter on the table between the couch and the armchair, Rami lit the joint. The rolled-up paper quickly burned up and the grass glowed away just as fast in the dimly lit, greenish orange room.

"The main high lasts just three minutes," he continued. "Winding down then takes about a half hour. And yet the brain feels as if thousands of years have passed." He handed over the joint and blew out the smoke. "You live through adventures and visions unfold in your mind."

"Thousands of years in three minutes," I summed up. Having examined the glowing end of the joint and knowingly knitting my brows, I took a deep drag. I held the smoke in for about ten seconds, and then, forming a ring with my mouth, I slowly blew out the smoke. It was strong stuff.

"Yeah, time is relative," I went on. "I once read that dreams that seem to take hours or days really unfold in our heads in a couple of minutes."

Rami took another drag.

"But the film of your life is a whole life."

"The film of life . . ." All at once my mind opened up. Rami hadn't even suspected that his short sentence was in fact an uncut diamond just waiting to be polished into a gem.

Getting high with Rami was always sweet. The grass affected him just the opposite way it did me. While he slowed down, I myself began to spin from the thoughts that flooded my brain—sometimes good, sometimes not so good, but always seemingly new and logical at any given moment. This of course also meant that conversations at such times were one-directional: my little presentations and my bright ideas remained but instances of psychological masturbation.

With a precisely aimed movement I flicked the butt out the open window. As the music flowed in slow waves through the room, my mind now sped up. Thoughts flew about in my head as I tried to catch them. "The last moment, the film of life," I mumbled to myself. Over many years I'd learned that a thought left inside my head would vanish without a trace by the time my mind cleared. A word spoken, however, could live to see the next day. And so I got up out of that squishy armchair, wrapped my fingers around the nape of my neck, and started to walk back and forth in front of the couch Rami was on.

"You say the film of your life plays before you in your final moment. That's what you're saying, right? But then what's that like?" In no time I answered my rhetorical question: "Like any film you watch. It could be good, and it could be bad too. Just imagine how lifelike this last film might be. Totally 3D in effect. You smell the smells, you taste the flavors, you feel it through and through. . . . You live it all again with every last fiber of your being." In my enthusiasm I was gasping for breath.

Reaching out for my phone, I turned down the music with a clumsy movement. Rami tried voicing his disapproval, but I didn't care. In the greenish yellow cloud of smoke I stood before him as a demonic prophet.

"So then . . . ," I began, louder, pausing for effect for a couple of seconds to let the wonder of the forming thought take shape. "A person's final moment can be good or it can be bad. And just as with salvia, it might . . . might be just a moment, but you experience it as an eternity all the same. What if this seemingly eternal moment is its very own heaven or hell, with a private entrance?" Rami gave me a blank stare. I wasn't quite sure he was all there as he kept sitting on the couch, but I went on nonetheless.

"That last moment is the final settling of accounts," I declared. "Get it? Over the course of your life you do all sorts of shit but don't admit it to a soul. Least of all to yourself. Like . . . like when you stuff a sandwich into yourself during Ramadan, knowing full well Allah is displeased and will one day call you to account. And—even if you don't bother with it right then—you're worried about the punishment you know will come. Just as you're worried about being called to account for all the prayers you skipped out on and about the consequences of the little and larger bits of evil you've done to others. All sorts of things like this pile up throughout your life, and meanwhile deep inside you an inner scale takes shape nice and slow: *I've lived a good life* or *I've lived a bad life.* Of course you don't want to face up to this. You always tell yourself: *I've got time yet, I'll fix things, I haven't yet fucked it all up.* . . . But when that last moment comes, there's no one left to hide from anymore. And you can no longer make amends for all you've fucked up. *Hisab,* Judgement Day, has come!" I shouted that last sentence while my brain kept spinning at an almost painful, breakneck speed.

"Of course, I know what you'll say to this," I said, suddenly raising an index finger into the air. "That all Muslims go to heaven. And if not . . . if you wind up in hell all the same for a bit on account of your sins, after a while Allah will lift you out of there, simply because you're Muslim." Of course Rami did not look at all as if he was about to say such a thing. I went on: "What if the judgment of God is none other than our own conscience? What if, when it comes down to it, you yourself are God? After all, at the end, in that final, eternal moment, you pass judgment on yourself. *Have I lived as I think I should have lived? Have I lived a good life? A moral life? A full life? Was I good to others?* You pose yourself a hell of a lot of questions and can no longer lie to yourself. No indeed. You for one won't show mercy to yourself just because you're Muslim."

Rami was probably still pondering something I'd said three sentences earlier while I drew circles faster and faster in the room. My heart all but jumped out of place, and my breaths came ever harder, but the moment felt exquisitely inspired to me. I felt beauty as the grand thought slowly took shape in me and through my words.

"If . . . if you lived a life that by your own standards was a good life, then you can take comfort in that and your bliss will be everlasting. You've made it to heaven. But if you lived a life you're not happy with, you'll never manage to escape that awareness. Never . . . never again. You'll never manage to fix the faults. And that is nothing other than the worst hell there is."

That was it. All at once the recognition glued my feet to the floor.

"Why, that's what hisab means! That . . . that you can no longer change a thing!" I faltered as a last thought now took shape slowly in my brain. "That final, eternal moment contains only either regret or contentment. That is your own heaven or hell! And you yourself are your own God."

When you're high, all sorts of shit usually piles up in your brain. This was different. The next day, as my head cleared, not only did the string of thought that had unfurled in my brain the night before not seem stupid, but it seemed outright brilliant. It was almost noon, but since it was Saturday, I was still lying in bed. I was still reflecting on the idea that had crystallized in me the previous night, and it filled me with boundless satisfaction.

I'd found the key to eternal happiness! My theory would, after all, stand its ground in all systems of thought or faith. It didn't matter what you believed in—in divine laws, in the laws of society, or in yourself. The point is to always do what you regard as right, so your conscience will, in the end, be at peace.

Of course this opened a dangerous gate. It meant that a jihadist—insofar as he really believes that he does good by killing innocents—goes to heaven the very same way. Still, my new insight helped temper the fears I felt in the aftermath of my father's death. After all, he always believed firmly in his own truth. On account of his huge self-confidence and his continual—likewise successful—self-justification, he didn't even have a clue how much pain he'd caused his parents or others.

One big doubt remained in me, however. What if the whole theory was false, if nothing was like I thought, and in fact it would be Allah passing judgment on me in my final hour? He probably wouldn't be too impressed with my godless thoughts. Finally I reassured myself that in this case, Allah—just as the Koran had said—was forgiving and merciful. And even the sheiks agreed that Allah does not mete out punishment for thoughts. Surely he wouldn't send me to hell for such an innocent thought.

On Sunday I crossed paths again with Rami, now in the gym.

"Do you remember what I was saying the other night when we were high?"

Rami had just been getting ready to do bench presses. Naturally he didn't remember a thing.

"Well then, listen," I said. "I'll now say it again."

The room was empty, but to be on the safe side, I now presented my thoughts in a somewhat muted tone. I spoke to him of the relativity of time; how that final moment lasts for eternity; how heaven and hell are determined by our own internal scale; how God is in fact ourselves; and how, ultimately, the followers of all the world's religions, and even atheists, get into heaven or hell on the basis of their own consciences.

"What is this shit!" he asked when I finished, knitting his brows. "You know full well that both hell and heaven are eternal." He shook his head disapprovingly. "Besides, what about 'Hum feeha khalidoon,' 'they'll live therein forever,' then what the hell would that mean? Not that they will remain there eternally? And that we ourselves are Allah! Are you Muslim at all?"

"Are you crazy?" I shot back. "What else would I be? It's just that I got to thinking."

"Then think less next time," said Rami. He lay down on the bench and, carefully placing his middle fingers on the two marks at the outer edge of the bar, took two loud breaths and gave the bench press his all. I stood behind him.

"*Astaghfirullah*," I mumbled quietly to myself to be on the safe side, while holding my upturned palms just below the bar as it moved up and down.

I was unmitigatedly happy. Father had gotten to heaven.

15

As the days got warmer, my mood got better and better. I was sitting about at a table out front of old Ashraf's kebab place with a tall glass of lemonade. I just happened to be noticing how the sunlight filtering through the red sun umbrellas was painting my freshly purchased, stylishly broad leather shoes, and meanwhile I was thinking I should borrow a phone charger from someone else sitting here. Finally I decided that there was no point getting to my feet just for that. I would charge up my phone in the car.

Three old men were chilling out at the table next to mine, slurping tea from tiny Turkish cups. I never did understand what sense it makes to have hot drinks when it's warm out, but for some reason old men swore they had a cooling effect.

"Don't defend them," said one of them, a balding oldster in a brown polo shirt, audibly stirring the sugar in his tea. "It was about time they were locked up."

"Do you think that fools anyone?" countered his similarly bald, thickly bespectacled friend. "Name a single terrorist who used to attend Sheik Taymullah's mosque! See how little you know!"

"That's not what this is about. A mosque is a mosque. But the law applies to everyone. They can go to a clubhouse, an association, or whatever they want."

"What about religious freedom?"

"What of it? All those fanatics who can't bring themselves to do an honest day's work will get up and go to a normal mosque. And that's that."

"Oh, the Constitutional Court will reject it anyway."

"Hell it will," said the other. "This Bollen isn't stupid. She's doing everything by the letter of the law. Just take a look at this." He picked up an oversized phone from the table, typed something into it, and then, squinting at the screen, began to read aloud: "All parties in Parliament support the amendment to the law on religious denominations. In its public statement on the matter, the Central Fatwa Council likewise called the bill acceptable and constitutional."

129

"Precisely," the third old fellow added. "Inshallah, this can only be for the good.

The oldsters' smart talk didn't exactly rivet my attention. All the less so because this bit of news had been making the rounds for weeks now: the latest installment of the New Loyalist Act permitted only state-sanctioned religious institutions to operate, while those organizations that were filtered out tried to stay in operation through legal loopholes—such as by establishing themselves as heritage clubs. That was the fate of Taymullah's mosque as well. Not that I understood the hysteria around the matter, since even before the elections three years earlier it was obvious that, if elected, Bollen would enact her program, the New Loyalist Act, and this was one of its key measures. Only that the grindstones of legislation move slowly.

My phone still had a half hour left on it, and on dimming the light, forty minutes. So I opened my favorite dating app, RVous, to again scroll through the past day's results, "14 matches." A new record. And I hadn't even posted a new picture of myself for a while. Previously, after searching for an hour, even in the best-case scenario I'd have just one or two matches. Ever since the refugees had been moved into the tower blocks in the north of the Zone, even ten was unheard of. While browsing the profiles, I was increasingly certain that it had been a good marketing strategy to post that picture in which I was sitting on top of the hood of my Honda. I'd brought the car home a month earlier. I'd always scoffed at those who posed with a car. But Husam had persuaded me that in the interest of attaining my objective, taking self-marketing a bit more seriously was nothing to be ashamed of. He must have really wanted me to get over his sister, and I let him talk me into it. Not that I needed a car all that much, but then I concluded that, if not now, when? I hoped a bit that as was the case with lots of my friends, I too would be in love with my car.

Since Mother didn't like to drive, I inherited my father's Mercedes. I decided from the outset to sell it. Whenever anyone asked why, I cited all sorts of emotional reasons: that I wouldn't be able to sit in it, seeing as how even without it I'd had a hard enough time of it getting over Father's death, and so on. The real reason, however, was far more mundane: I simply saw that Mercedes as something to show off with, something I didn't need. So I traded it in for an almost new black Honda, and deposited the difference into Mother's account. It wasn't the Honda's fault that, in the end, I didn't dare fall in love with it. My subconscious resisted, telling me that that could only lead to disillusionment and pain. Yes, in my youth I'd seen up close way too often how windshields shattered into thousands of pieces, how upholstery caught fire, how cars were devoured by flames.

Of course, I couldn't take my car home at once. When I finally did get it from the dealer, I had to take it for chipping right away, and that took a full day. Under a law passed three months earlier, a satellite tracking device had to be installed in every car. With that, the authorities sought to reduce the number of terrorist attacks using cars. Without a chip, not only would you be nabbed at a roadside check but you couldn't even fill up your tank anymore. To the owner, the only advantage of being chipped was that your car was practically impossible to steal. The disadvantage, though, was that through a satellite the authorities could take control of your car's electronic system anytime. They could close the windows, and if they wanted to, they could stop the vehicle in the middle of a highway with the clamp brakes.

I was just past thirty-one, and this was my first car. I hung Grandfather's misbaha from the rearview mirror, but then after a day of driving about like that, I decided it was better kept at home, in the drawer it came from.

Husam had been right. It was a good idea to post that picture of myself with the Honda. The sparkling clean body of the car radiated onto me, too. I gave the impression of being a serious young man making a good living, and that was attractive to the girls looking for dates. My profile was up on several apps. On the more conservative among them, the Honda did not up my odds. But my success on RVous was something else. Especially among those residents of the tower blocks in the Zone's northern end who were not primarily seeking a husband or romance. "African panther seeking her gallant knight." "I'm Leila, and I'd gladly spoil you."

In the intro texts, at least, there wasn't even a hint of girly romance. Following the rules of the market economy, once new, lower-paid workers came to the fore, those long plying the trade were compelled to lower their prices too, or else to hold onto their clients through bonuses and special favors. The guys were swimming in a sea of possibilities. Me too.

There at that table in front of old Ashraf's kebab place, I now sucked hard on the lemonade through the straw. The crushed ice spread in all its pleasant coldness through my mouth. Having thoughtfully browsed all the matches, I finally chose Yasmin, a girl with big brown eyes and a wide smile. According to her profile, she was twenty-one. I sent her a greeting, and she replied almost immediately. Figuring I'd start off humbly, I asked her only for a twenty-minute liaison.

After work I picked up Rami. We agreed that he would wait in the car: relations between the longtime residents of the Zone and the refugees inhabiting the northern tower blocks were not unclouded.

This was in fact the first time we'd gone there since those tower blocks had opened.

"For fuck's sake, the whole thing is in such order! Under us, everything is rotting away." So Rami grumbled as we looked for Number 12.

The neighborhood really was newer and cleaner than what we'd expected. The buildings had clearly opened to their residents not long before. There wasn't a sign of graffiti on the walls, and children were playing on the grass outside.

I parked in the lot by Number 12.

"I'm in front of the building," I texted.

"Press Number 66," came the reply at once. "Fourth floor, Apartment 4."

The building was new inside too—nicer than the one I'd grown up in. The painted walls were clean, and not even the elevator had any graffiti.

Yasmin opened the door. I recognized her immediately, but concluded that she knew how to manipulate photos. Her black cocktail dress did not hide her irregular shape. Her posterior was a bit thicker than I'd expected, but it didn't bother me, for just now it wasn't her posterior that I was interested in. As we stepped into the flat, her features melted away in the red lighting of the room, slyly masking even the finer faults of her skin.

"You came for the fifteen-minute program, right?" she asked with a smile. Her teeth gleamed white in the red light.

"Yes."

"With or without a condom?"

"Without."

"No problem," she said with an even wider smile than before. "But let's agree on the business side of things first. There will be a little extra fee without."

I didn't haggle. I counted the money into her hands, and to be sure, she counted it again. My earlier worries began to lift. Yasmin and her surroundings persuaded me that I'd come to a professional establishment. Nonetheless, I held my phone throughout, knowing that Rami was ready to jump at a moment's notice if any problem arose.

Yasmin took me by the hand and led me into the room. Placing a towel on a black leather armchair, she pulled down my pants in one sure motion and had me sit down in the armchair. With a damp cloth she carefully wiped me off.

"You can't cum on my skin," she warned. On seeing my oafish smile, she added by way of explanation, "Sperm is *najis*."

"But if it goes in your mouth, isn't that *najis*?"

"Only if on my skin," she said, shaking her head. "But I'll be skillful."

She was skillful. Not a drop went on her skin.

16

Bollen's followers announced their demonstration for a Saturday afternoon. Of course the civic organizations and trade unions organizing the rallies took pains to ensure the appearance of political neutrality, so they pointedly asked participants to take with them neither party flags nor signs referring to their political loyalties. They went on and on about how what was now at stake was far above party politics, and that they awaited that silent majority of citizens who'd had enough of terror, crime, and constant protests. A protest against protests.

Neither Bollen and top officials of her own party, nor the leaders of the other parties in the governing coalition, commented publicly on the preparations. It was a fact,

however, that they needed support, really needed support.

Opposition parties and all sorts of rights groups had been protesting for more than a month already over the treaty signed with General Abbas. Initially, tens of thousands had taken to the streets. Then, as usual, anarchists and youth from the working-class urban outskirts, many of them in black ski-masks, joined in too. So clashes with the police became the order of the day. By the time the "A Million for Peace and Security" demonstration supporting the government was announced, the peaceful, anti-Bollen rallies had dwindled, giving way to violence alone.

Since Husam had other plans, I took a microbus and then the subway downtown on my own. It was a weekend, but I wore an ironed shirt and linen pants, as if on my way to work. Of course, as usual I fucked up my timing, so instead of the 5 PM start time I got to the subway station closest to the city center only at 7. On checking the news, I was surprised to see the aerial footage. By then it was clear I hadn't a chance of getting into the main square. Even the boulevards leading there were packed with people kilometers deep.

At the subway exit a young woman, a volunteer wearing a "Peace and Security" T-shirt, pressed a candle into my hand. She smiled at me, and I forced a smile in return before heading forward into the crowd, which

134

was getting bigger and bigger at every step. Armored cars were positioned strategically on the streets, and I could not turn my head without seeing the green uniforms of the army or the black ones of the counterterrorism forces. Drones circled above the crowd like vultures.

I'll admit that it wasn't just curiosity that drove me. The video compilations on my favorite news portals often ridiculed Bollen's supporters, portraying them as a collection of pathetically simple, illiterate fools. I thought I'd see them for myself. I was disappointed. Standing all about me were agreeable, well-dressed citizens, candles in their hands and paper flags of the Pan-European Federation. There were blacks, whites, and browns, young and old, women and men. Some had brought their little kids or their dogs. According to the organizers there were three million people on the streets, and even the police estimated two and a half million. Analysts agreed that this was the largest such demonstration in the history of the republic, well exceeding the "peace demonstration against terrorism" that had previously been held for "national solidarity." Many were on hand, and they'd had enough. They wanted peace and security.

The whole story had begun with my favorite reality show, the civil war in the North African Union. Although the battles had been underway with varying intensity for almost ten years already, events had really gathered steam of late. I kept checking the interactive maps showing the ever-changing frontlines, I listened to analyses, and on my news feed I looked at practically every video uploaded by the soldiers or the militias. But then—as customary with reality shows—I grew bored with the war too. The whole thing had turned way too complicated, and after a while I couldn't keep track of who was on which side. The resistance groups were constantly renaming themselves, alliances being made and broken with less and less transparency. My acquaintances gave up far earlier than I did. My shares and posts saw fewer and fewer reactions, and in the end only Husam was left, along with those who, simply out of friendship, reacted to everything I shared. By then I was reading the headlines only at the major news portals. If those concerned civilian deaths, shot-up homes or mosques, or bombed-out schools and hospitals of one of the sides, that was enough to tell me that the other side happened to have the upper hand just then. In war, it's always the weaker side that complains; the stronger issues denials and marches on ahead, knowing that there will be time to explain things later.

The show then took yet another an exciting turn, and I again gave it all my attention. A young officer rose like a phoenix from the ruins of the war. His expression was one of determination, his countenance one that invited medals, his smile captivating. His war-honed elegance and his neatly trimmed beard were refreshing to eyes weary of seeing jihadists and mean-faced guerillas. General Abbas was hardly five years older than me. I envied the rotten bastard.

Abbas pushed forward with resolve. With his ascendancy it seemed that the decade-long civil war was no longer deadlocked, that a straight path forward would materialize, surely if slowly. Even the leaders of the Pan-European Federation welcomed this. Winter was over, and with spring the migrant season arrived, too. The situation was worse than ever before: tens of thousands were waiting on the opposite coast to depart. The Pan-European Federation decided not to sit there waiting for this to happen. Roused by the international backing, Abbas and his crew now considered themselves their homeland's only legitimate leaders, and they branded as terrorists anyone and everyone who held arms or who provided food or fuel to such people, and that's just how they treated them too.

From one day to the next, news of the torture in Abbas's prisons vanished from the headlines just as surely as atrocities against civilians. Meanwhile, the forces belonging to the newly internationally recognized countergovernment went on destroying Islamist positions, but soon in the shadow of drones provided by the Pan-European Federation, Abbas's forces made fast progress and took few prisoners. They uploaded brutal videos showing the consequences of precision aerial bombing of and battles against the jihadists. Of course, in deference to the sensitivities of European public opinion they sought to prove the legitimacy of the punishment: clips were introduced with videos taken from the phones of the liquidated jihadists, showing them committing barbarous acts against prisoners and civilians.

Abbas called for a summit with the confederation of tribes so as to assure them of his good intentions. He invited observers from the

Pan-European Federation and the Russians, too, to the event. He received the tribal delegation in a tent pitched in an oasis recaptured from the Islamists. To honor the occasion he changed from his military uniform into a jellabiya. His men served strong black coffee to all the other men negotiating among the pillows set in a circle on the ground.

So much for the twenty-first century, I mused with a laugh on first seeing the pictures. The foreign observers were clearly uncomfortable. Tight suit-pants had not been invented for sitting about on the ground.

An agreement was forged. The tribes swore a *bay'ah* to Abbas, who in turn offered them several ministerial posts in his new unity government. The civil war officially ended. As for the Pan-European Federation, it wasted no time in classifying the whole of Abbas's country as secure and fitting its coast guard with the most modern equipment.

Though peace took hold, terror attacks continued, giving Abbas the excuse to maintain a state of emergency. The Pan-European Federation opted to let the Arabs see to their affairs among themselves, in Arab fashion. An activist/blogger based in the North African Union reported numerous times that the bullet-riddled bodies of Africans were washing up on the seashore again and again. Then after a while, he too stopped reporting on anything.

Abbas became the Pan-European Federation's most faithful friend. Investments got underway, and a huge treaty in the energy sector also began taking shape. Aside from this, the forging of such promising ties was helped along by another conflict. Things in China were getting tense. European governments decided to establish various industrial facilities in North Africa. Within a short time, huge factories opened. Abbas killed two birds with one stone. Thanks to the European investments, he was able to ensure work for lots of people, increasing support across the fabric of society. This breathed new life into coastal tourist regions that had been on the decline during the decade-long civil war.

That's when something happened that led to the eruption of protests in Europe against Bollen. The counterterrorism treaty between the Pan-European Federation and the North African Union was clipping along so smoothly that, at Bollen's behest, the Federation leased from Abbas for ninety-nine years more regions in which to build colossal prisons to house terrorist suspects nabbed in Europe. That's when people took to the streets. Most were naturally not concerned about the futures of those arrested on suspicion of terrorism, but everyone understood this measure to mean that the governments of the Pan-European Federation had now given up on its citizens who'd fallen into crime. And what was the guarantee that in a couple of years common criminals would not be joining those terrorist suspects in the prisons of North Africa?

Needless to say, the prisons filled up fast. Bollen and other leaders had come to realize, of course, that few understood the language of the radicals better than Abbas's men. And so they turned over supervision of the prisons to them, with the Europeans sending only observers and interrogators.

We'd heard of one or two people carted off from the Zone on suspicion of terrorism, and at first that was it. Back then the net was full of videos and special reports on the humane circumstances enjoyed by the prisoners in those modern, super-secure prisons.

The real exodus ensued after the approval of the New Loyalist Act. Not that we knew exactly how many people had been sent from Europe to those prisons, but in the Zone rumor had it that the numbers reached as many as a few hundred in certain weeks. We never again saw special reports on the circumstances and "humane" prison life enjoyed by the detainees.

Maybe not by chance. No one among those transported there ever returned.

But all that happened only later. On that pleasant summer night, millions of candle flames professed peace and security.

17

One Wednesday in August I was sitting in the office and staring anxiously at my monitor. It was something like my eighth attempt to reach someone at a company based in the North African Union so he would answer a few simple questions. *Damn Arabs!* I thought. They were always the ones who meant the biggest headaches. The front desks of even big-name firms were staffed by good-for-nothing lowlifes hysterical about accepting even the tiniest bit of personal responsibility. By email it was simply impossible to communicate with them, since they didn't respond to messages even if they'd first promised explicitly by telephone to do so.

"Inshallah, we'll send the data this afternoon," promised a man who, by the sound of his voice, was about my age. Of course, they didn't send it. And then, after a bit, casting policy aside, by way of introduction I muttered my own name and said my company's—H&H—loud and clear. At such times I even dispensed with the use of Arabic. *If they don't believe I'm one of them, at least they could avoid tiring me out with that "inshallah" of theirs.*

Unreliability was just a minor matter. It riled me up a lot more that I couldn't get worthwhile information out of anyone. Even if I put to them just the simplest question—for example, which local companies they do business with—the secretary would transfer my call to the executive office, which then transferred me to the office manager, and then on to the deputy director's office, and finally to the office of the chair or the director. In the end I always had to ask the top boss for permission to get the simplest information. Of course it would have made a lot more sense to ask for that office to begin with, but under H&H policy you always had to start your snooping at the bottom of the ladder.

I could hardly wait for the day to be over. I'd just been chewing over my impression that in a few countries, dictatorships made complete sense, since some people need someone to tell them what to do. All at once every single phone began to buzz. That could only mean one thing.

139

"Emergency!" the terror-watch application's red-flashing message read, "Explosion at Bloc II of the KHD nuclear power plant."

A rumble passed through the office.

> The government, in coordination with the emergency defense command, has declared a state of emergency. The authorities ask citizens to go to the streets only if necessary. A general curfew will take effect from 7 PM.

"That's just over a hundred miles from us," said someone from the corner of the room in front of me. We all knew the radiation would reach us quickly. But why was it the terror-watch application that had told us? What did an accident in a power plant have to do with terror? A cold shudder passed through me.

> Counterterrorism Office: The explosion at Bloc II of the KHD nuclear power plant was a terrorist attack.

Oh fuck, that's all we needed, I thought, pleading deep down that for a change of pace, just this once, the attack would turn out to be the work not of jihadists but of some far-right group.

"Who wants to bet it's the jihadists," said Wladek from the other end of the office. He'd tried to say it quietly, but even his hushed voice echoed through the room. I knew that everyone around me was thinking the same thing. The mix of excitement and anxiety in the air was thick enough to cut. Everyone was looking on their phones for newer crumbs of information.

"I ask that everyone to return to work!" called out Xavier, the office manager, stepping out of his office. "Lunch break starts in half an hour." Though we seemed to obey, in the time remaining we logged not a single call worth making.

While scrolling up and down through the data table flashing white on the screen in front of me—the central office could check anytime what someone was looking at—on the phone in front of me on the desk I kept browsing the news, and meanwhile tried reassuring myself that an attack on a nuclear plant was not a simple knifing or gas attack, and it wasn't even technically a bombing. An operation this complicated exceeded the capabilities of solitary idiots who become radicalized online. But also those of the Caliphate, the Global Intifada, the Champions of the Sunna, and so on, which, thanks to the effective work of the secret services, had not pulled off a big one in at least six months. But the European Liberation Front and the other right-wing terror groups were capable of bringing off such an operation. When, not long before, they'd staged simultaneous bomb attacks against four offices of a refugee assistance organization, I'd quipped to Rami that this was at least serious work, and how could those idiotic jihadists lead a real caliphate if they couldn't even pull off a normal bombing?

"The right-wingers are tight with the cops," he replied. "It's simple that way."

He was not alone in his opinion. Many in the Zone figured that anti-Islamic groups got the inside dope from the police, counterterrorism, or both. Under this popular view, that was the only way to explain why they always attacked in places less covered by drones and surveillance cameras. A lot more people were in agreement that the police were not doing all they could to put the brakes on right-wing terror groups. Though there were raids and arrests, the number of vigilante attacks against Muslims did not subside.

Meanwhile everyone's phone began dinging again. Bomb attacks had hit three other countries of the Pan-European Federation: in one, a central power transformer; in the other two, major gas pipelines. Five minutes were left until lunch break, but no one cared anymore. Everyone reached for their phones.

The terrorists had now targeted not people, squares, buses, or subway lines but the power supply—power plants, gas pipelines, and transformers. It was clear as day that the attacks had been coordinated. Soon the first images of the scenes of the attacks reached us. The first one was a live video showing emergency defense personnel making their way through the front gates of the nuclear plant in gray coveralls. Another panned a blown-up, still-burning electric transformer building. And the third showed flames shooting out of a mangled gas pipeline above a pine forest stretching into the background. The emergency defense command had secured the area.

Though the gas utility had immediately shut off the valves, it took a while for the gas in the damaged pipe to burn away. The local military had sent out drones to check the length of pipelines. According to commentators, the perpetrators must have known just what they were doing. Gas and electricity supplies were cut to several dozen communities.

I sat back in relief. The action had white power written all over it. I couldn't imagine that Islamic radicals would have been capable of such precision. When an expert with one of the stations began conjecturing that the pipelines had probably been blown up with plastic explosives, an ethereal calm descended upon me. This method suggested that it was the nationalists' work.

In the lunchroom, I tried all the same to sit as far from Wladek as possible. I set down my tray at Badil's table. Badil was a Kurd. I'd never spoken with him before of politics or religion, but in the present circumstances I felt that we shared the same fate.

"The far right, no doubt," he said in a hushed voice while typing away at his phone with his right hand and, with the fork in his left, trying clumsily to tear away a bit of the chicken breast before him.

"Most likely," I replied. We ended this discussion right then, for Judith and another girl sat down at our table. They kept on blithely chattering away, as if not bothered for a moment that the gravest series of terror attacks in the history of the Pan-European Federation had just unfolded and might not be over yet. Judith was holding a minipresentation on why joints should be strained only gradually, and what sort of nutritional supplement is advisable for those who were into jogging.

"Take her advice!" I said with a smile. "She knows what she is talking about." They returned the smile, and I sank my eyes once again onto my phone.

The news update came an hour later: there was no radiation danger. The explosion had occurred at the entrance to Bloc II. But the state of emergency and the 7 PM curfew would remain in force. To our regret we thus had to work the whole day through. On the subway I leaned back with satisfaction. The nation had experienced terrorist attacks, but finally the Muslims weren't the scapegoats.

I was already home when the news appeared in my feed. I couldn't believe it. For a couple of seconds I just stared blankly before taking another look. The same thing was written there: "The Office of Counterterrorism and its partner agencies have confirmed that they suspect Islamist involvement." They even showed a picture of the nuclear plant bomber: one of the cleaners there, identified in the article only as Fatima K. Though as per the workplace dress code she was not wearing a hijab, her first name made her heritage clear. She had probably smuggled the explosives in by hiding them in the floor-cleaning machine, and catastrophe was averted only because her permission did not allow her entry to the facility's more sensitive areas.

The Champions of the Sunna claimed responsibility for the coordinated attacks. In a video posted by the group, a monotone *nasheed* served as a backdrop, while a hysterically chanting male voice declared that jihad had now stepped to a new level. After so many knife and vehicle attacks, the future now held in store a series of "quality" attacks similar to these.

An expert commentator on one channel tried calming the mood. He emphasized that only the bombing at the power plant involved serious planning, while the others only proved the jihadists' weakness. The terrorists had probably figured out that surveillance cameras and drones—equipped as they are with facial recognition and motion-sensing software—are effective at foiling urban attacks. Hence they set rural, relatively undefended infrastructure in their sights. The expert, of course, did not add that the effective foiling of urban attacks he'd mentioned involved primarily those whose skin color was darker than average: most successful such attacks in the past year had been carried out by light-skinned Muslim converts, while darker-skinned attackers had been nabbed in time.

That night my friends were not too active on the public portals. A momentary impulse led me to look at Wladek's profile. I saw that he'd commented on the story on one of the leading news portals about the statement issued by the Champions of the Sunna. He wrote, "The terrorist is Fatima K. Any other questions? I don't understand how she could have gotten such work. Doesn't that require national security clearance?" Within ten minutes of its posting, the comment had gotten more than two hundred likes. I recognized five of the names from the office. Judith was among them. I decided to call in sick for the second half of the week.

From outside, sirens were approaching. Their squealing echoed among the tower blocks. I stepped to the window. A convoy of four black military vehicles passed down the street. The last one slowed, and then carefully backed onto the asphalt island in the middle of the intersection.

No one among my acquaintances believed that jihadists were behind the attacks. Most laid the blame on anti-Muslim terrorist groups who were trying in this manner to incite anti-Muslim sentiment among the public and, yes, the government. Yet others believed the secret services had planned the attacks, seeking to exploit the general panic to have Bollen expand their powers. There were even some who believed Bollen herself was behind the attacks: even earlier she'd been pursuing strict policies, and now she was looking for excuses to limit rights even more. The most creative among my friends kneaded all three theories into one, convinced that anti-Muslim groups had carried out the attacks under the direction of the secret services, and that Bollen had known of everything in advance.

Proponents of all three theories agreed, however, that Fatima K. was either an innocent victim who didn't know that explosives had been hidden in her floor-cleaning machine, or else she was stupid and hadn't realized that the person she'd regarded as her jihadist contact was in fact an agent of the secret services. Several people expanded this possibility by claiming that the jihadist terrorist groups had been created to begin with by the secret services—or, according to others, by the Jews—or at least that the secret services kept those groups under their supervision.

An emergency press conference was announced for the day after the attack. Though I'd called in sick, I was in no mood to watch it solemnly on the phone, so I went to the Barak Café, next door to old Ashraf's kebab place.

I arrived a couple of minutes before noon. As the door opened, the din from inside struck my ears. The café was full. I must have been the youngest person there. The sweet aroma of the water pipes filled me with a homey feel. I sat down by a table beside the wall and asked for a jasmine tea. It felt good not to be alone. The press conference started right on schedule. The café fell silent. The barkeep even turned off the water boiler. Every important political leader was lined up behind Bollen, including the grand mufti.

"Our patience has ended," said the prime minister, her voice even firmer than usual. "Our community and our homeland have been attacked. We can't stick our heads in the sand. The Pan-European Federation is in battle. And the enemy is now within."

It was a strong start. A couple of those standing behind her nodded while the rest stared blankly straight ahead. Bollen spoke of the importance of unity and solidarity, and that it wasn't citizens' gender, origin, or religion that counted, but their loyalty to the state and to European values.

"Though Islamist terror groups are behind most of the attacks, our war can by no means be directed at either Islam or our Muslim compatriots," she continued. "The main pillar of our European identity is secularism, and we hold religion to be an inalienable private affair in which the state does not and cannot have a say. We stand in solidarity with our Muslim fellow citizens, with whom we battle hand in hand against radicalism. But the time for patience is over. All must decide whether to wage the war with us or against us." In the background, the grand mufti nodded most of all. Bollen went on: "The greatest curse of our age is terrorism, which has the whole continent in its hold. The leaders of the Pan-European Federation therefore agreed at their emergency summit yesterday that from now on all measures will be allowed in the war against terrorism."

She added, with unflappable resolve, "The perpetrators—and even those who have so much as considered committing terrorism—can count on the most severe punishment. Our government therefore proposes the New Loyalist Act. In coordination with regional and local authorities, we seek to implement security measures more sweeping than ever before. The terrorists will have refuge neither in their actual hideouts nor in the online world."

Bollen then summed up the details of the New Loyalist Act. The authorities would be able to subject to up to three months of preliminary detention anyone who is suspected by the secret services to have even the slightest of association with any terrorist group or who has supported such groups verbally, in comments online. Such detention could be extended, and its location would be one of the "relocation camps" in the North African Union. In addition, online activists would be monitored retroactively for five years, so the aforementioned regulations about terrorist suspects would apply in cases of past participation too. Suspicious activity on public portals, and even the possibility that someone has used the dark web, would be sufficient for detention.

Glancing around me in the café, I saw shocked faces everywhere. But only next did the truly tough part come.

"The government will, moreover, propose legislation to Parliament to prohibit dual citizenship with countries outside the Pan-European Federation," said Bollen. "In the scope of the New Loyalist Act, our nation expects complete loyalty from its citizens in these hard times, and in the case of dual citizens, we cannot be sure where their loyalty truly lies."

A loud murmur passed through the café. Bollen went on spelling out the details of the plan.

"From the point at which the new citizenship law takes effect, affected citizens will have a few months to decide whether to keep their original or their European citizenship. If they decide on the former, their European citizenship will automatically become an employment visa. That will have no expiration; so as long as the individual has a registered workplace, he can stay and travel freely on the territory of the Pan-European Federation. But if, within six months, someone cannot provide documentation of having worked officially for at least one month, the competent government agency will cancel their employment visa and he or she will have to move home. The legal status of minor children—regardless of their citizenship—would be that of their parents or guardians."

Bollen added that the ban on dual citizenship would not apply to everyone. Dual citizens of countries such as Canada, the United States, Australia, Russia, Israel, and Malaysia would be exempt. Not as if there were masses of Malaysian dual citizens. Having a Muslim country on the list was probably a way to hush suspicions of religious discrimination. There were a lot of Muslim dual citizens though. Later it turned out that nearly 57 percent of dual citizens in the Pan-European Federation were Muslim.

"Nothing will come of that, anyway!" said one of the old men near me, waving a hand dismissively. "If they took away the citizenship of millions and deported them, no one would be left behind to work."

"Don't you get it?" another hissed. "Work has nothing to do with citizenship. Millions of foreigners worked in the Gulf states back when the oil business was still big. And they didn't have citizenship. And then, when those countries no longer needed them working there, they took them and tossed them right out. And in a lot of cases even their fathers had been born there."

"But this here is Europe," the first old man said. His voice suggested that not even he was so sure.

My family and Rami's had nothing to worry about. Thank goodness, back then my grandfather had never taken the trouble to register his kids as dual citizens at his country's embassy. Maybe he'd neglected to do so out of laziness, and maybe he simply wanted the best for his kids. Father used to tell us that my great-grandfather, back in the home country, had to pay huge sums to the general in charge to ensure that his two sons, living in Europe, would not be required to enter the military in the home country. Perhaps Grandfather thought it was better to save his own children the trouble.

Marwan was not particularly moved by the announcement. His ancestors had come from Palestinian territories. Since they never had a state to begin with, it had never even come into consideration that they would have had other citizenship. Marwan was jubilant: "I love the Jews! May Allah protect the State of Israel for long!" He posted on his profile.

Husam, though, was understandably nervous. His parents had come to Europe, and while he and his sisters had been born there, his parents had registered them as citizens back home too. Up until now this hadn't carried any disadvantage to them. Since he had no brother, under the laws of the home country he was not required to do compulsory military service. When, from time to time, he traveled home, he used his European passport.

"I got the notice," he said when taking me to work one morning. "I have until November 30 to prove that I have no other citizenship."

"But you do."

"Not for long. On Monday morning I'll get the process underway."

"How does it work?"

"I don't know. That's exactly why I'm starting there."

"And Latifa?" I asked.

"Her husband is a natural-born European citizen," he said. "So she's got no worries."

Oddly, for once I found myself reassuring Husam.

There was general confusion. The officials of those countries most affected were not exactly quick to provide information to their citizens about what to do. And the news had made it clear that for Pan-European Federation citizens, citizenship elsewhere was a problem now facing millions. More precisely, how could such citizenship be renounced? It was none too clear. There were hardly any idiots among these millions who would not have chosen their pretty red European passport over a good-for-nothing document from somewhere else, whatever color it was. Husam, in any case, would do well to try sorting it out in person, even if that meant I needed to get to and from work by subway.

We may have been well into the twenty-first century, but online processing was evidently still a mystery at some embassies and consulates. They would be overrun on Monday morning by the many seeking to sort out their citizenship imbroglios. Some of those arriving after nine didn't even find room on the street outside. It looked like Black Friday just before the stores open. While I scrolled up and down the lists on my monitor at work, I kept track of news updates on my phone. I tried finding Husam in one of the crowds. But it was impossible to find him in that billowing sea of unfamiliar faces. In most locations the employees simply got scared and didn't even open up.

"Please be so kind as to submit your applications on our website!" said one employee who had removed his suit coat and was standing in front of the wrought-iron front door of an embassy in an effort to calm the crowd. A moment later he was stooped forward, hands on his bloody forehead. The rock, bottle, or whatever it was that had hit him nearly took out an eye. The police officers standing guard outside surrounded him and helped him escape back inside the door. Some in the crowd scooped up handfuls of stones from the base of trees outside and cast them at the embassy building. A few windows shattered, tear gas soon filled the streets, and the police saw to dispersing the crowd. It didn't take them long. Most of those waiting outside were women and old people who'd been caught off guard when the situation took a turn for the worse.

From the next day on, the police allowed onto the streets housing such embassies and consulates only those who could prove, with documents, that they had gotten appointments. Of course not many had. Indeed, the website had simply crashed at one such location. Those affected had just three months to see to renouncing their citizenship, so anxiety prevailed. To make matters worse, this period would include Ramadan too, when, as everyone knows, not even the grass grows in Muslim countries. The affected governments naturally agreed to post on the Internet those documents that needed to be filled out. Weeks passed, and there was not a trace of this. One article after another appeared saying that in more than one country there was no legal provision whatsoever for renouncing citizenship.

Meanwhile Parliament passed the bill banning dual citizenship. The Socialists and the Greens were no match for the Conservatives and the far right, and everyone waited for the Constitutional Court to attack the decision. It didn't. Analysts recalled that Bollen had first raised the idea of banning dual citizenship during her tenure as interior minister, and that a big legal debate had unfolded back then over the matter. It seemed that Bollen had learned from the experience, and that the legislation in its current form had been drawn up to make it legally beyond reproach.

Then one day an unexpected message came from the North African Union. "Human blood is not a slip of paper. You can't renounce it. The Homeland will not give up even one of its children." President Abbas had thus succinctly, terrifyingly summed up his thoughts on the matter. Arab and African governments were quick to hop on the bandwagon. The rumor was that secret border agreements had been born; that presidents, dictators, and revolutionary governments had agreed, in exchange for all sorts of infrastructure funding and quotas, not to give up their citizens. Moreover, within the scope of counterterrorism agreements, the Pan-European

Federation had comprehensive information-exchange agreements in force with every country in the Middle East and northern Africa. And that meant that Bollen's government knew the name of every last person in the citizenship databases of the partner countries.

The Internet was aflame, and people took to the streets in every large city of the Pan-European Federation. The government tried calming the public in vain. Meanwhile even the Conservatives' Muslim wing and the Central Fatwah Council defended the New Loyalist Act, arguing that the new measures equally served the interests of us all. Those with nothing to hide and who did honest work had nothing to fear. That understandably reassured no one. The protests intensified by the day and people became ever more despondent.

Then came the bombings—coordinated attacks that, a couple minutes apart, shook mass demonstrations held simultaneously in five large cities of the Pan-European Federation. Initial reports spoke of a least 150 dead and 250 wounded. A previously unknown far-right group, the New Templars, claimed responsibility. The interior ministers of the Pan-European Federation declared states of emergency across the federation's entire territory, the police withdrew previously issued demonstration permits, and a general curfew took effect after 7 PM.

Protests kept up unabated on the Internet, of course. Groups formed there that went by such names as "Europe Is Our Home," "We Are Not Afraid," "We Are at Home." Every such site was filled with pictures of the attacks and the victims. My acquaintances waged all-out war on the news boards. Some believed that the far right really was behind the attacks, and that its aim was to intimidate the Muslims and others of non-European descent living in the Pan-European Federation. Others were convinced that the "New Templars" were in fact jihadists who sought to turn the already tense, explosive public mood into civil war. And then there were those who insisted that counterterrorism or some other state security service was behind it all, trying thus to force the government to give it more money and power. Why, some went so far as to say that Bollen herself—with the complete agreement of the other European leaders—had given the order for the attacks so as to intimidate the public and bring an end to the demonstrations.

The truth never did come to light. Not that it really even mattered anymore. Whether or not the Pan-European Federation's leadership had anything to do with the latest bombings and the earlier attacks on the nuclear plant and the other utilities, one thing was certain: they were the only winners.

In the course of the previous four years, thanks to deteriorating public security and the economic crisis, the Conservatives and Bollen had seen their popularity waning steadily. It had seemed that the attack on the nuclear plant would be the last straw. People were scared and angry. They sought those responsible. Well, Bollen and her crew delivered the goods. Following the announcement of the New Loyalist Act, the Conservatives' popularity soared, hitting a historic high by revoking the European citizenship of millions whose parents or grandparents had migrated to Europe or who had done so themselves.

The opposition parties didn't stand a chance in the national elections the following spring. With the revocation of the citizenship of so many, the Socialists had lost their main voter base, and the voices of liberals were suppressed by the bombings. As for the Patriotic Front, it could no longer promise the public a thing the public wouldn't have gotten from the Conservatives. Bollen and her party captured 78 percent of the vote in the elections.

I was sitting at home alone on election night. The wind brought the sound of detonations through the open window. I couldn't tell whether I was hearing tear gas grenades, weapons fire, or explosions.

18

Even while browsing the ingredients of a new energy drink, I kept glancing up and wondering which line to stand in. In vain would I guesstimate which line had the fewest items in the baskets held by those ahead of me, or in which stood the least idiotic-looking shoppers. It would no doubt turn out that someone in front of me would either be more thick-headed than first it seemed or would have second thoughts about something he or she just bought, or else, quite simply, the self-service register would call it quits. It was now rush hour, when those on their way home from work flood into the supermarket all at once, and at such times every line creeps along at a turtle's pace anyway. Noticing others also panning the lines with their eyes, I suddenly ceased my efforts and, come what may, stood in a line behind some guy who looked my age.

Damnit, I suddenly thought, *the caramel chocolate*. I knew that rushing off now would do me no good. By then someone had stood in line behind me—a black man in a blazer and a turtleneck. The chocolate was not so important, after all. I already had a bar in my desk drawer at work; I'd only just begun it, so it would be enough for the next day.

I really should switch to ordering groceries online—came the usual thought that flashed through my mind at such times. But then, also as usual, I cast it aside at once. Not all supermarkets in the Zone delivered, and those that did were not famous for taking their best quality products, those with expiration dates still weeks away. Besides, I liked to pick out my own groceries. I'd inherited that penchant from Grandfather. Back in the day, when he used to take me to the market, he'd go on and on about how you could tell if fruit, vegetables, or meat was fresh, what was in season and when, and what was the best buy on which day of the week. I was just fourteen when he died, but by then Grandfather had planted in me the seed of the smart shopper.

There were four people ahead of me when my phone began beeping. It was an email from the HR department at H&H. With my feet I pushed my basket ahead of me on the floor, and I opened the message.

Dear Sir,

We are writing to inform you that, as the result of an investigation
by our legal department, we have concluded that your activity on
public portals is incompatible with the H&H's guiding principles of
employment and commitment to political neutrality. Under Section
342/238 of the Labor Act, H&H exercises its right to terminate your
employment immediately. We inform you also that you are eligible
for one month's pay, which will be deposited to your account on the
next business day.

We further inform you that your workplace email account has
been suspended concurrently with the termination of your employment. Within eight business days of the date on this letter you may request access from our IT department to the archived private messages
at that account. As for any personal items you may have left on your
office desk, you may request those from the H&H reception desk.

Wishing you all the best,

H&H

I was not surprised. After all, I hadn't held back one bit the past few
months. Until such public gatherings were banned, I had regularly gone
out to the protests with my chums. Since then our resistance had been
restricted to the online realm. I'd read everything I found on the net, and
I'd habitually shared and sometimes commented on the antigovernment
posts Latifa had shared. In fact I was really just surprised that they'd sent
the letter only now. I decided at once not to appeal. I wouldn't stand a
chance against the lawyers of a multinational. I'd rest up for a couple of
weeks—summer would soon be here anyway—so I could put my affairs in
order before looking again for work.

By now only two people were ahead of me in line. A young woman was
bungling away with the barcode on a bunch of plastic-wrapped bananas.
She kept trying to smooth out the wrinkled sticker so the scanner could
read it.

Picking up my basket from the floor, I headed back for the caramel
chocolates.

19

The commandos descended from the helicopter on long ropes. The rotor was buzzing loudly while the helicopter tried to land as close as possible to the building. The commandos were already dangling by the window. They were looking right at me now as I sprang out of bed. They could have kicked in the window at any time. The buzz of the helicopter got louder and louder. I groped about for the key and, my hand trembling, tried fitting it into lock from the inside. It turned. I tore open the door, jumped onto the bobsled, somehow shoved it away from the wall, and slid down the red tracks. Meanwhile the commandos had kicked in the wall and were already pursuing me. The helicopter buzzed toward the tracks, and my every last muscle was set to leap right out when I got down and ran into the woods. But when I hit the ground, I didn't even have time to stand on my two feet. Three pairs of hands gripped me simultaneously.

I opened my eyes. The contours of the furniture slowly crystallized before me from the dimly lit splotches they first seemed to be. Since I lived on the fifth floor, the light of the street lamps filtered only tenuously into the room. The dream had left me in a state of mute anxiety. But then again came that buzzing noise. From just outside the window. *A drone*—the recognition hit me. It had only been yet another nightmare.

Fuck it, I should have shut the window, I thought. Of course even in my momentarily muddled state of mind I knew, on second thought, that that would have been a bad idea. My AC had recently called it quits, so on these unusually warm early June nights sleep was possible only with the window open. I staggered to my feet and looked outside. The buzzing of the surveillance drones could be heard from close by, and the flashing blue lights of police cars beat back against the building walls. Indeed, two cop cars were parked in front of the tower block opposite mine, two black paddy wagons behind them. I looked at my phone: 4:23 AM. About what I had suspected. Raids usually happened between 4:00 and 4:30, when the targets were still asleep. Since such individuals were mostly religious, the authorities assumed they would wake up for morning prayers, so the cops

154

struck beforehand, since after that, closer to dawn, the subjects would be too alert and might escape. Two buildings away it had happened one morning that a young man about to be picked up jumped right out his window. He'd figured that since he lived on the second floor and there was grass underneath, nothing too serious could happen. Well, he hung out of the window, holding the railing, so his feet would be as close as possible to the ground. It was a bad idea. With a sprained ankle he tried limping away, but the drones pinpointed his location in no time, and the counterterrorism unit nabbed him, like that.

I closed the door and spied the street from behind the curtain. I was not alone. I saw curtains stirring in several windows of the building opposite. But the windows stayed shut. The New Loyalist Act had registered its effect. No one wanted to get involved in a thing. Back when I was a kid, folks would swarm onto the streets for every last little crap of a reason. If two cars had a fender bender, half the Zone would be teeming outside. If there was some police action, the locals—from kids to oldsters—would be stretching their necks to see what was happening. A while back there weren't too many street fights: whenever two guys fell at each other, they often moaned away deliberately until a few others gathered round and pulled them apart. This was a social ritual that allowed troublemakers to back out of conflicts while saving face. But by now all that had changed. People not only avoided getting mixed up in conflicts but went all out to avoid attracting even the slightest notice. If they saw anything at all, they turned their heads the other way and felt grateful that the trouble wasn't visiting them or some close loved one.

Meanwhile dark, hooded figures emerged from the building opposite, the phosphorescent emblem of counterterrorism shining off their backs even from afar. They walked in pairs, leading stooped characters whose hands were twisted behind their backs. As soon as they left, I opened the window again. Upset though I was by what I'd seen, I tried falling back asleep. I hoped not to have another nightmare. By then, such dreams were routine. The storyline was usually about the same: sometimes they came by helicopter, sometimes in cars, but they always came at night. I could think only of escape. But sometimes I was so frozen with fear that I couldn't even get up out of bed. At other times I managed to run off, slide down a slide, climb up some stairs, jump out a window. . . . But they always caught me in the end. There was no escape. I awoke drenched in sweat, my heart beating frantically.

That day's news feed included only a minor item about counterterrorism having raided three flats in the Zone the night before. In two, one man each had been caught on suspicion of terrorism, and five men had been taken away from the third flat. The latter—having had their employment visas revoked—had been residing illegally on the territory of the Pan-European Federation, and not even after the passing of the grace period had they reported to the competent authorities.

Barely a year after the New Loyalist Act was first announced, we'd reached the point at which the authorities no longer sent out warnings. Those facing deportation did what they could to avoid detection, but facial recognition cameras and drones positioned all over the city were of great help to the authorities in revealing their whereabouts. At first those who did not appear in time at designated locations received official notices that the authorities would arrive at their homes to transport them to relocation centers.

The warnings were dispensed with once and for all after a nasty incident. It happened in another city. Four police had wanted to detain two siblings. They arrived at their flat before dawn. Music could be heard from inside. Since no one came to the door even after lots of ringing, the police broke the lock. The entered the hall and, *boom!* Explosives had gone off.

It soon turned out that I recognized one of those arrested the previous night. An eighteen-year-old guy. His mom cried all over the Internet. No one liked her comments.

We then learned that his crime had been to play—an online game, that is. He'd belonged to a clan called Global Caliphate. The authorities took dead-seriously every single sign of terrorism or even suggested support for terrorism—especially since it had turned out that several who'd carried out attacks had communicated with each other in the chat rooms of online games.

All day long the guy's story was on my mind. By the time Rami and I met up in front of the gym that evening, I was shaking from nerves.

"We too had so many clans with dumb names back then. If I were a little younger, they'd now take me away too. For fuck's sake, it's a game, nothing more!"

Unable to say a thing, Rami just stared at the ground.

Another guy arrested the same night was two years younger. Just sixteen. Nope, you can't get mixed up early enough in terrorism. . . . They'd taken him away because he'd been following the video blog of a comedian popular among kids his age. In the most recent episode, which had aired three days earlier, this comic had goofed off in front of the camera dressed as a jihadist. The sixteen-year-old fan who'd been taken away had shared similar videos day in and day out on his own profile.

A couple of days later the kid's folks were also taken away. The authorities explained that as his guardians, they too were responsible for his acts. For my part, I suspected that the real motivation was this: after his son's arrest, the father, on his own online profile, had begun issuing threats. If anything happened to his son, he wrote, "the police will pay for it." The kid's older brother, who to his good fortune was no longer a minor and lived on his own, was taken into preliminary detention just long enough for every real and online activity of his to be checked. Following this incident, mandatory "family unifications" became increasingly common. Lots of minors were apprehended for all sorts of reckless online activity. Afterward—though usually they hadn't a clue as to their kids' doings on the Internet—the parents often followed. Those dragged off on suspicion of terrorism who still had minor children at home could choose between having some relative adopt them or having them sent to a state orphanage.

I opened my profile and turned off private mode everywhere I could. I then looked up a few really hard heavy metal bands and requested their shares. Just to be on the safe side. No way could counterterrorism see a satanist metalhead as dangerous.

20

Not even in the Zone did the name Angel Hill carry any positive connotations. The residential district, which in fact had nothing to do with any sort of hill, much less an angel, was but a dilapidated concrete jungle at the other end of the city. Way back when—maybe just around the time of the Strauss government—it had been built for freshly arriving guest workers. Then as the years and the decades passed, required maintenance work became less and less frequent before eventually ceasing altogether. The paint flaked off the formerly pastel-hued tower blocks, leaving only a somber grayness in its wake. Just what a good place the Zone was, I didn't even suspect until one day I wound up in Angel Hill with the guys. We went to a hip-hop concert where this kid we sort of knew was among the performers.

Even from the window of the elevated train the postapocalyptic tower blocks rose up into the sky with a repulsive gloominess, their faceless ugliness souring the otherwise idyllic pink sunset. As the train drew near, each station was more dilapidated than the previous one, and the local passengers' glances became glassier and glassier. Then we arrived. Had we been in a video game, this would have been the course where, just to be on the safe side, at the moment the automatic door slip open, I would have begun by lobbing a grenade. As we headed toward the club, it finally sunk in what a good place I live in. The heart of the Zone was, after all, the onetime city center, whose buildings had been rebuilt in their original style after the bombings of the world war. The row of shops, Strauss Square, and the park were full of life, and even the pastel pink and green forest of tower blocks now seemed to me much more livable and friendly than ever before. In contrast, Angel Hill was a concrete hell. As for the concert, it was nothing special; the locals weren't much different from the residents of the Zone. One thing was certain though: lyrics about hopelessness and violence came off sounding credible from the mouths of their rappers.

Later the low-cost rentals in Angel Hill became popular with refugees. Back then word had it that die-hard jihadists were hiding away in those bleak tower blocks, just waiting for the opportunity to stage attacks. It was also said that the residents' lives were under the purview of Sharia courts and local criminal gangs, and that police no longer even dared set foot in the area. How much of that was true, I don't know. Not much, I suspected. Indeed, sometimes I heard the same sort of thing about the Zone. Friends of my onetime colleagues from H&H and friends of those friends often shared such drivel. Most of them, of course, had never been in our neighborhood.

The lives of those in Angel Hill took an even sadder turn after the New Loyalist Act took effect. Once it turned out that dual citizens couldn't just give up their original citizenship, everyone realized how big the trouble really was. Unemployment among immigrants and their children was high. An even bigger problem: income for many derived from fishy, not quite legal businesses. To make matters worse, numerous companies dismissed employees who'd lost their citizenship, for the tax breaks they used to get for such "socially disadvantaged" workers no longer applied to them. So everyone waited anxiously for the first six months to pass: it was certain that masses of people would now lose their employment visas.

That's just what happened. Thousands in the Zone alone were deported. In Angel Hill, several times as many. Though they couldn't do a thing about it, not everyone was willing to give themselves up in silence.

Perhaps not even in her wildest dreams had Bollen considered that some would band together and choose resistance. And yet that's what happened. As the noose tightened, so did the despair and determination of those concerned. One late June morning, residents of Angel Hill awaiting deportation—nearly 400 of them, including some 150 children—moved en masse into a terribly dilapidated, by then sparsely inhabited building set for demolition. With enough food to last them weeks, they barricaded the entrances. They formed a committee that communicated with the world via video messages uploaded to the Internet. They demanded that the authorities extend their residence permits and reconsider the decisions to deport them.

Hopelessness breeds dumb ideas, I thought on first seeing the news. I wondered at their grit, and I understood their despair, but I didn't see what good they could expect from gathering in one place, thus easing their deportation. From that moment on I was certain they didn't stand a chance against counterterrorism.

Police and counterterrorism forces surrounded the building. They didn't dare break in, for those inside had announced that if they so much as suspected an imminent assault, they would set the building on fire. Rights organizations naturally announced a demonstration beside the building—Tower 82—and created profiles called Moriscos82 on every major public portal, where they collected images from inside the tower and news connected with the matter.

"A real reality show," Rami observed.

"Counterterrorism will vote out everyone at once," came the bantering reply from someone or other.

Thanks to the media attention, the government was compelled to deal with the tower affair. The government spokesperson—by then Bollen barely ever spoke to the press herself—declared in no uncertain terms that the laws applied to everyone, and anyone without a valid employment permit would have to leave the country. This, however, could not simply be solved with a nighttime raid. In the crosshairs of the cameras, the police could not do a thing without consequences. Not even supporters of the New Loyalist Act were certain to look on eagerly as sobbing women were wrestled to the ground and as children torn away from their parents were herded into a paddy wagon.

The standoff was on its fifth day when the authorities decided to get tough. They had the power and gas cut off, and notified those inside that water would soon be next—officially speaking, so those inside "could not do harm to themselves." And yet the measure looked much more like a wartime blockade than concern for those barricading themselves inside.

Once the electricity was cut, the phones of the tower inhabitants began to run low. They quickly realized that they'd do well to turn off their still-working phones and to only turn them on just long enough to take and upload new images. The number of videos emerging from within plummeted. Reporters and activists meanwhile moved into adjacent towers and, using drones, sent portable chargers to those in Tower 82. The crisis had been underway for a week and the squatters were increasingly in

Allah's Spacious Earth   161

the throes of despair. More and more videos of crying children appeared at Moriscos82.

One video showed a woman in a white veil, her eyes overflowing with tears. Her little girl—curly black hair, big brown eyes—was shrieking and sobbing away in her lap. Behind her was an open window.

"I swear I'll throw the child out!" the woman screamed in despair. "If Europe doesn't need her, she'll find refuge in heaven," she said, weeping, as the camera operator zoomed in on the little girl, who surely had no idea what was going on around her even as she soaked in her mother's despair.

"Allahu Akbar! Allah is greater than tyrants!" shrieked the mother.
"Allahu Akbar! Allah is greater than tyrants!
Allahu Akbar! Allah is greater than the police!
Allahu Akbar! Allah is greater than Europe!"

If the woman had been aiming to elicit the sympathy of the good citizens of the Pan-European Federation, she sure had missed her mark. Public opinion had already shuddered to see her threatening the life of the girl, and her howling of "Allahu Akbar!" was icing on the cake of bad impressions. A straw poll conducted by one of the Internet portals determined that the video had seen the percent of those sympathizing in some degree with those in the tower fall from the previous 72 percent to under 50. The Patriotic Front urged that the building be immediately stormed.

On seeing the outrage sparked by the video, a group of Christian organizations issued a statement on the Internet offering to transport children under ten to reception centers and to help them find permanent adoptive parents if those in Tower 82 would rescind their blockade. So even if the parents had to leave the Pan-European Federation, a path to citizenship would at least be open to their children. Muslim civic organizations also joined in, saying the kids would wind up in moral—meaning Muslim—families in which their appropriate rearing would be guaranteed. The shocked residents of Tower 82 rejected the offer.

Finally the child in the video escaped, for it was her mother who jumped out. In a video that was filmed from a distance, a figure in black, her head veiled in white, could clearly be seen in one of the windows on the seventh floor, thrusting her way outward, then plummeting to the ground. In the air she wriggled like a caterpillar, turned away, and slammed into the concrete at a forty-five degree angle from her thinner, white end—presumably her head. I might even have had cause to be grateful to her: The image of her falling and then striking the ground was to become a recurring motif of my nightmares in the weeks that followed, thus sneaking an exciting bit of variety into the suffocating monotony of the scene of my apprehension.

"Voting-out show," Rami commented online about the video, but then after I told him off in a private message, he quickly deleted his words.

Then came the next, and yet another. A couple minutes later a video arrived in which one of the women about to commit suicide said good-bye and announced in a hysterical voice that she preferred a "martyr's death" to enduring humiliation. Just what she meant by it, she didn't say. And that was a mistake. Someone with the State Migration and Integration Office who was following the events from the studio of the government broadcasting station offered the off-the-cuff expert opinion that a Muslim woman cannot decide on her own about her own death, since from childhood on she has been raised to regard her life as subjugated to the male members of her family—first to her father; then to her oldest brother; and after her marriage, to her husband. After following through a bit more on this analysis, the expert, whose glasses sat with thick-as-hell lenses on a mouse-shaped head, concluded that the three woman must surely have been forced to jump by their male relatives.

"But how can anyone capable of this sort of thing possibly be integrated into European society?" asked the program host, visibly repulsed.

"As the chart here also shows, in the case of the ideology of Islam it is extremely challenging to realize equality between the sexes as understood in Europe," replied the expert, and that was that.

In no time the police spokesperson said this at a press conference: "We will examine the circumstances behind such deaths with the utmost thoroughness. If a suspicion of murder or incitement to suicide proves true, the perpetrators will face the most serious legal consequences."

Hardly had a half hour passed when the Central Fatwa Council issued a statement, citing the arguments of religious scholars of yore, declaring that those leaping from the tower—insofar as they did so on their own, naturally—were not martyrs but suicides. The difference was literally heaven and hell.

After this incident the authorities left nothing to chance. They stretched a trampoline all around the tower and declared an operational zone in a two-hundred meter radius, including the two adjacent towers. They shooed journalists away from the area, ordered a complete news blackout, and cut off mobile phone communication.

Then all hell broke loose. Fire erupted on the fifth floor of Tower 82. Since power had earlier been cut, it could hardly have been caused by a short circuit. Clearly those inside had made good on their earlier threat. No one knew how many people were on the lower floors and how many on the upper ones. The news broadcast videos provided by the authorities showed firefighters as they surged forward past the barricades by the doors and emerged carrying coughing women and children on their shoulders. At least 150 people perished from the fire and smoke—among them, eight firefighters, which likewise did no good as far as public sentiment toward those who'd barricaded themselves inside was concerned.

"The tragedy has shaken us all," the government spokesperson began his press conference, to which he wore a black suit and black tie. "We thank our firefighters, rescue workers, police, and counterterrorism officers for their self-sacrificing work, without which who knows how many more fatalities there would have been. Our government will do everything to ensure the speediest recovery of the injured." He looked about at the press corps and went on: "But the country will not let itself be blackmailed. Its laws and regulations apply to everyone, and not even the most brutal method of protest can be cause to suspend the laws approved by Parliament. The protestors who barricaded themselves in Tower 82 will not be exempt from laws applying to them. Those not in possession of residence permits are presently in closed centers awaiting their departure from the territory of the Pan-European Federation. Moreover, eight individuals have been charged with multiple counts of murder and attempted murder, and thirty-two with endangering minors. Four people have been charged with planning a terrorist attack. Since the suspects do not have residence permits, once their conditions have stabilized they will await their proceedings in the designated overseas detention camp.

After the fire, those protests supporting the protesters of Tower 82 that had gathered pace on the Internet were cut, it seemed. And the police continued their raids.

Although government communication after the events in Angel Hill left no doubt that everyone would be held to account for rules and regulations, Bollen and those around her must have sensed that they could avert similar occurrences in the future only by making some concessions. Total hopelessness breeds despair, and desperation spurs people to radical acts.

The solution came in President Abbas's visit two months later. Abbas had arrived in the Pan-European Federation. He visited capital cities, held talks with leaders, shook hands, and looked at factories. His visit attracted general interest. What with his theatrical gestures, he'd already been a favorite of those on the Internet, hundreds of memes having arisen out of his quotes and his unmistakable mimicry. I too awaited his joint press conference with Bollen as if it were a new episode of some funny vlog.

"It fills me with pride to be able to stand here," Abbas began his speech. Pressing two clenched fists to his chest, he really did look as if he were filled with pride.

"On this day we signed a historic agreement with the leaders of the Pan-European Federation, bearing in mind the interests of both our peoples. The comprehensive economic cooperation treaty was born in the spirit of mutual respect and coexistence."

From beside him behind the podium Bollen listened with the help of a translation machine. She wore a dark blue two-piece outfit and a white blouse.

With flowery turns of phrase, Abbas praised the exceptional ties between their countries, as well as the Pan-European Federation's wisdom and good intentions, thanks to which the decades-long civil war in his homeland could come to an end. He then spoke for a few minutes about the importance of European investments.

"Under the agreement signed today we expand our cooperation. Our people will offer more territories for European development projects."

A map now appeared on a screen behind him and, using his finger, he pointed out where those territories were.

"As previously, now too our people will lease the territories for ninety-nine years for a token sum and will also open its doors to immigrants arriving from Europe. Thanks to the huge factories, the expansions, and the new investments, we will be able to receive those wanting to work in numbers never seen before." Looking with satisfaction about the room, he added, "Those who want to can lead respectable lives and find secure livelihoods in our homeland."

"Our people respect Europe's secular laws. Prime Minister Bollen and the leaders of the Pan-European Federation have meanwhile assured us that Europe, too, will respect our homeland's new constitution, written in the spirit of Islam. In the Koran, God says in His Surat al-Ma'un, Charity, 'As for the orphan, do not oppress him, and as for the petitioner, do not repel him.' This is a truth that not only we, Muslims, profess to, but so do all humanists in the world."

I couldn't help but smile. It was common knowledge that Abbas's humanism did not apply to his domestic opposition, especially not his African Muslim brothers arriving from the south. Those who managed to cross the mine-strewn desert were locked up in camps by government troops or militias loyal to the government. Rumors had it that the government's local officials were up to their necks in the slave trade underway on an industrial scale in the country's southern reaches.

"Since we are Muslims, we await with open arms those Muslim brothers of ours who have lately lost their European citizenship and do not wish to return to their original homelands. Among us you can find a new home!" Here, Abbas theatrically opened wide his arms as if ready to embrace all the world's Muslims. "And the same way we await those Muslim brothers of ours who, though they have not lost their European citizenship, feel that Europe is no longer the most suitable place for them and their children. Beyond work and a livelihood we can offer them even more: North African Union citizenship. Thanks to our homeland's dynamic economic development, our citizens partake in an ever expanding web of social benefits. We open our arms and say: welcome to your new home, our brothers and our sisters! Allah's earth is spacious!"

The announcement came as a shock. Who, after all, would decide against Europe in favor of a recently war-ravaged, blood-soaked North African Union ruled by a notoriously iron-fisted sadist? In the case of the masses who'd been deprived of their European citizenship and were awaiting deportation this might have been a somewhat understandable decision. Indeed, civil war was still raging in many of their home countries, with perhaps not a single surviving relative under the ruins back home. For them, the North African Union might indeed have been a good decision. But what of those who didn't have to leave? Why would they choose to give up the lives they'd built for themselves in Europe? While the situation here was in fact worse and worse, while life was ever more uncertain, this was, after all, our home. This is my home. This is where everyone important to me lives; this is where I've lived all my life. I wouldn't leave for all the money in the world.

The first posters appeared a couple days later. Satisfaction radiated from the man's eyes. The confident repose of those who'd gotten somewhere in life. He looked about my age, his muscular frame taut underneath his light green polo shirt. Sitting on his arm was a smiling little girl with curly black hair who looked about three. Both were looking straight at me. Right up next to them was a woman with a lovely face—his wife, I suppose—staring into the distance with a wide smile. Snow-white apartment buildings shone in the background, contrasting sharply with the blue sea. Underneath, the green caption:

A NEW LIFE—THE NORTH AFRICAN UNION

The poster glowed warmly against the gray concrete wall. *How nauseatingly idyllic*, I thought.

Several versions of the ad now populated apartment building walls in the Zone. In one, old men were smoking hookahs in an atmospheric seaside café; in another, a businessman decked out in a suit was adjusting his gold cuff link. Elsewhere, seemingly well-off parents were playing with their happy children on a modern playground amid newly built, neat-looking apartment blocks.

A NEW LIFE—A FUTURE BY DESIGN

The ads—A NEW LIFE was the recurring motif—were constantly popping up online as well as I read the news, listened to music, and streamed videos. Though on account of the New Loyalist Act it could not appear all over the streets, the online campaign even included videos in which women in niqabs, or full-face veils, were strolling along palm-tree-lined paths alongside their bearded, moustacheless husbands pushing baby carriages.

The government was, it seemed, doing all it could to render President Abbas's offer attractive to as many people as possible.

Finally I clicked on one of the ads. Browsing through the details, I more or less saw those bits of information Abbas had covered in his speech. A separate menu item served up the latest on the constantly expanding list of job opportunities and approximate salaries. President Abbas had not been fibbing: I was amazed to see a virtually endless list of job ads that had something for everyone, regardless of gender, age, or work experience. And the salaries seemed friendly indeed.

Too idyllic. I kept browsing. What followed was an exceptionally long explanation of the details of traveling to, establishing residency in, and becoming employed in the North African Union, details dappled richly with regulations. How to apply for citizenship? It was all there. The process was surprisingly simple and really did carry lots of advantages. But then, amid the barely comprehensible legalese, I found the gist of it: since the struggle against terrorism was a declared goal of the North African Union as well, it too expected complete loyalty from its citizens, as did the countries of the Pan-European Federation. So all those seeking North African Union citizenship would have to give up their European citizenship.

Furiously I slammed my phone on the bed.

It's simply impossible that anyone would choose the North African Union over Europe.

I was wrong. As time passed, more and more distant acquaintances decided to move, even some who had to give up their European citizenship
to do so. Desperation had reached the level where even the faint promise
of security was enough for some to give up their life thus far. Even though
whispers were rife that the European governments paid out substantial
sums to Abbas for every Muslim moving from the Pan-European Federation, that didn't interest people in the least.

21

"Wonderful, Nasim!" said old Ashraf. "Then we'll go together!" Though his shop had been run for quite a while by his son and his grandson, Basim, Ashraf himself still sat all day long at the table opposite the old TV. He read the news on his tablet, chatted with the older patrons, and bitched about his son and grandson.

"This good-for-nothing was last in a mosque when he was a kid," he said to me, pointing a finger at Basim, who, behind the glass counter, was opening a fresh batch of eggplant salad. "But you . . . you're a good kid. If only your granddad could see you!"

I was sorry that I hadn't kept my trap shut, that I'd let it slip that I was on my way to the mosque. Like Basim, I too had last been in the mosque when I was little, and deep down I celebrated myself as some hero for finally having gathered the strength for a visit. I'd begun the week with a slight fever, and I sensed that I was coming down with something. So I called in sick for Friday. Oddly enough, the moment I emailed my boss, I felt better. By Friday it was as if I was a new person. Maybe my insides were protesting the new workplace. When, at the start of the summer, I'd been kicked out of H&H, I'd figured I'd allow myself a few weeks to rest up. The few weeks finally became nearly six months. Companies outside the Zone didn't even bother replying when I applied, and at first I was of the mind that I didn't have to take just anything. The months passed, and by November I'd used up my very last savings while still getting no replies. So it was that in early December I said yes to an offer in the Zone, which an acquaintance of my mother had made sometime earlier. I became an administrator at a firm representing various apartment blocks. I hated every minute of it. The only thing worse than the nerve-racking paperwork was the on-site work, in the course of which residents showered their every grievance and dissatisfaction upon our necks.

Nor did my nightmares cease. Sometimes I could barely sleep. My head was constantly spinning with questions and doubts. Not as if it seemed too logical, but I felt it would be worth my while going to the

169

mosque. Maybe I'd get a few answers. Since I was officially sick that day, I also had the time.

Proud as I was at my resolve, and not wanting to give myself an opportunity to change my mind, I said to old Ashraf that I was on my way to the mosque. Definitely a mistake.

Old Ashraf walked slowly. Leaning on an old-fashioned cane, he stamped ahead with plodding determination, so I found myself nosing along beside him at the same, turtlelike pace. I had only myself to blame.

"Not even eight hundred years was enough for our sort to get over our downfall," he said out of the blue.

"Excuse me?"

"I saw a documentary film about the Islamic Empire. *Mashallah*, it was so big that when one caliph looked up at the sky and saw a cloud, he said, 'Go ahead and float wherever you want, for wherever you give rain, that will water the Muslims' lands regardless."

"Ah . . ."

"Mathematics, astronomy, philosophy . . . , we were the center of the world. But then . . ."—he waved his hand dismissively—"What became of us after that? Colonies. Doormats. So then that's what we haven't been able to get over ever since."

I nodded. It's best not to argue with the elderly. In the best-case scenario they won't get what you're saying, and in a worse case they'll charge even deeper into the thick of their words.

"The nationalists came, and then the Islamists, and now these rotten jihadists. They say they're better than the others, but . . . same difference. You think they're anything special?" Having posed this rhetorical question, he waved a hand again, dismissively. "They're all the same. They brood about the past, blaming others for the end of the golden age. They hate everyone when they should really be looking at themselves. This is why all the Muslim countries are so shiftless."

As we made our way over a crosswalk he fell silent, but then he went on.

"I arrived with one suitcase. I didn't bother about politics; I just worked. I got up at dawn every day and hurried to my restaurant. If those people back home had done the same thing, by now their countries would be better than Europe!"

"Well, yes," I said. My feet were practically itching from the slow pace.

"Europe will keep getting worse. It's now that they are really feeling their decline. The center of the world has long been in the Far East. I once saw a Chinese map on TV. Get this. China was in the middle! To its right, America; to its left, the rest of Asia, whose furthermost little offshoot is Europe. It was only this big," he said, pressing his thumb and index finger together and raising his hand in the air, stopping dead in his tracks for effect. "Europe is no better than us either. By now they're frustrated and aggressive too." Raising a finger by way of warning, he added, "And just like we did, they're blaming others for everything."

"We'll be late, Mr. Ashraf," I said to urge him on. I sensed that he was right, but it was bad to hear it all the same. "I've still got to *wudu*," I said, referring to the ritual washing before prayer.

"Why, you didn't do that at home? Shame, shame," he said, shaking his head. "It would have been better there. You see so many new faces at the mosque these days. So many carpetbaggers. There's nothing worse than foot fungus. But don't you worry, I'll recommend a good ointment. Worked for me."

Slower than time itself we alone were trudging by the row of shops. But we were getting close. The sight of the two police cars and the black armored troop carrier filled me with hope that we would soon arrive.

The square in front of the mosque was empty. On account of the ban on public gatherings, those arriving went in the door quickly and expediently. A minor tumult formed only at the screening gates and retina check just inside the entrance. The guards said not even a word to old Ashraf. They examined even me only superficially.

Reverse ethnic profiling was not entirely unjustified. The shooter who, many long years earlier, had first set in motion the avalanche of attacks against mosques was, after all, an Arab. A brown-faced, dark-eyed, scruffy character no one in the world suspected of a thing. The incident had occurred in a mosque similar to Al-Nour in another district. The twenty-five-year-old had sat through the khutba near the *minbar*, or pulpit, and he had stood up with the congregation for prayer. He waited for the second *sujud*, half prostrated himself along with all the others, and then suddenly sprang up. First he aimed at the imam, and then he emptied the barrel of his Glock 26 into those around him. Some tried to flee; others, frozen in shock, waited to die. Using the chaos to his advantage, he reloaded and took aim at those trembling on the floor. He shot on target twenty-four times in all, saving the last for himself. Thirteen dead and five wounded.

Though the first reports suggested that the European Liberation Front was behind the attack, it quickly turned out that the perpetrator was a lone wolf. His name was Michael Haddad. An Arab Christian who'd arrived in Europe as a child refugee after his family had been killed by Islamist militias. Back then there wasn't yet strict screening of such immigrants, but on account of his faith and his origins no one would have suspected anyway that he represented any sort of threat.

When it came down to it, the unsuspecting were right: he really wasn't dangerous to Europeans. Haddad had timed a video to appear on the net the night of the attack. In it he spoke at length about how Islam had ravaged his native land, the Christian Middle East, and he also recounted how in the refugee camp Muslims—most of whom, he said, were jihadists who hated Christians with all their hearts—had humiliated him account of his religion. He showed his lower arm, on which dark spots were scars caused by the cigarettes of his fellow refugees. This alone was suspicious. Some commentators observed that Islamists consider smoking a taboo, so something wasn't right about the story. Of course, few were bothered by this. In a statement it posted on the Internet, the European Liberation Front welcomed the attack, calling it shameful that while European youth lived in the spell of hedonism, Haddad, from the Middle East, had given his blood for the survival of Christian Europe. Yet another underground organization posthumously named "Our Fellow Soldier Michael" its honorary member and established a profile for him titled "Died a Hero." "Muhammad's bastards," came a cyborglike male voice in their video, which spread like wildfire. The mim glowed red-hot against a black background. "Our patience is over. You people can no longer rest easy. From now on, the mim not only will bloom above your doors but will be burned into your foreheads too."

Haddad's example was contagious. Earlier there had been attacks now and again, but in the months to come, assaults against mosques using weapons and Molotov cocktails became the norm. Those at Friday prayers were targeted by helmeted attackers arriving on motorbikes, veiled women were shot on the streets, and Muslim-owned shops were set ablaze. Previously unknown underground terror organizations claimed responsibility. Later the New Loyalist Act spared not even anti-Muslim terrorists. They too were regularly subject to raids and arrests.

Though it was impossible to protect every possible target, every last mosque commissioned a security firm, whose men screened those arriving for daily prayers. From then police cars were always parked by mosques. The worshippers, though, were by no means in agreement over whether the police were shielding them or protecting others from them.

"*Assalamu alaykum* (peace be upon you), my friend," said someone, placing a hand on my shoulder, as I stepped into the washing room. The mustachioed man was a refugee I myself had told about al-Nour.

"I'm grateful for your advice," he said. "I've been coming here ever since."

The encounter came in handy. Never had I been able to remember the order of washing before prayer. Nose or mouth first? Ears or head? Back in the day I'd always done as my grandfather did. Since then I hadn't gone to prayer. I let the mustachioed man go ahead of me, winning time by talking, waiting until he sat down on one of the white-tiled seats in the washing area. I then sat down beside him and, watching the order of his movements out of the corner of my eye, I too began to wash. *Now we're even*, I told myself. I'd earned a hasanat for pointing him to the mosque, and now somewhere a check mark was being made for him, too, in the column of good deeds.

I sat in the back on the red-gold woven rug. The prayer room was only half full, and I was surely the youngest. I caught sight of Abu Sa'id from a distance as he was whispering to an older man near the minbar. Old Ashraf was to the right, leaning up against the wall while waiting for prayer to begin. Listless, glassy eyes stared fixedly toward the minbar. By the time I realized what was happening, the sheik was already on his feet, leaning against his cane. Not as if he particularly needed this at the age of fifty or so, but since the Prophet had used a staff, well, he, like so many other sheiks, abided by the sunna. The muezzin's voice resounded. The sheik cleared his throat, and the deep clicking of the speakers signaled that he'd turned on the microphone.

"*Al-hamdu lillah summa al-hamdu lillah,*" he began. Having issued this greeting of praise and thanks to Allah, he switched languages.

It struck me that nothing had changed since I'd last been there, with Grandfather. The khutba unfolded slowly, the sheik speaking of the divine gift of inner peace and its preservation, while I buried my head between my knees to conceal my yawns.

"The members of the congregation have expressed their concerns to me over the measures our government has taken," came the words in the sheik's voice that all at once struck my ears. "Some criticize our leaders for, as they claim, wanting to chase Muslims away from their homes. But what is the truth? What is the response of Islam in such hard times?"

All those glassy eyes stared fixedly at the minbar.

"O, believers! The greatest responsibility of the true Muslim is obedience to the will of Allah. And what does obedience mean? Obedience means that a Muslim cannot accept a worldly command that is counter to Allah's will. Above all, a Muslim must be sure both in his mind and his heart that he acts in a manner dear to Allah. What is he to do who is unsure he can do enough to fulfill what the Dear and Wise One expects? We can find the answer only in Allah's unadulterated words, in the Koran. The Dear and Wise One says in the *Surat al-Nisa* . . ." The sheik now read in Arabic, rolling his tongue over every letter of every word while quoting from the holy scripture. As if mimicking a dialogue, he posed a thunderous question he then answered in a quavering, fearful voice. He then raised a finger toward the sky and again pumped up his voice. The drawn-out second *a* in the name of Allah echoed through the mosque before he once again switched to a fearful tone and, quavering anew, diminishing the stress. Allah's unadulterated words were followed by the usual two-second pause. The men sitting beside me stared in resignation toward the minbar.

"How have you people lived?" the angels will ask. "Did you fulfill Allah's commands as good Muslims? There won't be any waffling in response to the angels' questions. Then you can say all you want about how weak and oppressed you were on Earth, but you will do so in vain. In vain will you explain how, when working eight or ten hours a day, you didn't even have time to go for coffee, much less to pray. In vain, that the boss threatened to fire anyone who tried justifying their lack of productivity with the month of fasting at Ramadan. In vain, that you couldn't put a hijab on your wives, girls, and little sisters because otherwise they wouldn't have been allowed in school or into workplaces."

The sheik paused for a moment, glanced over the congregation, and then continued.

"'Was Allah's earth not spacious enough?' the angels will ask. 'Could you not leave your places of residence so as to live according to Allah's wishes?' Indeed, the only reward for such explanations can be hell. May Allah protect us from that."

"Allah's earth is spacious, and it awaits those who fear that in their present home they are unable to fulfill his will."

When everyone then stood up to start in on the prayer in orderly lines, I quietly slipped out the door. The security guard followed me with his eyes but said nothing. My nights, I knew, would be no calmer on account of this answer.

22

The Tawhidis simply vanished from one day to the next.

One particularly cold Saturday afternoon in October, police sirens broke the rhythm coming from my earphones. I quickly tore the music from my head and pressed my palms to my ears so the sirens would not pop my eardrums.

This must be one helluva raid, I thought. The convoy was suspiciously long. The light on the cross street had already turned green, but traffic was frozen. I pulled the zipper on my jacket right up to my chin while staring at the metallically glistening police cars and black paddy wagons disappearing into the distance to the north. I figured they were preparing to fold up some drug lab or illegal sanctuary for refugees. I was wrong. Twenty minutes later I learned that this time the target had been the clubhouse used by the Tawhidis as a mosque. It was Saturday afternoon. Practically everyone was there, so the police packed the whole bunch in one fell swoop into the paddy wagons.

By then I was at Rami's.

"What nonsense!" said Rami while reading the news. "Everyone knows the Tawhidis don't commit atrocities. They're bigoted idiots, but not terrorists!"

"They don't have to be terrorists," I replied. "Under the New Loyalist Act anyone can be accused of terror. Even before, lots of folks were concerned about the Tawhidis. What's surprising is they've avoided trouble until now."

"I feel sorry for them," said Rami. "I have a lot to thank them for."

By the time Rami closed up shop and I set off for home, the first details came in the news.

The Office of Counterterrorism has arrested 112 radicals in the northern section of the Zone. According to a statement by Counterterrorism Spokesperson Arthur Kowalsky, there are grounds to charge the suspects with violating the New Loyalist Act and engaging in activity against the state. The investigation is underway, and further arrests can be expected.

As the music rumbled away in my ears, I'd barely noticed my fingers turning numb from the cold and nearly freezing to the phone. But now I dropped the phone into my jacket pocket, breathed into my palms, rummaged through my pocket with my unfeeling fingers for my keys, and then stepped in the door.

Earlier, in March, my car had happened to be in the garage, so I was bouncing along on the way home in a minibus when my phone dinged.

"Come by if you can," Rami had messaged me.

"Is something wrong?" I asked.

"In person," came the reply.

Rami was not in the habit of being secretive. After getting off the bus I turned in his direction. By then he'd been working for a while in a store along the row of shops that sold nutritional supplements. The delivery company he'd worked for earlier, as a driver, had laid him off. Under the new regulations commercial drivers had to pass a background check to continue their work. Rami was caught up in the filter. "We are writing to inform you that risks were determined in the course of screening your profile," came a succinct official notice from a government agency. "We will not extend your commercial driving license. Your Trust Score is 70. And we require a score of 90." The agency was not responsible for explaining the decision. Driving was Rami's bread and butter, so he didn't leave things at that. He appealed, requesting access to the documents pertaining to the background check. But it turned out that the agency was not obliged to produce them. Rami was dejected. The owner of his favorite gym felt so sorry for him that he offered him a job as a sales clerk in his nutritional supplements store until he managed to find a new job. When it came down to it, Rami had just the right look. He'd always taken working out more seriously than I had, and over the years he'd worked himself into quite an impressively buff guy.

He happened to be telling two spindly young men about a new protein supplement when I stepped in. He nodded my way, cut his little presentation short, and as the glass door closed behind the would-be customers, he stuck his phone under my nose.

"What do you think?" he asked, visibly excited.

A girl in a white hijab started back from a profile photo. Though her nose was a bit odd, her face seemed, on the whole, attractive.

"Well, it depends how much," I said with a shrug.

"Go fuck yourself. She's not a whore."

"Sorry," I said, raising my hands. "The dating app confused me. You know the sort of girls it's full of these days." Rami gave me a prickly glance, shrugged, and showed me another couple pictures of the girl.

It turned out that Rami had happened upon Layal two weeks earlier. Since then they'd been talking nonstop and had already met three times in person.

"I've been waiting all my life for this woman."

"What does she do?"

"She's attending a language course."

"All right, but what's her line of work?"

"Cleaning woman."

That didn't sound like a good catch. Rami knew that, too, so he began explaining the situation.

"Oh yeah, I didn't even mention . . . ," he went on, in a voice suggesting reluctance to say what he was about to say. "She doesn't have a normal work permit. With her protected status she can apply only for certain designated types of employment."

It was all I could do to resist breaking out in a grin.

"I see," I replied with a poker face, but deep down I was howling with laughter, and if this hadn't been about my friend, I would have immediately posted that Rami, the great antirefugee swashbuckler, was in love with a refugee.

"She's different. She really is an angel. Twenty-four years old and still a virgin." His enthusiasm was apparent.

That she was an angel, I would have been ready to believe. That she was a virgin, I wasn't quite so sure. Everyone knew what refugees go through by the time they reach Europe.

"Her little brother guards her like a bulldog," Rami went on, as if suspecting what was going through my mind.

"Aha. But then how are you able to get together?"

"She tells them at home that she's going to her language class, but meanwhile we meet by the apartment blocks in the south part of the Zone. No one around there knows her."

"If things develop that way, I'll give you a key to my flat," I offered. It had happened before that Rami had had dates at my place. But this time he stared at me furiously.

"If you weren't my best friend, I'd sock you in the face right now."

"I meant well."

"I won't say it again: Layal is an honorable girl!"

I was compelled to believe what he was insisting. From Latifa's example I too knew that there were girls you didn't want to fuck but to marry. And the fact that Layal was not an easy catch was a good sign.

All in all, it was good to see Rami so enthusiastic. He hadn't had a girlfriend in more than ten years. The first and only love of his life had been an Albanian teenager. When they began getting close, she still had a boyfriend. Some white guy, a sort of first love. Zamira—that was her name—must have gone out with the kid out of rebellion because, in contrast with her brothers and cousins, he was a real gentleman. Kind, courteous, and attentive. She told Rami she'd fallen for him because they could talk of really deep stuff. It was her ex's loss that she could do so with Rami as well. Rami also had his buff frame going for him, as it gave him a manly presence. Zamira had, after all, grown up among manly men, so despite the rebel in her, deep down she was drawn to them. Rami did not have to woo her for long. Three dates was all it took.

Rami felt like the king of the world. He was convinced that his success was due to his exceptional personality and irresistible allure, and of course to the fact that his prick was the biggest there ever was. He then fell flat on his face. It quickly turned out that the girl had used him only as something to grab onto while exiting her former relationship. Not two months went by before Zamira found a man even more exceptional, more irresistible, and better-endowed than Rami: Ziyad, one of Najib's cousins. At first Rami wanted revenge, but he fast realized that it would be best not to make trouble with Ziyad or, more precisely, with his large extended family. And since Ziyad always referred to Zamira behind her back as his whore, Rami also acted as if she'd been nothing more to him than a booty call. Why, he went so far as to do high fives with Ziyad after this or that good laugh. I alone knew what a deep mark it had left in him.

Layal changed everything, however. It seemed that Rami had finally landed with someone deserving of trust. In secret I, too, began following the girl's profile. Her shares, picture, and comments really did make her out to be as Rami described her. Of course, the suspicion kept stirring in me, for it was not at all unheard of for a Muslim girl, alongside the good-little-girl profile she had under her own name, to have another, wilder one her family knew nothing about.

Soon enough I was able to see Layal in person myself. Rami let me see her from the car as they met by the south apartment blocks and together walked into the park. She wore a white hijab, a stylish leather coat, a long skirt, and sneakers. Though she really seemed shapely, from a distance I wasn't struck by whatever it was that had left my friend smitten. *Obviously this is what they call chemistry*, I thought to myself.

Rami's enthusiasm endured. Every time we met, he always talked about Layal. My conscience, however, did not let me leave it all to him.

"Not that I want to steal your mood," I began on one occasion, if in a slightly roundabout manner. "But hasn't it occurred to you that she only wants to get you hooked? After all, for a refugee you're not a bad catch." No sooner had these clumsy sentences left my mouth than I realized he might take offense. Fortunately that's not how he took it.

"First, there's nothing wrong with a woman wanting a secure relationship. I've already had enough of the emancipated girls around here. Second, Layal is not the sort of girl who always has a guy pay her way. She barely has money, but she insists on sometimes getting the bill if we sit down somewhere."

I learned that back home Layal had originally studied English language and literature. She'd wanted to be a teacher, but the war had gotten in the way of her plans. She'd lived with her family in a popular lower-middle-class district of a large city. Her folks died when a stray missile struck their building. Their home was uninhabitable, so she and her brother moved in with an old relative on the city outskirts. In the ever deteriorating situation, her little brother had to pass through a series of checkpoints every day to get the chemical company where he worked as a clerk. That was not without risk for a young man of military age. Though he was a civilian, both the rebels and the government soldiers always gave him the rundown. The route to work was barely six miles, but sometimes it took him as long as three hours to get there, and occasionally he slept in the office after work to save going through the process again.

Meanwhile the rebels seized several major highways. As supplies started running low in the city, food prices went through the roof. The chemical firm closed its doors, and what funds Layal and her brother had left began running dangerously low. Three years after the fighting first erupted, they hardly had anything left, and the end of the war was still nowhere in sight. That's when their greatest fear came to pass: Layal's brother got a draft notice. They didn't know anyone who might help; nor was their money enough to bribe the general concerned to ensure that Layal's brother wouldn't be sent to the deadliest front. Their sole choice was to flee. They sold their father's shop downtown and their car. Businesspeople with ties to the various militias naturally exploited the situation, buying everything for pennies. Even so, the money was enough to come to terms with someone who smuggled people across the border, and an elderly relative of theirs agreed to send it after them in installments. They'd arrived in Europe illegally three years earlier. Since they were able to prove that they really had come from a region affected by war, they could take an oath to uphold the values of the Pan-European Federation, whereupon they were granted a temporary residence permit, with which they took jobs in the trades designated by the government. Layal was a cleaning woman at a hospital while her younger brother worked in construction at the airport.

The romance proved lasting. Even months later Rami behaved like a lovestruck kid. We couldn't even talk normally anymore. Just when we'd get into some topic of conversation his phone would ding and ding and ding, whereupon he, with an imbecilic grin, would type out his reply.

Though I was getting really tired of this, I would not have told him so for all the money in the world. And then, as time passed, I found myself feeling jealous for his attention. That is to say, Rami started saying less and less about what the two of them were up to. They now had their own inner world where I did not belong.

"I'll get engaged to her," said Rami when I stopped by the shop one day. At first I could hardly catch my breath. Then I somehow gathered the strength to squeeze out a clumsy *mabrouk*. With a forced smile I listened to him go on and on about how happy he was, and how of all women he could imagine only Layal as the mother of his children. There was no point in questioning his decision, I sensed. The decision had been made, and I would have risked my friendship with Rami by not supporting him in his plan. So I warmed up to the idea.

Rami had a big challenge ahead of him, however. Umm Rami was by no means an easy woman to deal with. She was the sort of woman who was unable to accept that her son had grown up. She'd call Rami even at work, and she didn't let up on the leash even after her son turned thirty.

Rami therefore spoke first with his father, who laid the groundwork. Abu Rami knew his wife's weak points well. He spoke to her of Layal as the true embodiment of the old values of home, who would be not only their son's wife but also his parents' new daughter. Umm Rami softened up sooner than hoped for and took charge of matters right away. Tradition had it that the mother and other woman family members of the man wanting to get married went to the girl's home to introduce themselves. But Umm Rami decided that on account of the exceptional circumstances—and because, of course, we live in a modern era—it would be best for the two families to meet in a restaurant. That's what happened, and fortunately everything went well. Both Layal's little brother and Umm Rami gave the marriage their blessing. The engagement happened not long after, in the course of another family dinner.

Rami and Layal did not want to put the wedding off for long. For my part, I was certain that Rami was, by now, as horny as could be.

"For fuck's sake," growled Rami while staring at a computer monitor. "Why the hell can't they design a page that makes sense?"

As usual, I'd dropped by the shop. There were no customers at the moment. So Rami was trying to make headway online on the administrative side of the marriage.

"To request a date for the wedding," he explained, "first I've got to create a Digital Citizenship Gateway. But I just can't figure out where to click."

Stepping up beside him, I knit my brows while also staring at the web page. I made as if I too was trying to figure it out, but in fact I was only extending him emotional support. Such online interfaces quickly drove me mad too. The roundabout instructions; the long forms to fill out; the random error messages—in the blink of an eye they set me in a rage, and after a couple of minutes I would most gladly have stomped all over the monitor. Despite this, out of solidarity with my friend I stared ahead with Rami for a while.

"I think it would be best if you went to City Hall," I finally said, and he nodded in resignation. At least we had no trouble finding the office hours, and requesting an appointment took but one click. He could go the next morning.

The following afternoon I stopped by again at the shop. Rami's grimace did not bode well.

"They need Layal's birth certificate," he said with a sigh. "I'm supposed to somehow prove that she's not married. Get it? Her birth certificate! Not a chance."

"Why don't the two of you try at the embassy?"

"At the embassy of a country with a civil war going on? They couldn't be bothered."

In silence we stared blankly ahead.

"I've got it!" I exclaimed.

"What?"

"When it comes down to it, for the two of you to be able to move in together, you don't absolutely need a marriage recognized by the government. It's enough if you marry in a Muslim ceremony."

"That's it!" he said, giving me a hug. "I'll ask the sheik at Al-Nour for an appointment." He did a search for the phone number, and a moment later was already typing his request into his phone. The mosque answered right away. Two days later he could go meet with the sheik. Rami was in heaven.

"No go," came the message a couple of days later. Rami had spoken with the sheik, who politely but quite firmly informed him that Al-Nour could certify only marriages recognized by the state. Hope was lost.

The same day I stopped by again at the shop to cheer him up. Though I had no good advice to offer, I figured it would help a bit at any rate if I listened to him lamenting. I was pretty down as I opened the glass door, which had ads pasted all over it, and stepped inside. To my great surprise, however, Rami was grinning from ear to ear. He happened to be with a customer. The moment the person went out the door, Rami got to the heart of the matter.

"Al-Nour can go to hell," he said. "I solved it another way. You were right. What matters is that there should be some sort of marriage. Do you know Adnan Karim?" It was a rhetorical question. How could I not have known the onetime boxing legend and the Zone's most popular Tawhidi boxing coach?

"Well, I called him up and asked if they could handle it. He asked Sheik Taymullah, who said yes right away! We'll get married in a week!"

Finally it was solved, though I still had something to take care of. I could not let my cousin and best friend get hitched without a stag party. I sent word out to a group of people that included, well, everyone we knew who lived and breathed. Time was short, so pulling off a big party was not going to happen. And there was always the possibility that a sudden curfew or ban on public gatherings would leave all the planning up in smoke. So the choice fell to Rafiq's billiards hall. I planned the stag party for the day before the wedding. It was a Friday night, so everyone came. The marriage itself was a mere formality. Rami went to Sheik Taymullah together with Layal's brother, her sole guardian, and in front of two Tawhidi witnesses they signed the marriage contract. The next day Rami and Layal moved into the studio apartment Rami had rented in the southern part of the Zone. Over the course of the next two months I often dropped by to visit them. All my earlier reservations faded away. Layal was in fact a charming girl. Well-informed and intelligent, she had been able to retain her splendid sense of humor despite all the horrors she'd experienced. I grew fond of her, and I know the feeling was mutual. For his part, Rami was in the clouds.

They were taken away two months after the wedding. It turned out that Counterterrorism had had the Tawhidis under surveillance since months before the raid on their mosque, tracking every movement, as well as those of anyone and everyone who came into contact with them. Raids aimed at their broader network saw more than two thousand people arrested within about a month of the mass detention of the Tawhidis. Rami and Adnan's conversations had been bugged too, and in the course of the raid on the mosque the authorities found the marriage contract. Rami and Layal were accused of violating the New Loyalist Act and committing a crime against the state. Under the law they were not married, so they could not stay together. Layal's protective status was revoked immediately, and since civil war was raging in her homeland, she was deported to a migrant camp on the territory of the North African Union. Rami was meanwhile transported to another relocation camp.

23 Only the immediate family gathered, but even so, the living room at Rami's parents' place was full. As soon as we heard the news, I picked up my mother in front of her building and we went right over to them. My sister and her husband agreed to join us after work. Rami's parents and his sisters were beyond themselves. It was already well past noon, and though I hadn't had breakfast, I couldn't even think of food. Since we found no hopeful information on the Internet, the room was in the grips of a suffocating silence.

"I told him not to marry this woman," Rami's mother said with a sigh, in a broken voice. Her eyes were red from tears. Her hair, gray strands amid a preponderance of black, hung in a disheveled ponytail. I just stared numbly ahead. I hadn't been ready for this. Having already seen the storm clouds gathering over our heads, I'd looked on quietly as the storm began to stir and claim victims. But that it would reach my family too—not even in my worst nightmares would I have thought of that.

Counterterrorism had phoned Rami's parents at 9:30 AM. The man at the other end of the line, who'd introduced himself as some sort of operations manager, informed them of the facts: Rami and the woman refugee in his company had been arrested on well-founded suspicion of activity against the state. He added that since not even Rami had denied the accusations, their validity had been borne out. Rami's mother said she wanted to see her son immediately, but the investigator dryly informed her that in the event of an accusation of terrorism, they are unable to provide information as to the whereabouts of the detainee. He then added that the place of Rami's detention was immaterial in any case, since the proceedings would occur on the territory of the North African Union, naturally in accord with the laws of the Pan-European Federation. And Rami would be transported there together with all the other suspects on the next flight out. Before hanging up he said only that the family could find all information on the official webpage of the Office of Counterterrorism.

As the head of the family, my uncle could not allow himself to show his despair. With a determined look he browsed on his tablet, trying to find something in the legal regulations to cling to. The situation was not encouraging. Since the New Loyalist Act had come into force, an accusation of terrorism—indeed, any ties to groups conspiring against the state, or even the well-founded suspicion of such ties—was tantamount to having already been found guilty of a serious crime. In contrast with matters of public law, in such circumstances the authorities were not even obliged to justify the charges. The press and inquiring relatives were shooed away "in the interest of the ongoing investigation," and the documents pertaining to the case were, on account of national security interests, classified for thirty years. All sorts of experts at news sites explained that Counterterrorism and other such government agencies worked with undercover agents, secret informants, and classified digital data collection methods, and so justifying individual cases would put the terrorists at an advantage and deal a serious blow to the fight against terrorism.

Before long my uncle happened upon the phone number of an NGO specializing in the cases of terrorism suspects. He called them at least fifty times before getting through. The voice at the other end of the line was a young woman's. She too confirmed that in the present circumstances nothing could be done, that the proceedings would be held in courts built beside the European prisons in the North African Union.

"We want a lawyer right away!" my uncle proclaimed.

At length the woman explained the regulations. The point was, previously it had been possible to hire a private attorney, if at some expense. Since the New Loyalist Act had come into force, however, those detained on various charges of acting against the state could no longer request their own attorneys. Since every matter that can be connected to terrorism qualifies as a state secret, the cases of such suspects were handled by specialized lawyers' chambers established at the location of the proceedings. So Rami would have to make do with his appointed defender.

"The good news, though, is that attorneys are already examining the conditions for establishing a legal organization specializing in such cases, which . . . ," began the woman, but my uncle interrupted.

"Forgive me, but 'already examining the conditions' is not enough for us," he said, having lost his patience. My aunt just stared ahead with glassy eyes.

"But we have groups all over the country that facilitate weekly meetings with those whose loved ones have been arrested in such circumstances. If you tell me your address, I will give you the contact information for the group closest to you."

"It's not therapy that we need, but help!" my uncle shouted, and slammed down the phone.

"I did this with my son . . . ," Rami's mother said through her tears in a fading voice. My mother hugged her, drawing her near with her own eyes now closed.

I alone knew that she wasn't the one at fault. I had suggested to Rami that he try at Al-Nour. Had I not mentioned that, then no doubt it wouldn't have occurred him to go to the Tawhidis, and he'd still be here. Instead he was perhaps already on his way toward some camp where he'd spend his next few years locked up with religious fanatics and criminals. What then?

I stared ahead in silence. The sense that I was responsible for it all weighed upon me unbearably. I kept staring at the wall and tried casting away the thought. *Everything is written in advance*, I thought to myself. *Maktoub*.

I wanted to believe that a person's fate is written in advance. My mother jolted me out of my musing.

"Nasim, you had a friend. A police officer. What was his name again?"

"Nizar."

"Ask him if he can look into it."

"I haven't seen him since the funeral," I said. "Besides, he's just some simple cop. That's not enough for this."

"Abu Sa'id!" my uncle cried out. "He's got serious contacts. If anyone, he can take care of it."

For my part, I didn't understand how a businessman, no matter how much money he had, could help in such a situation. But it was a fact that had been proven more than once: his hand reached far.

"If anyone," my uncle repeated, "then Abu Sa'id can take care of it. He always worked with the police and Counterterrorism, you know."

This surprised me a lot. But then I remembered.

"Yes, when I went to his office one time, I saw a picture in which he's shaking hands with the chief of police."

"Don't be naive," said my uncle. "You know it's about more than this. Who do you think the police got information against the Boufikara family from?" he asked, giving only a wave of the hand in reply to my puzzled look. "You were still young. And who did the authorities have to thank for the fact that riots always stopped after a couple of days? From whom did they practically always find out on time which foolish kid wanted to buy a weapon?"

I didn't say a thing. Just why riots used to die down long ago, I too could have had a clue as to that. The picture now really did take shape, but I didn't reveal my surprise, because the fact that Rami and I had been there rioting back then remained a secret. Not that that would have counted for a thing in the present situation. "Abu Sa'id is a snitch?" I asked, taken aback.

"He's not a snitch," said my uncle, turning toward me suddenly. "He's a zaim. The difference is huge. One serves them; the other works for his own people. Your father worked with him. He could have told stories of such things. But he always was a discreet man. I myself put together the story only from words spoken by the by."

My uncle picked up his mobile from the table. He looked up the number and called.

"It's ringing!" he said, and raised his right hand to signal that we should be silent.

"Salaam, Abu Sa'id!" he said into the phone. "You've got to help." Try as he did to be calm, his voice was still trembling from nervousness.

"Salaam, my brother," we could hear the staid voice at the other end of the line. "What's the matter?"

"They took away Rami!" my uncle replied, and as he spoke these words his voice faltered. His wife broke out sobbing in the background, and my mother and the girls put their hands over her shoulder, trying to comfort her.

"Let's talk about it in person," said Abu Sa'id in the same staid voice. "I'll go over to your place. I'll leave right away." He hung up.

"Everything will be OK," my uncle said, turning to his wife. "If anyone, then Abu Sa'id can help."

The next half hour passed in tense but hopeful waiting. No one said a thing.

To occupy myself I looked at the news on my phone. I tried to squeeze as much as I could out of the dry official statements and out of articles on nationwide raids, alongside which I looked at everything marked with the relevant hashtag. But then, unable to take the suffocating silence anymore, I stepped out to the balcony. *Maktoub*, I murmured to myself, still browsing the news.

The portals were chock full of news of arrests, raids, mass deportations, and the successful apprehension of those suspected of terrorism and crimes against the state. As if the whole world was about only this. My throat seized up more than ever before. I thought again of Rami. I remembered how terribly relieved we'd both been when, after the New Loyalist Act came into force, it turned out that since we had no other citizenship, we didn't have to fear a thing.

How the hell could we have been so naive? I wondered. By now it was clear that those who'd been deprived of their citizenship had fared better. Their lot was at least clear, after all, for removing them from Europe had been easy. The danger hanging over the heads of citizens, however, was an accusation of terrorism, and the consequences of that were unpredictable. North African Union citizenship was another option. At the moment I could not have said which was worse.

I wasn't blind; I could see that the situation was getting worse and worse. My recurring nightmares also spoke of this. Until now, though, I'd tried fooling myself into thinking that as long as we didn't do anything out of line, as long as we were working, and as long as we quietly lived our lives, then there would be no trouble. But now the horrible recognition came crashing down on me: the mīm was branded on our foreheads. Of course we could always go ourselves. "Allah's earth is spacious."

Abu Saʿid kept to his word. A half hour later, the black Mercedes SUV stopped in front of the apartment building. No longer did Abu Saʿid shave his head as thoroughly as he used to, so one glance at his scalp confirmed that he was balding naturally too.

The doorbell rang.

Rami's mother brought tea and a bowl full of chocolates, while my uncle opened the door.

Abu Saʻid greeted my uncle with a hug. He shook my hand, placed his left hand on my shoulder, and gave me a commiserating stare. My uncle offered him a seat, and his wife served him tea in a tiny glass cup.

My uncle, being the head of the family, told the story in its every detail. Abu Saʻid just stared, gloomily.

"The situation is very difficult," he said. "Lots of people have been taken away from the Zone in recent days. Most have been like your Rami. They never even set foot in radical circles." He took a gulp of his tea, and then spoke at length about those whose parents had turned to him for help lately.

"What to do, then?" asked my uncle, barely concealed impatience in his voice.

"I'll think through what we can do. I carry Rami's fate in my heart and will handle it as a matter of utmost importance."

He bid farewell to my uncle with yet another hug. Looking me in the eyes, he shook my hand reassuringly with his right hand while patting my shoulder with his left.

"When should I call you, Abu Saʻid?" my uncle asked.

"I'll call you. Inshallah."

Inshallah. That night I couldn't get to sleep. I kept pressing my phone until my eyes began to sting from the illuminated screen in the dark. Reading about the how the arrests had unfolded, I tried reconstructing what had happened to Rami. I read at least fifty anonymous accounts by those who'd witnessed their loved ones being taken away. Usually four Counterterrorism men came. They would break the lock at a building entrance but then ring the doorbell once at a flat. If those inside asked who it was, they only said they'd come from the police. Thinking there was some trouble in the building or that some neighbor was up to no good, the occupants opened the door. The Counterterrorism men then forced their way in. On identifying the target individual or individuals, they tied their hands behind their back with plastic cuffs and sat them down. While two Counterterrorism men whisked the family to one location, the other two watched the targeted individuals. They ordered everyone to keep their hands readily visible and to stay put during the process, and then informed them of their rights. Then they removed the cuffs from the targeted individuals and gave him fifteen minutes to put their most important possessions into a bag.

Around 1:30 AM I gathered my strength, dropped the phone beside the bed, and turned off the light. Many years of experience had taught me that at such times this was the least bad solution, for even if I didn't get to sleep, at least I'd rest my eyes in the dark.

For a long time I lay there in bed, eyes shut, before sleep finally came. Not as if it brought peace after the day's distressing events. The familiar story line played itself out yet again. They came for me. Frantically I tried to run away, but there was no escape. Meanwhile it occurred to me that I hadn't even packed my most important possessions. I began flinging them into a large bag, which, however, had no bottom, so everything fell on the floor. When black-gloved hands gripped my shoulders, I always woke up.

The next morning, after a strong coffee, I decided to pack my bags. Never had I collected anything in particular, so I had no irreplaceable objects of sentimental value. Sure, a good while back I'd had it in me to save all sorts of odds and ends, figuring that someday they'd be good for something or other, but when I moved away from home, all my superfluous possessions had stayed behind at my parents' in two big boxes. I had no shackles now, and that filled me with a sense of liberation. I concluded that if I had to go, it would be best to take a new one of everything. So I ran down to the row of shops and bought six pairs of boxer shorts; six pairs of black socks (one thick and five thin), five plain charcoal gray T-shirts, two hooded sweatshirts, and a pair of dungarees. Just to be on the safe side, I also bought a new pair of sneakers to replace the worn old ones. Then I stopped in at the supermarket and bought a bottle of body wash, anti-hair-loss shampoo, two toothbrushes, and a tube of toothpaste for sensitive teeth. Back at my parents', to my surprise, everything fit in my gym bag. That really was it?

In the afternoon I stopped at Mother's place with a bag of oranges. We talked, and then I headed home. I decided I'd sleep that day, and so I bought a bottle of whiskey in a store. Not even for a minute did I have a guilty conscience. Some religious thinkers say alcohol is haram only if consumed for pleasure. I only wanted to sleep. I turned on a film, and by the time it was over, a good third of the bottle was missing. I recalled that my father had always listened to a recording of the Koran while drinking whiskey. But I no longer remembered the name of his favorite muezzin. It was already too late to call my mom, so I randomly selected a sheik, and then hit play on the *Surat al-Jinn*.

I once read that according to brain researchers, a person's brainwaves unconsciously assume the rhythm of any music the person happens to be listening to. This might be the reason certain Muslim sheiks regard listening to music as displeasing to Allah, for music distracts believers' attention from Allah, inducing in the listeners instincts and feelings that displease him. Hence many Muslims listen to the Koran in lieu of music. I'd read that in the days before Islam, the deserts of Arabia were the world of the djinni. According to the Koran, the world of the djinni is similar to that of people. There are good and bad, Muslim and non-Muslim djinni, who conjure up doubts and strange thoughts in human hearts. It is not good to say their names, since then they'll raise their heads and worm their way into human souls. But people can keep them at bay by reading and listening to the Koran. The holy scripture approaches the soul on all levels of thought, filling it with boundless tranquility, and thus protecting believers from the djinni also dwelling within them. Father was right. The Koran really is something else with whiskey. The djinni went off to sleep.

In the middle of the night, my eyes open. I look out the window. I see the minibus quietly coming to a halt in front of the apartment block. Four men wearing black riot gear approach the entrance with determined steps. I can even hear the clicking of their lock breakers as they get through the door and its iron bars. The first thought that passes through my mind is to flee to the roof. But why? The drones are already buzzing around the building. Not that I hear them, but I know it always happens like this. My brain is working away ever more feverishly. All at once I remember the slide. Maybe I can escape on that. I run back and forth in the flat but can't find the way down anywhere. Suddenly I recoil. I see the clothes I've packed. That's when the real panic hits me. I haven't prepared! There's so much I haven't put inside. My friends, the playground, old Ashraf's kebab place, pot-smoking nights, Latifa's smile. . . . Hysterically I throw my things off the dresser. Suddenly everything becomes so important; I've got to pack it all into the bag. Meanwhile noises filter in from outside: the Counterterrorism men are already coming up the stairwell. I start losing my mind; my belly shrivels up. That's when I notice Grandfather's misbaha. My fear goes up in smoke. A perfect calm envelops me. They knock on the door. I take the misbaha in my hands and slip it into my pocket. I raise my bag, step to the door, and open it.

"Good evening. . . ." The retina-scanning gun in the commando's hand flashes green. "Mr. Nasim! Can we go?"

"Yes, I'm ready," I reply with a smile.

I wake up well rested. The clock says 5:31 AM. Surely they won't come today. Maybe tomorrow. But that doesn't matter; there will be enough time for everything. *Maktoub.*

There's just one old debt I've got to settle. I wake up, find my shoes, and head off. Today, for the first time in more than twenty years, I will go up once again to the lookout tower.

Glossary

Ahl al-Bayt: The family of the Prophet Muhammad.

Al-hamdu lillah summa al-hamdu lillah (*Al-ḥamdu lillâhi thumma al-ḥamdu lillâh*): Praise be to God and still more praise (the traditional words at the start of a *khutba*).

Allahu Akbar!: God is most great.

Assalamu alaykum: Peace be upon you.

Astaghfirullah: I seek God's forgiveness.

'aris: Groom.

ayran (*'ayrân*): A yogurt drink.

bay'ah: An oath of allegiance to a leader.

da'wah (*da'wâ*): A convocation, summons, or invitation; proselytizing.

Fatiha (*Fâtiḥa*): The short first sura of the Koran, used as an element of the five daily prayers and on other occasions, such as funerals.

habibi: My dear.

hajji: Someone who has been on a pilgrimage to Mecca.

halal (*ḥalâl*): That which is allowed, permissible, or lawful, particularly food and drink.

haram: Forbidden.

hasanat: Divine credit for good deeds.

hijab (*hijâb*): A head covering worn in public by some Muslim women that leaves the face exposed.

hisab (*ḥisâb*): Computation; reckoning; accounting; Judgement Day.

houris: Women with beautiful eyes described as a reward for the faithful Muslim believers in heaven.

Hum feeha khalidoon (*Hum fî-hâ khâlidûn*): "There they will live forever," a phrase that occurs frequently in the Koran (e.g. 2.25).

inshallah: If Allah wills; God willing.

Isha: The last of the day's five prayers.

jellabiya: A traditional long, loose-fitting Sudanese and Egyptian outer garment native to the Nile Valley.

jizya: A tax levied by Islamic states on certain non-Muslims.

khutba: Sermon given in a mosque.

mabrouk: Congratulations (literally "blessed").

maktoub: "It is written," already written, inevitable.

Mashallah: "What God has willed," used to express appreciation, praise.

mim (mîm): The Arabic letter *m* (ρ), which starts out as a hook and ends as a tail hanging down.

misbaha: Prayer beads.

minbar: The pulpit in a mosque.

mufti: A professional jurist who interprets Islamic law.

mukhtar (mukhtâr): The head of a village.

najis: Ritually unclean.

nasheed: Song or hymn.

niqab: A full-face veil worn by some Muslim women that leaves a gap only for the eyes.

qiyam (qiyâm): That portion of prayer when the faithful are standing up, hands folded on the chest.

shahada (shahâda): The Muslim profession of faith: "There is no god but God, and Muhammad is His messenger."

Sharia (sharî'a): The canonical law of Islamic tradition.

Sahaba (ṣaḥâba): The companions, disciples, scribes, and family of the Prophet Muhammad.

Subhan Allah (Subḥân Allâh): Praise be to God.

sujud (sujûd): Prostration to God, or that part of prayer when the faithful prostrate themselves, touching their foreheads to the floor.

sunna: The established practices of Islam, passed on as an oral record traced back to the deeds and sayings of the Prophet Muhammad.

Surat al-Jinn: "Sura of the Djinn," chapter 72 of the Koran, with twenty-eight verses.

Surat al-Ma'un: "Sura of Charity," chapter 107 of the Koran. In chapter 20 General Abbas is paraphrasing rather than quoting.

Surat al-Nisa: "Sura of the Woman," chapter 4 of the Koran.

taharrush: Harassment

ummah: Literally "community," a synonym for *ummat al-Islām* (the Islamic community), and commonly referring to the collective community of Islamic peoples.

Wa alaykum as-salam wa rahmatullah wa barakatu: And upon you be peace, as well as the mercy of God and his blessings.

wudu (wuḍû'): Ritual washing before prayer.

zaim (za'îm): Leader.

zakat: (*zakât*): Charitable donations, tithing, one of the five basic pillars of Islam.

Omar Sayfo is a Syrian-Hungarian academic, a journalist, and a frequent traveler to Muslim neighborhoods across Europe. He is a researcher at Utrecht University and a previous visiting researcher at the University of Cambridge. Besides his academic works, he published articles in *The New York Times, Foreign Policy,* and others. His first English monograph, *Arab Animation: Images of Identity,* was published in 2021 by Edinburgh University Press.

Paul Olchváry is the translator of more than twenty books of Hungarian literature, mostly novels, including György Dragomán's *The White King* (Houghton-Mifflin) and *Budapest Noir* (Harper Collins). He has received translation grants from the National Endowment for the Arts and PEN American Center. Born in 1965 to a Hungarian family in New Brunswick, New Jersey, and raised near Buffalo, New York, Olchváry lived in Hungary for many years after the Cold War. He is also the publisher of New Europe Books and the editor-in-chief of *Hungarian Cultural Studies.* Since 2010 he has lived in Williamstown, Massachusetts, with his son Ákos.

Printed in the USA
CPSIA information can be obtained
at www.ICGtesting.com
LVHW091223151223
766489LV00004B/387